"Dr. Branch claims that 'Plays capture the drama of theology in the making.' That is certainly true in her compositions, where she employs the scriptural idiom in dramatic format to invite both performers and audiences to see themselves as part of the greatest story ever told."

—**ANDREW DEARMAN**
Professor of Old Testament, Fuller Theological Seminary

"Dr. Robin Gallaher Branch has taught on the college level, written for the Society of Biblical Literature, and published an important book on contributions of lesser-known women in the Old Testament. Dr. Branch is an excellent scholar; in addition, she is able to write so that the average person understands the message being conveyed. Her *Six Biblical Plays for Contemporary Audiences* is a delightful look at Bible stories and helps us see these rich stories in a playful light."

—**JOHN B. "MIKE" LOUDON**
Pastor, First Presbyterian Church, Lakeland, FL

"Robin Gallaher Branch has written six plays which Christians will enjoy enacting as their audiences gain fresh insights into the significance of familiar biblical texts. The profound scholarship displayed in her annotations enables her to understand accurately the background of these texts. She correctly depicts Elizabeth and Mary as young teenagers at the time they were wed. She empathetically describes their emotions: Elizabeth while suffering the anguish of barrenness and Mary while living under the suspicion of being an adulteress. Her plays based on characters from Proverbs and on the parts of the body of Christ personified display wit and humor."

—**EDWIN M. YAMAUCHI**
Professor of History Emeritus, Miami University

"These biblically based plays remind us of Jesus' method of teaching the multitudes through stories rather than directly through lectures. Robin does what Eugene Peterson said (using words from an Emily Dickinson poem) about Jesus with the parables—'Tell it slant.' Her technique works equally well with audiences that do not have a background of biblical knowledge and with those who think they know all about the Bible."

—DAVID A. BOWEN
Assistant Minister, Mid-Adults; Memphis Fellows Teacher,
Second Presbyterian Church

"Dr. Branch's plays serve as a wonderful tool to take a closer look at what REALLY happened in familiar Bible stories. As I read each play, I used my imagination and reason to ponder and question how I might receive a divine pronouncement—something that definitely would interrupt the routine of my life! Two characters in particular—*Lady Wisdom* and *Mary*—encouraged me to respond daily to God's freely offered wisdom and redemptive plan."

—ELIZABETH DICKINSON
Lawyer

"Dr. Branch's plays are theatrical windows into biblical narratives and human nature. Characters embody an array of emotions—from joy to fear and cockiness. *Funny Bone Finds a Home* is humorous. An audience or reader may chortle over the dismissive declarations of one member of the Body of Christ: 'I don't like being around you . . . I'd rather be out playing golf with unbelievers!' Yet upon reflection, Head's words may mirror an interior attitude that needs examination."

—JULIA THOMPSON
Secondary Education English Literature, AP, CP, and ESL Teacher

"Dr. Branch's plays reflect her expertise as a biblical scholar and seasoned teacher. They are by turns humorous, tense, and profound, while teaching about the theology, cultural contexts, and critical issues around the texts dramatized. Four of the plays even include copious footnotes! These plays will be especially welcomed in college classrooms, where they can enliven class sessions without sacrificing content."

—JAMES BUCHANAN WALLACE
Associate Professor of Religion, Christian Brothers University

"In these plays, there are touching depictions of faith (and its lack): the moment we see the animals running to meet God, contrasted with Adam and Eve as they hide . . . Mary's courageous faith as she attempts to explain her predicament to Joseph, without knowing how he will respond . . . the faith of the disciples as they see what Jesus' resurrection means to all men . . . the faith that the Body of Christ is called to be one in their differences, in imitation of the Lord in His Trinity . . . Robin has laid out these moments for our contemplation, worship, and for the good of our souls. However, the most moving of these moments I found in the story of the Incarnation as told through the eyes of Elizabeth. Here we encounter something truly rare. We are moved by so many moments in the play, entitled *Astonishment and Joy,* but none more than the grand inclusive gesture that is its final tableau. Through Elizabeth's prophetic application of pronouns an astonishing reality is revealed: that the entire Church, both male and female, is, to her Lord, a *bride.* For this and these plays we owe Robin thanks."

—JOHN MASON HODGES
Director, Center for Western Studies

"Entertaining, yet poignant. Funny, yet heartbreaking. Astonishing, yet delightful. Enraging, yet revealing. And now, let's talk about Dr. Robin Gallaher Branch's latest development: her book, *Six Biblical Plays for Christian Audiences*; prior to that, I was referring to the Bible. Dr. Branch captures all of these experiences and emotions we engage—or perhaps should engage— as we read through the Bible in a way few other means can: by the use of dramatic theater. Already a fan of her first book, *Jeroboam's Wife*, I eagerly anticipated the arrival of *Six Biblical Plays*, and it did not disappoint. Dr. Branch's careful, methodical scholarship underlays all her work and aims to excite all her readers' senses. She brings them as close as they can get, through both scholarship and imagination, to the flesh-and-blood (-and-spirit) reality of life in Old Testament times. Further, Dr. Branch aims to give those who read her books or receive her plays a deeper appreciation for the multifaceted cultural and historical elements of what biblical narrators assumed, but to which we are not necessarily privy. Yet, she also gently but boldly helps us consider the theological implications, whether glorious, comforting, or disturbing, beyond what may be obvious at first glance of the texts. At once entertaining, instructive, and illuminating, *Six Biblical Plays* will benefit individual readers, classes, and groups from young to old, and congregations through reading, performing, or viewing these plays. They, along with their attending questions for discussion, are simple enough for young viewers and participants and new believers, yet nuanced enough to engage and challenge older and mature Christians."

—**NATALIE R. W. EASTMAN**
Author, *Women, Leadership, and the Bible: How Do I Know What to Believe?*
A Practical Guide to Interpretation

SIX BIBLICAL PLAYS
for
CONTEMPORARY AUDIENCES

SIX BIBLICAL PLAYS
for
CONTEMPORARY AUDIENCES

Robin Gallaher Branch

Foreword by John Goldingay

CASCADE *Books* · Eugene, Oregon

SIX BIBLICAL PLAYS FOR CONTEMPORARY AUDIENCES

Cascade Books
An Imprint of Wipf and Stock Publishers
199 W. 8th Ave., Suite 3
Eugene, OR 97401

www.wipfandstock.com

PAPERBACK ISBN: 978-1-4982-3084-1
HARDCOVER ISBN: 978-1-4982-3086-5
EBOOK ISBN: 978-1-4982-3085-8

Cataloguing-in-Publication data:

Names: Branch, Robin Gallaher, 1948–

Title: Six biblical plays for contemporary audiences / Robin Gallaher Branch.

Description: Eugene, OR: Cascade Books, 2016 | Includes bibliographical references.

Identifiers: ISBN 978-1-4982-3084-1 (paperback) | ISBN 978-1-4982-3086-5 (hardcover) |
ISBN 978-1-4982-3085-8 (ebook)

Subjects: LCSH: Bible plays, American. | Bible. Old Testament—Drama. | Bible. New
Testament—Drama. | Title.

Classification: PS3523 B64 2016 (paperback) | PS3523 (ebook)

Manufactured in the U.S.A.   06/09/16

"When Mary Tells Joseph: A Play Based on Matthew 1:18–19," *In die Skriflig/In Luce Verbi* 47.1
(2013) 12pp. http://www.indieskriflig.org.za/index.php/skriflig/article/view/92

"Astonishment and Joy: Luke 1 as Told from the Perspective of Elizabeth," *In die Skriflig/In Luce
Verbi* 47.1 (2013) 10 pages. http://www.indieskriflig.org.za/index.php/skriflig/article/view/77

"Funny Bone Finds a Home: A Musical Featuring the Body of Christ, "*In die Skriflig/In Luce
Verbi* 47.1 (2013) Art. #113, 17 pages. http://www.indieskriflig.org.za/index.php/skriflig/article/
view/113/2367

"He is Risen! A Play Based on Acts 1: 1–12." *In die Skriflig*, 44.1 (2010) 229–58.

"Life's Choices: A Play Based on Eight Characters in Proverbs," *Christian Higher Education* 4.1
(2005) 57–69. Also published in *Society of Biblical Literature, SBL Forum for February/March*
(2006) 8 pages. http://www.sbl-site.org/publications/article.aspx?articleId=488

To the older women in my life who have shaped it

- My mother, Gwen Gallaher, for constantly quoting Romans 8:28, 31: "And we know that all things work together for good to them that love God, to them who are the called according to his purpose . . . If God be for us, who can be against us?"

- Clara Evans Gallaher, my grandmother, who fiercely loved her grandchildren and gave us spectacular summer memories

- Azalee Freeman Bradley, my grandmother, who led the women of her church with skill and humor

- Cindy and Vera Freeman, my great aunts, who taught me the enduring qualities of family loyalty

- Margaret Gallaher Lee, my aunt, who generously befriended me

- Agnes Waser, who taught me to pray for my enemies

- Alma "Layton" Lerum, my godmother and endearingly known by the nickname my father gave her. She taught me the joy of doing simple tasks

- Rowena Tebbe, a prayer warrior and a growing Christian in her nineties. Her consistent life teaches the efficacy of persistent, regular prayer

- Mary Wheeless, another nonagenarian friend. Known for her gifts of hospitality and encouragement, she welcomes me and others. What a lovely tradition we share of a glass of Chardonnay with dinner and then our evening chats!

- Margaret Parks Gallaher, my great grandmother whom I never knew. She also loved the Bible. One day I found her handwritten comments next to Isaiah 41:10: "Fear thou not; for I am with thee: be not dismayed; for I am thy God: I will strengthen thee; yea, I will help thee; yea, I will uphold thee with the right hand of my righteousness." She wrote, "This verse has been our family's hope for generations."

Contents

Foreword

John Goldingay

DRAMA CAN GIVE THE Scriptures access to people in a way that complements reading and preaching. Several books in the Bible can easily be adapted for dramatized reading or dramatic presentation, and their stories then have that extra entree both to the people who take part in the reading or the performance and to the people who listen or watch. Esther, Ruth, and Jonah are examples. Maybe Mark wrote his Gospel for performance in a Roman theater.

Job is the one book that is more obviously structured for dramatized reading or performance, and each time I have watched it performed or have listened to it read, I have felt like tearing up my lecture notes on Job with their neat summaries of the various perspectives in the book. The words themselves that have been read out are much more profound and have much more impact.

I was therefore excited when I came across Robin Gallaher Branch's dramatization of Proverbs, in which she takes the material in the book about laziness, drinking, gossip, and so on, and turns it into character sketches. I have often used this dramatization in classes on Proverbs. It's one of those simple ideas that make you think, "Why has no one done it before?"

There's lots of material in Proverbs from which to construct those character sketches. With Mary and Joseph it's different. Yes, what was it like when Mary told Joseph about the angelic visitation? The silences of the Scriptures are sometimes as stimulating as their words. Here is an imaginative answer to that question, with lots of footnotes that in their own way are as interesting as the dialogue itself. The same applies to the plays about Elizabeth and Jesus' Ascension, while the imaginative drama about the Body of Christ has the imagination working in yet another way.

Yes, enacting a story makes it more real. It brings out the possible emotions of the people involved. It takes you outside of yourself and into another person. Paradoxically, fictionalizing the story brings home its factuality. While Dr. Branch often had children in mind in writing her dramas, dramas resemble stories in the way they reach adults in at least as significant a fashion.

Acknowledgments

A BOOK REQUIRES MANY people to bring it to pass. Consequently, many need to be acknowledged and thanked.

- Julia and David Thompson, lifelong friends and fellow pilgrims. I sat under their big backyard tree, comfortably shaded and singing praises. With my hymnbook in hand, I looked for tunes for *Funny Bone Finds a Home: A Musical Featuring the Body of Christ* and joyfully composed.

- The Rev. Dr. "Mike" Loudon for inviting me to be Scholar in Residence at First Presbyterian Church in Lakeland, Florida, in 2012. My happy months there gave me thinking time and the chance to direct three of my plays.

- Annatjie Verhoef, organist at Gereformeerde Kerk in Potchefstroom, South Africa, who asked me to do a sermon on Ascension Day for children. Her invitation led to the play, *He is Risen: A Play Based on Acts 1:1–12,* and to a lot of fun!

- Linda Fryer for her powerhouse clothes and wise words

- Gail McQuade for her lovely ways of strengthening the biblical concept of God's goodness

- Evelyn Lupardus for being the living model of Funny Bone, a great blessing to the Body of Christ

- Peggy Barkley, my friend, former student, and sister in the Lord, for her wisdom during a season of transition

- Anne Sayle, a lovely artist, for her constant encouragement and delightful poetic nature

- Dianne and Brad Champlin, noble actors and friends who immediately were game to be Mary and Joseph in a radio drama presentation of *When Mary Tells Joseph: A Play Based on Matthew 1:18–19.* They performed it in 2014 at Second Presbyterian Church in Memphis, Tennessee. Dianne has the high, soft voice needed for Mary, and Brad has the strong, loving, loudness of Joseph. They honored me by trusting me as playwright, friend, and director.

- Esmari Linde and JC Potgieter also agreed to play Mary and Joseph at a production of *When Mary Tells Joseph* at Gereformeerde Kerk in 2013. Both were students in the Faculty of Theology at North-West University. They fell in love during our rehearsal time. I rejoice that my play was part of their courtship. I watched with joy as they explored their growing love through their roles on stage.

    A delightful memory from our work together was how loved both are by the North-West students and faculty and by the believing community. At tea outside one Sunday after church, three of Esmari's friends cornered me. They introduced themselves. Each was very pretty. We exchanged pleasantries. One said, "Did you know that Esmari sings?" I nodded. We continued talking. A second friend said, "Esmari has a wonderful voice." I smiled. I asked them about their studies. A third exclaimed, "We love to hear Esmari sing!" I put down my cup, looked at the three, and smiled. "I think I understand! You three would like Esmari to sing during the play!" They nodded and grinned.

    That Monday during rehearsal, I mentioned the incident to Esmari. "They're very loyal," she said. I told Esmari that the Magnificat, which is summarized in the play, often is sung. I encouraged her to make up her own tune and sing those words to Joseph and the audience. She said she would try. During rehearsals, she worked on various original tunes. Her voice indeed was lovely and easily filled the church hall. On the night of the play, she sang with all her heart. Her voice honored the Lord. The audience, spellbound, experienced the beauty of praise during her singing and a visitation of the Lord's presence during the play.

    Another happy production memory was the way JC, a very handsome and manly man, learned the simple grapevine dance step and performed a rendition of it on stage during the play. He trusted me as a director.

- Nancy Cook for her prayers and encouragement over the years

- Chuck and Nancy Coe for their prayers and support

- The Rev. Dr. Andy Dearman, for watching my career in biblical scholarship over the decades and for writing oh so many letters of recommendation!

- The Rev. Mike Stokke, a pastor at Second Presbyterian Church, for seeing me roughly every six weeks for a year for what I called "an accountability session." These sessions centered me during a bewildering time in my life. I also am grateful to Heidi Stokke, Mike's wife, for her consistent prayers.

- Mike Warner and Jerry Williams, elders at Second Presbyterian Church, for praying for me daily in the mornings for months for a good job and for provision. Their prayers gave me hope.

- Eddie Foster, on staff at Second Presbyterian Church, for leadership in helping me to get outside funding for the Kilian McDonnell Fellowship to the Collegeville Institute at St. John's University in Collegeville, Minnesota. Thanks also go to Gail Stevens, likewise on staff at Second Presbyterian, for directing what she calls "God's supply" toward that fellowship; and to Samuel Meztger, organist at Second Presbyterian, for verifying that the tunes in *Life's Choices a Play Based on Eight Characters in Proverbs* are in the public domain.

- Joan Sommerfield, my friend for decades, who is known for tucking small gifts in envelopes

- Various staff and faculty members at Christian Brothers University in Memphis, Tennessee. Thanks go to IT Services, and especially for the help of computer techs Clinton Yelvington and Eddie Gallarno; and to Dr. Teri J. Mason, Faculty Services Curriculum Coordinator, College of Adult Professional Studies, for her friendship and excellent insights on teaching.

- The staff at the Collegeville Institute—especially Jan Schmitz, Carla Durand, and Dr. Don Ottenhoff—for creating a time for imagination, research, reflection, and writing in a lovely space with a view of a lake!

- Allegra Inzer, Paula "Polly" Ragland, and Blanche Tosh, literary friends all, for proofreading the manuscript

- Br. Aaron Raverty, O.S.B., Ph.D., St. John's Abbey, Collegeville, Minnesota, for his encouragement and copyediting skills

- Maggie Lee Peterson, my elegant cousin, for her generosity

- Dr. Greg and Patti Hollifield for practical Christian friendship and many times of fun

- Jim Tedrick, K. C. Hanson, and Ian Creeger, new friends at Wipf and Stock, for their guidance and editing expertise

- My beloved Faculty of Theology at North-West University. My thanks for your encouragement and insights on creative works.

Introduction

OFTEN AN OLD TESTAMENT or New Testament survey course is just that: It gives an overview of portions of the Bible. Yes, students get their feet wet, but they do not swim in the depths of the Bible's marvelous truths. I started writing plays because I wanted my students to learn biblical principles.

I found that plays enable me and my students to take a breath, look at a specific text together, discover some of its multi-faceted beauty, and meanwhile have some fun. The hard work of producing a play lets me get to know my students on a different level. We share sweat equity, so to speak.

I discovered that plays facilitate many aspects of learning. For example, plays teach in non-threatening ways. Like Jesus' parables, plays can showcase both praise and reprimand. A member of the audience or cast may experience what Christians traditionally call "conviction"—that is, when a point of the play or parable becomes uncomfortably personal. I remember a telling incident just before *Life's Choices: A Play Based on Eight Characters in Proverbs* was videoed at North-West University in Potchefstroom, South Africa. My cast members were my students in the Faculty of Theology. The play had been so well-received during a student/staff/faculty devotion that arrangements were made to video it and use it as part of the ongoing curriculum for Old Testament.

As usual, we cast and director joined in prayer beforehand. When we finished and just before going into the video production room, the student who played Satisfied Husband said this: "We all have learned a lot from doing this play. But what I think we'll carry with us throughout our lives is this: Not one of us will commit adultery. We've seen its consequences."

I was stunned. That "take away" effect from the play had not occurred to me. I rejoiced at the greatness of the Lord's good work through his words and our diligence.

Plays promote creativity. I often schedule dramatizations of *Garden Variety: A Dramatization of Genesis 3* in different classes throughout a semester. It's become a popular teaching tool. I encourage the participants to develop their characters and to enjoy them. Students are given the play at an earlier class and asked to choose a character. I have been surprised that the character of the Lord God is often played by a woman. Hesitant students particularly enjoy the fun of being the wind and bird sounds.

Other characters stand out as well. I remember two in particular. One was a tall, shy basketball player. He sat in the back of the class; his quiz scores showed he lacked good study skills. I was concerned about him. During the assignment of parts, he indicated he had no interest in participating. However, others persuaded him to play flaming sword, the part that closes the drama. He agreed. Pretending he was flaming sword, he ran back and forth and then ran around the tree of life and the tree of the knowledge of good and evil. The class loved it and applauded him. He was thrilled. I was thrilled.

The second standout character in *Genesis 3* was a top student who told me he wanted to be a dog. I said fine. The Lord God's practice was to come to the Garden in the cool of the day to talk with the woman and the man. On the day that the woman and the man ate the fruit of the tree of the knowledge of good and evil, the Lord God came as usual. Extemporaneously, the student playing the dog bounded out from the "shrubbery" (the other students who were pretending to be the plants whose leaves were pulled by the man and the woman for garments). Barking loudly and expressing exuberant joy, he ran fast on all fours, took a leap, and landed in the Lord God's arms! Luckily, the student playing the Lord God this time was a man and big enough to catch him!

I'll never forget that incident, for my student playing the dog understood something crucial in Scripture: The natural love of a creature for the Creator.

Plays create space for fun. I've learned to expect laughter, goofs, and (in my case, at least) character growth. Plays have made me more flexible. My actors for *Funny Bone Finds a Home: A Musical Featuring the Body of Christ* were nonagenarians and octogenarians. These residents of Florida Presbyterian Homes in Lakeland, Florida, arrived at rehearsals with walkers, canes, and scooters—and used them (of necessity!) on stage. Foot poked Nose with his cane during the stage altercation. Ear banged the horn of his scooter. Walkers served as dance partners. Rehearsal schedules accommodated doctors' appointments, family visits, and (of course!) afternoon naps.

Just before a performance, Unpresentable Parts lost her glasses. She searched everywhere—her pockets, the changing room, her purse. Without her glasses, she could not read the verses from Song of Songs that put her squarely in the Body of Christ. We retraced her steps. Heart, Funny Bone, Piano Player, and Hand helped. We mimed the makeup counter. "I took my glasses off to put on my make up and put them on the counter," Unpresentable Parts said. "Then I lost them."

The women searched their purses. "I've got them!" one exclaimed. "I put them in my purse by mistake. Sorry!" The women all exchanged hugs, leaving the changing room ready and eager to give the audience a fine performance.

Plays meet some needs. They reach some people. Plays do not take the place of good preaching, but they allow for those other than a preacher to offer their gifts to the Lord in worship. A good play leaves an audience with a strong impression—whether laughter, a new insight, something to think about, or weeping. The frequency of the latter always surprises me. When I've played Elizabeth from my monologue play, *Astonishment and Joy: Luke 1 as Told from the Perspective of Elizabeth,* people have cried. One man, a seasoned history professor, openly wept during its presentation at a faculty assembly meeting. He told me later, "I didn't realize what she went through." Older women also weep openly during presentations of *When Mary Tells Joseph: A Play Based on Matthew 1:18–19.* They are rock-solid Christians who have walked with the Lord for decades. They certainly understand Mary's predicament and reflect on it in personal ways. They tell me they weep for her and for themselves.

My plays show extensive research. In 2013 I sat next to a Brill editor at a luncheon at a resort near Nijmegen, Netherlands. After hearing that I write plays based on academic research, she said, "I believe you are the only one in the world doing that." Probably so.

Plays facilitate imagination. My plays seek to combine my God-given gifts of imagination and research skills within the boundaries set by the text. I visualize it this way: The text is a rectangular picture frame and inside that frame are my imagination and my research. The text itself is so wonderful in its surprises, scope, and insights on God's character that it is an honor to work "within" it! I believe that good preaching and good playwriting share this rule: Honor the text and let it speak to the people.

Plays capture the drama of theology in the making. Mary did not realize she was participating in a crucial part of the theology of the New Testament, the doctrine of the Incarnation. Surely she must have treasured Gabriel's closing words to her, "For nothing is impossible with God" (Luke 1:37). Adam and Eve did not know their disobedience would lead to so much sorrow and enmity and to separation from God. The disciples who watched Jesus rise into the clouds received the promise that he also will come back in the same way (Acts 1:10–11). The squabbles of Corinthian believers produced sound teaching on the importance of diversity in the church and on how to handle quarrels among members of the Body of Christ (1 Cor 12:12–27). The book of Proverbs teaches via exaggeration, a tool showing the broad, general results of repeated choices over a long period of time. Elizabeth testifies to the marvelous ability of God to answer prayers in creative, miraculous ways that leave her (and us!) stunned. The stories of the characters in my plays hallmark God's gracious work in individual lives. Like my six handsome disciples/actors in *He is Risen! A Play Based on Acts 1:1–12*, we too can be amazed, humbled, joyful and overflowing with thanksgiving at the goodness of God.

Prayer surrounds my plays—from their research through their writing, into their publication and throughout their rehearsals and performances. Invariably, the Lord shows up in all stages in the process. With a lovely finesse, he blesses everybody; he blesses the work of our hands (Ps 90:17). Plays have humbled me, for they point me to the faithful, ongoing kindness and greatness of God.

Prayer likewise surrounds your reading of these plays, dear reader. May the Lord bless you in marvelous ways. May the Lord quicken his gift of imagination in you. May this book and its insights change your life.

Chapter 1

Garden Variety
A Dramatization of Genesis 3

Text: *New International Version*

Characters:

Narrator	Wind and bird sounds
Serpent	Tree of the knowledge of good and evil
Woman	Tree of life
Man	Animals slain for their skins
Lord God	Two cherubs (cherubim)
Fig plants for covering	Flaming sword
Person who reads the italics	

Note: This play was written as an in-class teaching tool. It also can be performed in a worship service. If done in a classroom setting, read the lines slowly. Allow pauses for emphasis. Let the extras—the wind, birds, trees—participate with actions. Enjoy the story. Let the characters develop. Think about the meaning of the actions and the words. If done as part of a worship service, the lines should be memorized and said slowly.

Narrator: Hello and welcome. I am the Narrator for this drama, a play based on Genesis 3. This chapter in the Bible is commonly called The Fall. But the word *fall* does not appear in the text. Nonetheless, the story tells how sin entered the world.

1

The story has lots of characters. I will read the narrative portion. My fellow actor who is standing next to me will read some additional information discussing dramatic elements. In our scripts, this information is in italics. Throughout the play, you may notice some repetition. Repetition is a writing technique for emphasis as well as an aid for memorization. The additional information slows down the text. It gives both the actors and those of you in the audience a chance to consider what is happening.

Let me introduce the other characters; each will come forward and bow. The serpent, woman, man, and Lord God. The tree of the knowledge of good and evil and the tree of life. Fig plants for covering. Animals that crawl around on all fours and are slain for their skins. Two cherubs; they're also called cherubim. And a flaming sword that runs in at the very end of the play; it's a great part and closes the drama. Throughout the drama you will hear the sounds of the wind and the birds. You'll observe that they know what is happening. We'll discuss the play afterward. Questions for discussion are provided.

Now let's get to the play. The scene is the Garden of Eden. Imagine it! It's absolutely beautiful! The Garden is a happy place for the plants, animals, trees, and two people. The Lord God visits daily in the cool of the day. There are two trees in the Garden. Both have fruit. The first is the tree of the knowledge of good and evil. The second is the tree of life. The trees sway and flap their branches throughout the drama. The birds and the wind express happiness at first and other emotions as the play progresses.

Now let's have some comments from the one we call the Person Who Reads the Italics (PWRTI).

PWRTI: *(The wind and birds express sounds of cheerfulness and happiness. Trees and plants enter, smile, find places, and wave their branches and leaves. The animals come in as well. The animals frolic a bit on the floor on all fours. The scene is one of happiness and good will.)*

Narrator: (Genesis 3:1) Now the serpent was more crafty than any of the wild animals the Lord God had made.

PWRTI: *(The serpent enters. The woman and man enter. They walk around both trees. The fruit on both trees is visible. The serpent also walks around. The serpent studies the woman intently. The serpent looks only briefly at the man. The serpent might have a sneer in its voice. Or the serpent might seem to be quite reasonable. Both responses are backed up by scholarly debate. How the serpent presents the question determines, in large part, the direction of the story. The serpent comes to the woman and addresses her directly.)*

Serpent: "Did God really say, 'You must not eat from any tree in the garden'?"

PWRTI: *(The woman thinks about this for a while. The man is silent, looks bored, and does not answer or comment. He sighs as if he does not care or as if he has other things to do. The woman sees this and answers the serpent herself.)*

Woman: "We may eat fruit from the trees in the garden, (3) but God did say, 'You must not eat fruit from the tree that is in the middle of the garden, and you must not touch it, or you will die.'"

PWRTI: *(The wind and birds make sounds as if they are a bit concerned. The trees sway and their leaves shake.)*

Serpent: (4) "You will not surely die,"

PWRTI: *(The serpent is emphatic about this. The woman is surprised. The man shrugs his shoulders as if he is not really listening intently.)*

Serpent: (5) "For God knows that when you eat of it your eyes will be opened, and you will be like God, knowing good and evil."

PWRTI: *(The wind and birds express sounds of some concern. The woman again looks quite surprised. She walks around the tree of the knowledge of good and evil. She pats its trunk. She picks its fruit, looks at it intently, and holds it. She touches the fruit but does not die! The woman smiles. The man folds his arms and crosses his legs. He continues his attitude of non-involvement.)*

Narrator: (6) When the woman saw that the fruit of the tree was good for food and pleasing to the eye, and also desirable for gaining wisdom, she took some and ate it. She also gave some to her husband, who was with her, and he ate it. (7) Then the eyes of both were opened, and they realized they were naked; so they sewed fig leaves together and made coverings for themselves.

PWRTI: *(The man and the woman eat the fruit. They express surprise! Their eyes are suddenly opened, so to speak, and they see that they are naked! They want to cover themselves. They are embarrassed. They are ashamed. They look around for plants, find them, and rip off the plants' leaves. The man and the woman frantically try to sew the leaves together. They try to cover themselves. The wind and bird sounds during this part are very shrill and concerned. The trees shake and flap their leaves. Then the man and the woman are startled because they hear the sound of the Lord God in the Garden. The man and the woman try to hide. The Lord God enters the Garden.)*

Narrator: (8) Then the man and his wife heard the sound of the Lord God as he was walking in the garden in the cool of the day, and they hid from the Lord God among the trees in the garden.

PWRTI: *(The animals come to the Lord God and frolic with joy around his feet. The Lord God greets them and pats them. The Lord God looks around for the man and woman.)*

Narrator: (9) But the Lord God called to the man,

Lord God: "Where are you?"

Man: "I heard you in the garden and I was afraid because I was naked; so I hid."

PWRTI: *(The wind and birds express sounds of much concern. The Lord God ponders the words of the man.)*

Lord God: "Who told you that you were naked? Have you eaten from the tree that I commanded you not to eat from?"

Man: "The woman you put here with me—she gave me some fruit from the tree, and I ate it."

PWRTI: *(The wind and birds express sounds of great alarm. The man has said this in an accusatory tone. He points toward the woman. The woman hangs her head in shame; she covers her face; her shoulders slump. The Lord God considers the man's words and attitude. The Lord God then looks at the woman.)*

Lord God: "What is this you have done?"

PWRTI: *(The woman still hangs her head. She raises it and looks at the Lord God. She speaks slowly.)*

Woman: "The serpent deceived me, and I ate."

PWRTI: *(The Lord God considers this. He is very angry. He walks around. He is thinking. The man and the woman look at each other and are very concerned. The Lord God turns to the serpent and speaks forcefully. The wind and birds emit mournful sounds. Then they fall silent. The trees are "petrified" and stop waving their branches. All creation seems to stand still.)*

Lord God: "Because you have done this, cursed are you above all the livestock and all the wild animals! You will crawl on your belly and you will eat dust all the days of your life.

PWRTI: *(The serpent falls immediately to its belly on the floor and slithers away toward the bushes to hide.)*

Lord God: (15) "And I will put enmity between you and the woman, and between your offspring and hers; he will crush your head, and you will strike his heel."

PWRTI: *(The wind and birds express sounds of shock and amazement. The man and the woman gasp. The serpent hides deeper in the bushes. The Lord God turns next to the woman.)*

Lord God: "I will greatly increase your pains in childbearing; with pain you will give birth to children. Your desire will be for your husband, and he will rule over you."

PWRTI: *(The woman hangs her head and wrings her hands. The man is quite afraid. He tries to mask his fear with anger. He separates himself from the woman by walking away from her. He raises an angry fist in the air. He lifts a defiant chin to the Lord God.)*

Lord God: "Because you listened to your wife and ate from the tree about which I commanded you, 'You must not eat of it,' cursed is the ground because of you; through painful toil you will eat of it all the days of your life. (18) It will produce thorns and thistles for you, and you will eat the plants of the field. (19) By the sweat of your brow you will eat your food until you return to the ground, since from it you were taken; for dust you are and to dust you will return."

Narrator: (20) Adam named his wife Eve, because she would become the mother of all the living.

PWRTI: *(The animals come forward and God kills them. God skins them and makes clothes for Adam and Eve. God clothes Adam and Eve. The wind and birds express sounds of sorrow. The trees flap their branches, but with no enthusiasm. The sounds and action show distress and anguish. Nothing is the same in the Garden. Everything has forever changed.)*

Narrator: (21) The Lord God made garments of skin for Adam and his wife and clothed them. (22) And the Lord God said,

Lord God: "The man has now become like one of us, knowing good and evil. He must not be allowed to reach out his hand and take also from the tree of life and eat and live forever."

PWRTI: *(The tree of life flaps its branches. God drives out Adam and Eve from the Garden. They freeze upstage. God commands the two cherubs to come forward and to guard the tree of life. A flaming sword enters and comes in front of the tree of life. The sword flashes back and forth, prohibiting any from approaching the tree of life.)*

Narrator: (23) So the Lord God banished him from the Garden of Eden to work the ground from which he had been taken. (24) After he drove the man out, he placed on the east side of the Garden of Eden cherubim and a flaming sword flashing back and forth to guard the way to the tree of life.

PWRTI: *(The wind and birds express sounds of great sorrow. The trees flap their branches in sadness and without energy. The man and woman weep from outside the Garden. The sword flashes this way and that. The Lord God leaves. There is silence.)*

Staging Note: Without smiling and in silence, the cast members come to center stage, join hands, and bow. They exit.

QUESTIONS FOR CONSIDERATION AND DISCUSSION

1. What was the Garden of Eden like at first, from your reading of the story?

2. What is the most important point of the story in your view?

3. Who is to blame and why?

4. What are some themes and subthemes of the story?

5. What does this story teach us about the man? The woman? The serpent? The Lord God?

6. What do you "take away" from the story as something applicable to your life?

7. Why is this such an enduring story throughout the centuries, and why is it such a troubling story?

8. How did it feel to act it out? How is acting it out different from reading it aloud or silently?

9. What did you learn from the experience?

10. How does this story tie in with the New Testament?

11. What other texts do you suggest might work for this particular style of acting?

CHAPTER 2

Life's Choices

A Play Based on Eight Characters in Proverbs

INTRODUCTION

I wrote this play in response to questions from students in my Old Testament classes about how to interpret the book of Proverbs.[1] I wanted my students to see that Proverbs is not primarily a book of promises but a book of principles. These principles, if followed over a long period of time, produce results. As I read and reread Proverbs, I saw that it contained many types of characters who made choices about how to live. These choices became the habits that characterized them.

These principles that became choices and then became habits led to patterns of success or failure in life. I saw that Proverbs teaches via stereotypes and hyperbole. It exaggerates to make a point. Male and female stereotypes like those in this play cross its pages.

Proverbs also encourages a lifelong pursuit of wisdom and an enjoyment of wisdom's qualities. One of God's attributes is wisdom. Gradually I saw that pursuing wisdom, as Proverbs suggests, really means pursuing God. How delightful this is! God delights in being found! Scholars agree that a major theme of Proverbs, the fear of the Lord (Prov 1:7; 31:30), is not only a prerequisite of wisdom but also an attitude of the heart and a way of life.

My prayer is that you enjoy this play, learn from it, and even act in it! By all means analyze the marketplace of ideas it presents. I humbly encourage you to heed the choices it offers.

I wrote the play in South Africa while I was on my Fulbright Fellowship at North-West University in Potchefstroom. Consequently, *Life's Choices* has a South African setting. It takes place on the Bult, a busy area of coffee houses and bookshops near the university. *Bult* is an Afrikaaner word meaning *small hill*. The time is morning.

The play's Vaudevillian style makes use of the hyperbole present in Proverbs. You will notice the long speeches of the actors, especially Satisfied Husband. Long speeches reflect the genre of Wisdom Literature, and Proverbs is one of the books in Wisdom Literature. Much of the dialogue is based on Scripture references from Proverbs. These texts are given next to each character's description.

The actors wear nametags. The set is minimal: Ladders, tables, big black blocks. Simple Youth, a First Year student at the local university and the play's hero, faces many choices. He meets Sluggard, who avoids living by trying to sleep all day; Drunkard, who totes a big wine bottle and looks for a fight; Satisfied Husband, a magistrate (judge) who constantly talks about his noble wife, the Proverbs 31 woman; Adulteress, a lonely, beautiful woman obviously looking for men; Gossip, who delights in breaking up friendships; Lady Folly, a brazen, brittle woman who likes the easy way; and Lady Wisdom, an elegant teacher and forceful leader who invites the townsfolk to her banquet. Which lifestyle will Simple Youth choose? Throughout the day, Simple Youth listens to their stories and ultimately makes a decision that will set the direction for the rest of his life.

Scene: The Bult in Potchefstroom, South Africa. Among the shops on the Bult are several coffee houses, nice restaurants, bookstores, beauty salons, a grocery store, and a wine shop. The shops reflect the trendy combination of youth and academics that is common near a major research university.

TIMES AND MUSIC AND COMPOSERS[2]

Early Morning

Maple Leaf Rag   Scott Joplin

Mid-Morning

Minuet in G   J. S. Bach

Noon

Mexican Hat Dance   Felice Partichala

Early Afternoon

Waltz of the Flowers   Peter I. Tchaikovsky

Late Afternoon

Can Can   Jacques Offenbach

The End

Humoresque   Antonin Dvorak

CHARACTERS

- **Lady Wisdom** (Prov 1:18–19, 24–31; 5:4, 9, 15–20; 6:6, 13, 32–35; 8:7–8, 10–18; 9:1–6, 9–11; 26:14). Dignified, gracious, courtly in bearing, Lady Wisdom speaks wisely; she knows the people of the town and accurately assesses them. She wears slacks and a solid color, long-sleeved top. Her clothes are name brands. She is quality. She is a lady. She is beautiful.

- **Lady Folly** (Prov 1:7, 22; 9:13–17; 10:1; 17:24–25; 18:2; 19:13; 21:20). Loud, brash, sloppy in bearing. She displays open dislike for Lady Wisdom. She chews gum, and in this way draws attention to herself. She also knows the people in the town; however, she uses that information for blackmail. On stage she twirls her hair, paints her nails, and looks bored at times. In a word, she's cheap. Not only does she wear imitations, she is an imitation. However, she is beautiful in a brassy, hard, over-painted way. As a character, she's fun to play and memorable.

- **Drunkard** (Prov 23:29–35; 20:1). He slouches around the stage. He burps. He waves a bottle. Sometimes he seems sober. He staggers. He has alcohol breath, which nobody likes. He looks very slovenly. He has bruises and his shirt is miss-buttoned. Both Drunkard and Sluggard have day-old beards, an effect that can be achieved by rubbing burnt toast on the face.

- **Sluggard** (Prov 10:4–5, 26; 15:19; 18:9; 19:15, 24; 20:4; 21:25; 22:13; 24:30, 34; 26:13). He sleeps on the floor or wherever he wants. He snores. He loudly turns over. He looks very unkept and sloppy. Like Drunkard, Sluggard has undesirable qualities. He scratches himself.

- **Teddy**, a big Teddy bear, is a silent character on stage. Sluggard and Drunkard sometimes use Teddy as a pillow. Sometimes the actors toss Teddy back and forth. Be sure to let Teddy take a bow at the end of the play. Teddy is on stage when the play begins, propped up at the base of a ladder and facing the audience.

- **Gossip** (Prov 17:1; 16:28; 17:9; 11:13; 26:20; Ps 50:20). She is a busybody, always going hither and thither. She likes whispered conversations, knowing winks, and secret conferences. She goes from person to person on stage. She might mime a cell-phone conversation. She carries a tray and acts as a waitress. Beware of Gossip! Her tongue is lethal; she enjoys destroying lives.

- **Adulteress** (Prov 2:16–18; 5:3, 9, 20; 6:24, 28; 7:5, 10–13, 21). She is beautiful and expensively, somewhat provocatively dressed. Her countenance is hard; she has a cunning look about her. She openly flirts with all the men and instantly sizes up Simple Youth. She wears a boa that she uses in her flirtations; it can hang from Lady Folly's ladder. If the boa drops feathers on stage, leave them. Adultery always leaves a trail.

- **Simple Youth** (Prov 1:8, 11–19). This young man is the "hero" of the Book of Proverbs. He is easily led; at this stage in his life he lacks discernment and discretion. He is gangly and unsure of himself. He is dressed in casual clothes. He wears a baseball cap. He has few lines, mainly because the book of Proverbs is written as advice to him. But he is a good listener and engages in high-fives and bantering with the townsfolk.

- **Satisfied Husband** (Prov 19:22; 31:10–31). This man is the husband of the Proverbs 31 woman. He is prosperous, assured, humorous, well spoken. Because of his prominent position, people listen to him, and he likes that. You will notice that he is a bit pompous. He wears a suit and carries a briefcase. A nice tie and fedora complete his costume.

- **Sign Person**. This is a fun part. Although it can be played by a man or a woman, I tend to think of Sign Person as a woman. She is stylishly, modestly dressed, probably in a short skirt and leggings, a tank top, and a colorful blouse. She also wears a nametag and enters with the other characters. She does not speak during the play, but like Simple Youth watches everything intently. She carries six signs. While the other characters are entering talking, she goes straight to the stage and puts three signs downstage stage right; they are Mid-Morning, Early Afternoon, and The End. She then puts three signs stage left; they are Early Morning, Noon, and Late Afternoon. She stays stage left.

Some Stage Directions: *The lights are bright. The stage contains two ladders downstage, stage right and stage left. Upstage left are big black blocks that the characters use for sitting and speaking. Balancing them stage right are a table and chairs for Gossip's waitressing duties. Lady Wisdom uses the ladder stage right quite a bit. It may be higher than the other one, if desired. There are two chairs and another table downstage left. The two tables have tablecloths and flowers on them, for they represent two coffee houses on the Bult. There can be a large sign on the back wall simply saying* Bult. *In front of the sign is a bench or three straight chairs that form a bench. Drunkard and Adulteress end up there frequently.*

The tune Maple Leaf Rag *announces the play's beginning. The characters enter from a door at the back or side of the auditorium. They make conversation and general noise. They greet the members of the audience and engage them in hellos and handshakes. Sluggard goes downstage, stage left. He lies down facing the audience. Drunkard collapses against a wall facing the audience or lies across the "bench" chairs upstage. Lady Folly and Lady Wisdom take separate paths up to the tops of their ladders. The ladders represent the high places of the city. Satisfied Husband sits in a chair, stage right; he may carry a briefcase. Gossip, a busybody, fusses over everybody; she carries a tray with cups, for she serves as a waitress. She stands behind the table, stage left. Simple Youth enters looking dazed, maybe sipping a soda. Adulteress slinks across the stage, taking in everything, calculating her moves. She alternately drags or dangles the boa. Lady Folly climbs up the other ladder, stage left. Simple Youth sits with his legs over the stage.*

Early Morning

Sign Person walks across the stage from stage left to stage right. *Maple Leaf Rag* is playing and she and the characters keep time to that music. Goodwill abounds. She carries the sign, **Early Morning** for the audience to see. Throughout the play, Sign Person can develop her character to include locomotions like skipping, twirling, or hopping, and emotions like joy, laughter, concern, or even boredom if Satisfied Husband talks too long! She should bring a smile to the audience each time. Once she is at stage right with her other signs, then Lady Wisdom begins talking. The music stops.

Lady Wisdom (*She climbs to the top of the ladder, stage right, and delivers the opening remarks. She gestures expansively to the audience.*)

I am Lady Wisdom. I invite you all to a banquet. I've prepared my meat and mixed my wine. Here! I'm calling to you from the highest point in the city. (*She smiles at Simple Youth.*) You who are simple, come! Come! Eat at my banquet! Drink my wine! I'll teach you to live and to walk in the way of understanding. (*She smiles at Satisfied Husband and he looks pleased.*) Wise men, I invite you as well! For you long to be wiser still! You know that wisdom comes from instruction! The foundation of my teaching is respect for the Lord. The fear of the Lord is the beginning of wisdom. Getting to know the Holy One is the beginning of understanding ourselves. I invite you to know me, Lady Wisdom. Through me your days will be many, and years, happy years, will be added to your life.

Simple Youth (*Remembering his manners and standing, he bows toward Lady Wisdom.*) Thank you, Lady Wisdom. I am new in Potchefstroom. I came to get an education. Is that the same as wisdom? (*The characters listen, smile, and laugh.*) My parents are sacrificing a lot to send me to university. My father gave me much advice. He told me to remember his instruction and commanded me not to forsake my mother's teaching. He told me there would be many choices! He said I would see many lifestyles! He's right! They're here on the Bult! I've already been asked to take part in a carjacking and to waylay people on the N12 highway. But I said I had to study! (*The cast laughs.*)

Lady Wisdom *(Welcoming him with approval.)* You made the right decision to leave those ruffians alone! People like that who plot to get ill-gotten gain end up dead themselves.

Gossip *(A busybody, Gossip cannot be still. She constantly listens, sneaks up on people, winks. Two of her mannerisms are short little steps and "leading" with her nose. Meanwhile, Adulteress comes up to Simple Youth. She walks around him. He watches as she circles him. He is interested. She is interested.)*

Wherever I go there is strife. That's because I enjoy telling the truth about people. I make a point of separating friends. Once they know the truth about each other, they shouldn't be friends! After all, I am the Gossip! *(She flutters away.)*

Adulteress *(She talks both to Simple Youth and Satisfied Husband. She knows she is beautiful.)*

I am the wayward wife. I use beguiling words. I seduce. My husband has a huge belly that falls over his belt. I ignore the covenant we made because I cannot stand him. I have found other friends. Exciting friends. They love death and think they can escape it. I know the paths and the dances that lead to death. I cultivate smooth speech. My lips drip with honey. Come, youths and real men! *(She looks at Simple Youth and Satisfied Husband.)* Give me your strength! Let's enjoy a wayward life together! Come. Come. Let my seductive words convince you of the pleasures of life with me. Come. Let my smooth talk lead you where I know you really want to go. *(Both men, mesmerized, start following her.)*

Lady Wisdom *(Breaking the mood with her words.)* Yes, her lips drip with honey and her speech is smoother than oil, but the way of death she advocates is as bitter as gall. In the end, she turns on her lovers with actions and words sharper than a two-edged sword. *(Flustered, Satisfied Husband and Simple Youth go to one side of the stage while Adulteress goes elsewhere.)*

Mid-Morning

Sign Person crosses the stage carrying the sign, **Mid-Morning**. She keeps in step with the dancers as they dance to *Minuet in G*.

At each dance interlude, the characters are, on the whole, cordial and friendly to each other. After all, they have to live in the same town!

(Dance #1) Minuet in G.

The characters move in a simple kind of dance formation. They walk toward center stage, clap another's hands, turn, and form lines perpendicular to the audience. The women line up on one side, the men on another. They bow and curtsy and dosey-do around each other. Opposite corners can also bow and curtsy to each other. Teddy can tag along.

When the dance is over, the characters go to different sections. Only Sluggard and Lady Folly remain in the same places. Lady Wisdom goes upstage. Gossip goes up to her waitress station; she and Lady Folly like each other a lot. Satisfied Husband returns to his chair and puts his leg up on it and talks from a standing position to the audience. He indicates he does not want to be around Adulteress. However, as an attractive man, he frankly likes her attentions.

Satisfied Husband *(Booming. He can use the whole stage for this speech.)* I'm what you would call a satisfied husband. I have a happy marriage, mainly because my wife works so hard at it. I admit that. *(Laughing at himself.)* I am the husband of the Proverbs 31 woman. She consistently amazes me. Actually I am amazed she chose me. I do not deserve her, and everybody knows it! *(He laughs again.)* You know the proverb that says, "He who finds a good wife receives a blessing from the Lord." Well, the Lord has blessed me and blessed me for years with this woman. *(Expansively.)* Let me tell you about her and about our life together. My wife truly has a noble character. The basis of her character is that she fears the Lord. Together we worship and obey the God of Israel. All our life together she has brought me good. Never has she brought me harm or shame. My total confidence is in her.

Lady Wisdom *(Approvingly.)* The whole town knows that Satisfied Husband and Noble Wife enjoy each other. They are a happy couple. *(Adamantly.)* They do not commit adultery. They keep themselves for each other alone. They rejoice in each other.

Their children are blessed. He compliments her and calls her a graceful deer. They work at their marriage by saving themselves for each other. He is captivated by her love! *(Satisfied Husband nods in agreement.)*

Drunkard *(Waking up. Yawning. Sloppy. Scratching and burping. He slurs his words a bit.)* It's when I'm alone, when everything is quiet that I see strange things and my mind imagines confusing things. That's when I really need another drink. I like drinking so much that when I get in a fight, I don't even know I've been hit.

(He goes to Satisfied Husband pointing a finger, getting in his face. He is belligerent, accusatory.) You! You have your nice house and your big car and your good job! But are you happy? I say you're a hypocrite! I'll laugh in your face and mock you! I have my bottle here, and it's all I need. Yeah, I'm happier than you are. *(Satisfied Husband flinches at Drunkard's bad breath and backs away.)*

Lady Folly *(She has a loud, abrasive voice and an undisciplined, uncouth manner. She winks, motions with her hands, plants seeds of evil in the thinking of all who hear. Her tone is arrogant. Throughout the play, she and Gossip are friendly. They lead each other to various characters. Lady Folly sees Simple Youth as a new convert to her ways—maybe even as a conquest!)*

(Beguilingly.) Hey, Simple Youth! I call out to you! *(He comes to her side.)* What's the value of discipline, I ask you? Nothing! Every person puts on his trousers one leg at a time. There's no difference between us. None. *(She plays with Simple Youth's baseball cap. She leads him to the bench. She seductively crosses and uncrosses her legs. Simple Youth, fascinated, watches her.)*

You know me. I am at the door of my house, my big house. I don't like my neighbor, Lady Wisdom. We happen to reside in the same neighborhood at the top of the hill. She acts as if she's the only elite one, but I'm elite, too. *(She rises. Simple Youth also stands. Lady Folly links her arm with Simple Youth's arm, and they walk toward her ladder.)*

I call out to all that my way is the best. The easy way is the best way. I call out to all who are simple to come to me. I have special favors for those who lack judgment. Come up to my house! I'll really show you how to live. We'll laugh at how hard others work and how much effort they exert. And for what? For nothing! Follow my way and be rich. I know how to get rich quick. I know how to win the lottery! Look at my big house. *(Seductively.)* I'll show you how stolen water is sweet to the taste and food eaten in secret is delicious!

Lady Wisdom *(Snapping the spell Lady Folly has put on Simple Youth and the others.)* Oh, I hate all who speak with such pride and arrogance! Her speech is perverse! Her behavior is that of a scoundrel and villain, for she winks with her eyes, motions with her hands, and plants evil and deceit in hearts. Wherever Lady Folly goes, she stirs up dissension! *(Lady Folly tosses her head and flounces away.)*

Noon

Sign Person crosses the stage bearing the sign, **Noon.** She participates in the dance as she crosses the stage.

(Dance #2) Mexican Hat Dance

(Lady Folly and Lady Wisdom look at each other with distaste and hatred. The characters do another "dance" in that they come to center stage, clap hands, turn, cha-cha, and two-step to the music's rhythm. They then turn and go to other places. All characters take part. Sluggard and Drunkard burp loudly and enjoy it. Gossip goes downstage as does Lady Folly. Satisfied Husband goes up to the ladder, stage right. Drunkard goes to sleep or snoozes on the bench of two or three chairs, upstage. Teddy participates in the dance.)

Sluggard   *(He yawns, belches, rubs his face. His shirt hangs out. He is disheveled and has bad breath.)* I'm Slothful the Sluggard. It's eight o'clock. No. It's noon! Too early to get up! I don't care about getting money. I like the easy life. I like to go to the KFC. I certainly don't like working on the farm during the harvest! That's hot work! I prefer sleeping. *(He stretches and scratches, actions that make others uncomfortable.)*

Once I had a job as a courier. But it was hot work and my boss wanted me to hurry. It's not in my nature to hurry. I stopped for coffees and met my friends. They were right along the way. But my boss fired me and said I was like vinegar to his teeth and smoke to his eyes! *(He goes to Lady Folly and she comforts him. They walk from stage right to stage left arm in arm. She tries to avoid his bad breath.)*

(Sluggard whines. He shares his woes.) I crave a big car. I need a big car. I deserve a big car. Life is terribly unfair to me that I don't have one! So often my way seems to be blocked with thorns. Oh, woe! Life is terribly unfair to me! *(Lady Folly pats his hand and comforts him. He decides to sleep and finds Teddy. Sleep represents escape.)*

Lady Wisdom *(Shaking her head.)* Truly as a door turns on its hinges, Sluggard turns on his bed! *(Exasperated.)* Go to the ant, Sluggard! Learn the ways of the ant and be wise!

Satisfied Husband *(Quickly intervening. He tries to cover an awkward situation and Lady Wisdom's open rebuke by calling attention to himself and talking about his wife.)* Err. What you say, Sluggard, makes me want to keep talking about my wife. Everybody knows my wife enjoys hard work. She has an amazing energy level and cannot be still. She never eats the bread of idleness. She spends her time working instead of gossiping. She looks forward to Monday mornings! *(The other characters, except Lady Wisdom, are a bit bored by his praise of his wife.)*

As a seamstress, she is well-known here in Potch, in Potchefstroom. She makes garments of wool for winter and linen dresses for summer. She enjoys working with her hands. Merchants in town know her as one who looks for bargains of good quality. They save their best for her. We at home eat well because she knows how to cook. We laugh together about this proverb from America: "Kissin' don't last but cookin' do!" *(General laughter. He pats his stomach.)*

Gossip *(She moves around like a busybody. She has a little two-step walk and leads with her nose.)* I think it's my duty in life to repeat a matter over and over throughout Potchefstroom. After all, people should know the truth about their friends and neighbors, don't you think? Sometimes I betray a confidence. But people really should know what's happening here in Potchefstroom, don't you think? *(Emphatically!)* I am the Gossip. And I do my job!

Lady Wisdom *(Shaking her head.)* Truly, the power of death and life resides in the tongue. Gossip spreads death. But my mouth speaks what is true. My lips detest wickedness. All—yes, all!—the words of my mouth are just. Not one of them is crooked or perverse!

Early Afternoon

Sign Person carries the sign, **Early Afternoon,** across the stage and participates in the waltz, using the sign as a partner.

(Dance #3) Waltz of the Flowers

(The characters dance as partners. Lady Folly and Adulteress try to get Satisfied Husband, but he bows and chooses Lady Wisdom. Gossip and Sluggard pair off. Lady Folly nabs Simple Youth. Adulteress ends up with Drunkard but quickly flicks her boa and leaves him. The characters all smile. Teddy becomes the partner of Adulteress. The characters turn and go to different parts of the stage.)

Adulteress *(Taking charge. She puts Teddy down. She tries to be the center of attention at all times. She starts her speech with her hands on her hips.)* I cannot stand staying at home. There's nothing to do! So I dress up and survey the crowd. I go to street corners. I go to the Bult. *(She talks to Satisfied Husband and Simple Youth.)* I'll kiss you in public and call your name again and again! Let my words captivate you! I know you can walk on hot coals in an affair with me! Your feet will not be scorched! Who will ever know if we sleep together? Your wife is as dense as a doorpost, and my husband is away all the time! *(She plays with Satisfied Husband's tie. She seductively pulls the tie and him after her. Intrigued and mesmerized, he follows her.)*

Lady Wisdom *(Again snapping the mood of easy seduction that Adulteress creates.)* The man who commits adultery lacks judgment;

whoever commits adultery destroys himself. *(Satisfied Husband "wakes up" and hurriedly leaves Adulteress. He quickly puts distance between them on the stage.)* His life from then on will be filled with blows and disgrace; his companion becomes shame. The jealous husband will never be his friend or business associate. No amount of money can repair what adultery takes from a marriage.

Sluggard *(Waking up mad.)* You know what I'm really good at? Tearing down things others build. I like the easy way! Vroom! It's gone! Takes no time at all. Then I can go back and sleep. Yeah. I like deep sleep.

(He ponders his life.) You know, I like sleeping better than eating, yeah, better than eating. Sometimes I'll be eating and then won't even bring my fork to my mouth. It takes too much effort. Harvest is such a bore. I refuse to plough my father's field. He can do it himself. He was born to be a farmer. He does work I don't enjoy. *(Adamantly. He holds up his hands.)* See these hands? I don't want calluses! I refuse to let my hands get calluses! I refuse to work! Besides, there could be a lion outside in the field! A fierce lion along the road I travel! After all, this is Africa. Besides, I could be murdered in the streets—even in Potchefstroom!

(Resigned. Defeated.) Who cares—I certainly don't—that thorns overrun my field and my stone wall collapsed when a truck slammed into it? I like to fold my hands in rest and take a little nap. People say poverty will come on me like a robber, but I don't believe them. *(Before he settles into a nap, he gets Teddy from Drunkard.)*

Lady Wisdom *(Sad for the first time in the play. She says these lines slowly, with resignation.)* At the end, Sluggard, your life will end with a groan. You'll wake up one day and realize how worthless your life has been. *(She feigns an improvisation of Sluggard but keeps her dignity.)* You'll say, "How I hated discipline! How my heart spurned correction! I have come to the brink of utter ruin—and everybody in Potchefstroom knows it! They've been laughing at me for years!"

Lady Folly *(Venomous. Spiteful. Her face contorts in rage.)* I despise Lady Wisdom. I hate everything she says. I hate her knowledge. I delight in airing my own opinions. My mother says I have brought her grief because I am a foolish daughter, but I do not believe her. *(She snaps her fingers and looks at the audience. Gossip nods in approval.)*

Late Afternoon

Sign Person dances across the stage carrying the sign, **Late Afternoon.** Simultaneously, the characters line up, join arms for balance, and start kicking to *Can Can.*

(Dance # 4) Can Can

(The characters form a line. They do another "dance," but this one includes kicking, knee lifts, turns, footswitches, and laughter. Teddy is tossed. They separate and move around and up to where they are comfortable. Lady Wisdom ascends the high ladder again. Simple Youth stays on the main level. Adulteress continues to flirt, but to no avail.)

Satisfied Husband *(He may move around on his lines all over stage. He sings some of the words, for he has a great voice!)*

My wife leaves our bed before first light. Her duties begin early. She prepares our breakfast and makes sure our help in the house and on the farm eat a good breakfast, too. Yesterday she left our small holding in Potch early for the Cape because she wants to buy property in the wine district. An agent called her and told her about a small holding near Stellenbosch. The irrigation is good and the access to the main highway is, too. She bought the vineyard quickly and will expand it. Right now she manages our multiple fields and works at her books far into the night.

The lights are so often on in our home that our friends driving by joke that she never sleeps. I'm in bed by 22:00! I tell them my wife has a lot of energy. She works on her sewing projects at night. She weaves beautiful rugs and wall hangings. Her work hangs here in the rector's office at the university. It also hangs in the government buildings in Pretoria.

I love to take her for dinner at Neptune's, here in Potch. She turns heads! Her outfits, which she makes herself, are usually some shade of purple. I tell her she is a royal wife. A quilt she made covers our bed.

Her volunteer work extends to the poor. She works in an outreach to HIV/AIDS victims. She spends an afternoon a week ministering to their needs—feeding them and bathing them. She says she feels close to God when she does this for other human beings.

Gossip   *(Sighing and bored. She interrupts by bustling about. She does not really listen to Satisfied Husband. She likes to talk.)* Lots of times more people need to be involved in a quarrel. After all, it concerns more people than just two! Everybody is kinfolk in Potchefstroom! So I just keep a quarrel going and going until everybody has had his or her say! I know what to do! And I am for equality! I talk about my brothers, too! After all, I am the Gossip! And I do my job well! *(She is very proud of herself.)*

Lady Folly   *(Approvingly.)* I like your attitude, Gossip! We can be friends. I like to hear all the dirt on people! I've heard that your mother is very bitter. She says she is sorry she gave birth to you! She says that listening to you is like living with a constantly dripping water pipe. But I like you! Let's wander all over town and eat like pigs! *(They swagger off together around stage, arm and arm as conspirators.)*

Drunkard   *(He gives an incredibly loud belch. It startles everybody and embarrasses Lady Wisdom. He is belligerent in attitude and full of self-pity.)*

I am Drunkard. Let me tell you my story. I have so much woe. I have so much sorrow. Just give me space or I'll fight you. I'm used to fights—see these bruises? Look at my eyes—they'll tell you that I can drink any one of you under the table. *(He goes around to the men on the stage.)* Yeah. We'll see who can linger over wine or the hard stuff the longest!

Lady Wisdom   *(Speaking sadly. Suddenly a bit tired.)* Drunkard, you have rejected me for years. You have spurned my call and all my rebukes to you. So when calamity overtakes you, as it surely will, when it sweeps over you like a whirlwind, you will be devastated. Then you will look for me, but I will hide from you. You will not find me. Because you have hated knowledge and do not choose to fear the Lord, you will eat the fruit of your own schemes—and die. *(There is silence on stage. Everybody knows she is right.)*

Satisfied Husband *(Again breaking the mood. He tries to diffuse awkward situations.)* I'll admit it freely: Much of my respect in Potch and much of our mutual wealth as a couple come from her work. I'm a magistrate and, yes, respected here in Potch. My job gives me standing and responsibility in the community. *(Proudly.)* I am a judge.

(Expansively.) But I am able to do my job well and devote my whole heart to it because of my noble wife. I trust her completely. My love for her grows daily. As we age together, I see her lovely face as exhibiting strength and dignity. When she speaks, I listen, for she is wise.

Our children, and we have seven, look happy. *(Lady Folly and Gossip gasp and primly twitter when they hear he has seven children!)* They do well in school. They have good manners. Last week we celebrated her birthday. She turned fifty. During the speeches, our children told stories expressing how much they love her. I praised her—though in measure because she looked embarrassed.

When she spoke, she held my hand and praised God for his goodness to us. She quickly led us in a hymn of thanksgiving. That's the way she is. She gives God honor. But I am seeing that he delights to honor her.

Simple Youth *(He bangs on the table, speaks loudly, and gestures with his hands and arms. The other characters look surprised, for they have ignored him most of the day. They have become used to his silences. He points to the other characters. He pauses frequently for emphasis.)* Hey, guys! I've listened to all of you! Thank you for welcoming me to Potchefstroom! I see your lifestyles! I'm making a choice! *(He turns to Lady Wisdom.)* Thank you, Lady Wisdom, for the invitation to your banquet. I accept! I want to learn your ways! *(He bows to Lady Wisdom.)*

Lady Wisdom *(Lady Wisdom is thrilled. She pauses and speaks slowly. She extends her invitation one more time.)* To all of you I say this: Life offers you a choice between Wisdom and Folly. *(She and Lady Folly exchange glances. Lady Folly raises a haughty chin.)* I urge you with all power in me to choose my instruction instead of silver. Value my knowledge rather than the choicest of gold. Again, I invite each one of you. Come, come to my banquet!

(Lady Folly reacts with disdain. She mimics Lady Wisdom by also gesturing to everybody. Adulteress, Sluggard, Drunkard, Gossip slowly join her by the stairs during this last scene. They speak and then join her. They try to lure Simple Youth one more time, each with a key line. Simple Youth gradually becomes more and more certain that his choice of Lady Wisdom's way is the best. He stands taller and taller as he refuses each character's way.)

Lady Folly *(Beguilingly. She plays again with Simple Youth's baseball cap.)* Simple Youth, I'll show you the easy way! *(He retreats from her and straightens his cap. She glares at him.)*

Sluggard *(His words still slurred.)* Simple Youth, why work hard? We can tear down things others build! *(Simple Youth smiles sadly and pats him on the shoulder. Sluggard ambles away.)*

Adulteress *(Showing her charms and speaking with a silky voice.)* Simple Youth . . . *(He rejects her, and she is offended.)*

Drunkard *(Staggering and holding his beloved bottle.)* Ah, let's go have a drink! *(Simple Youth says no, but with compassion, for he sees Drunkard as a very sad character. Drunkard staggers away.)*

Gossip *(Fussing at Simple Youth and shaking her finger at him.)* Simple Youth! People will talk about you if you go to her banquet! *(Simple Youth throws back his head and laughs. He has grown up!)*

(These characters—Gossip, Lady Folly, Adulteress, Sluggard, and Drunkard—go upstage stage and "freeze" with their backs to the audience. Simple Youth and Satisfied Husband remain with Lady Wisdom. They walk with her slowly from upstage center stage to downstage center stage.)

Lady Wisdom *(The two men kneel on either side of Lady Wisdom, their profiles to the audience. Lady Wisdom puts her hands on their shoulders. She delivers her speech facing the audience.)* Ah, Simple Youth and Satisfied Husband, the wisdom I give you is more precious than rubies. Nothing you can possibly desire compares with my gift of wisdom! In me, reside counsel and sound judgment. I give understanding and power. By me and me alone, rulers make just laws and kings reign. By me, nobles rule the earth. With me are enduring riches and honor. I love those who love me. Those who seek me, find me. Yes. I love those who love me. Those who seek me, find me.

Sign Person comes across the stage for the last time carrying the sign, **The End**.

The characters assemble in a line and dance to *Humoresque*. During the music, they dance and bow. Teddy takes a bow as well.

QUESTIONS FOR CONSIDERATION AND DISCUSSION

1. Which character appealed to you the most and why?

2. What did you learn from taking part in this performance either as an actor or as a member of the audience?

3. Satisfied Husband chooses to go to Lady Wisdom's banquet. But what if, as a busy and prominent man, he had decided not to attend? What might that decision indicate in his life?

4. What are the attractions of Lady Folly?

5. What are the attractions of the lifestyle Lady Wisdom offers?

6. Why do you think Sluggard and Drunkard choose to remain in lifestyles that will eventually lead to death?

7. Which character would you like to play on stage?

8. What is the book of Proverbs teaching us today about life?

Chapter 3

When Mary Tells Joseph

A Play Based on Matthew 1:18–19

INTRODUCTION

This play looks at a summary in the biblical text, Matt 1:18–19.[3] The summary discloses that Joseph learns of Mary's pregnancy and chooses to divorce her. The play, based on this summary, investigates a way he may have learned of her pregnancy, that is, from Mary herself.[4] The play combines both scholarship and the standard literary features of a drama—character, conflict, plot, setting, point of view, tone, and dialogue.[5] The play encourages and engages the imagination of the cast and the audience.[6]

CHARACTERS AND SPECIFICS

Announcer: He or she is a modern person in modern dress

Mary: A young woman betrothed to Joseph; she is intelligent, pretty, and graceful

Joseph: A carpenter in Nazareth; he is bearded and handsome and a bit older than Mary

Time: Daytime. About 4 BC

Place: The carpentry shop and home of Joseph in Nazareth of Galilee, a Roman province

Set: A carpenter's shop with wooden tools and wooden imple-
ments like a yoke for oxen and a shepherd's staff. Wooden saw-
horses with lumber on them are upstage left and upstage right
and are part of Joseph's home and shop. Simple wooden tools
are spread on them. Two wooden benches adorn center stage.
There is ample room to move around the wooden furniture on
the stage.[7] An imaginary door is downstage left. A black stage
curtain marks the horizontal upstage boundary of the single
room stone house.

Costumes: Mary and Joseph wear sandals and old, loose, long clothes.
Mary wears a graceful head covering. Joseph's hands are those
of a working man.

THE PLAY BEGINS

*(Mary is upstage left with her back to the audience. Joseph is
stage right with his back to the audience. Both are frozen. The
Announcer enters carrying a Bible. The Announcer greets the
audience warmly.)*

Announcer: The Holy Scriptures contain many silences. Often a writer
squeezes together events and summarizes them. The scriptures in both testaments are known for their brevity, their con-
ciseness. This play investigates one such silence in the Gospel
of Matthew.[8] The silence involves when Mary tells Joseph she
is pregnant with the Son of God.[9] This short play relies on
supplemental information about the birth of Jesus the Messiah from the Gospel of Luke.[10] Listen to the summary from
the Gospel of Matthew.[11]

(The Announcer opens the Bible.) Matthew 1:18–19.[12] "This is
how the birth of Jesus Christ came about: His mother Mary
was pledged to be married to Joseph, but before they came
together, she was found to be with child through the Holy
Spirit. Because Joseph her husband was a righteous man and

did not want to expose her to public disgrace, he had in mind to divorce her quietly."[13] *(The Announcer closes the Bible.)*

The scene is the home of Joseph of Nazareth. *(Joseph turns to the audience and quietly starts working.)* It is a small stone house with a dirt floor.[14] The door is over there. *(The Announcer gestures stage left.)* Joseph is a carpenter. The time is around 4 BC. Herod is king in Judea. The Romans occupy the land. *(Mary turns and walks toward the imaginary door, downstage left, and starts knocking. The Announcer turns and smiles.)* Ah, someone is at the door.

(The Announcer walks stage left and opens the door. If the Announcer is a man, he bows to Mary. If the Announcer is a woman, she nods her head. Mary enters; she wears a headdress/cowl gracefully over her head. The Announcer leaves and returns either to a seat in the audience or goes off stage. The imaginary door remains open.)

Mary:	*(Mary enters Joseph's shop.)* Shalom, Joseph.[15] May I see you for a moment?[16] *(Joseph stops, turns, puts down his tools, smiles. He quickly comes to greet Mary.)*
Joseph:	Peace to you as well, Mary.[17] It is wonderful to see you.[18] *(They are a little awkward with each other. Joining hands they twirl around center stage. They obviously want to run to each other's arms but do not.)* I am so glad you are back from visiting your relative Elizabeth.[19] You left so suddenly[20] and you returned yesterday, is that not right? *(Joseph tenderly removes her headdress/cowl from her head and lets it fall gracefully on her shoulders.)*
Mary:	Yes, I did. It was a good trip.[21] Elizabeth is pregnant and is due any day now.[22]
Joseph:	I had heard that! What awesome news! And at her age![23]
Mary:	*(Encouraged.[24])* Yes! The Lord is truly moving again in the lives of his people!
Joseph:	*(His shoulders sag.)* Israel has waited so long! We are so oppressed by the Romans! *(He makes a spitting noise in disgust. Mary notices. She is calm and gentle. She moves slightly away.)* The Messiah truly needs to come! *(Mary nods a bit knowingly.)*

Yes. Well. Tell me about your trip.[25] Won't you sit down? *(He smiles and steps closer to Mary.)* I'm sure you told her about our wedding.[26] It's next month![27]

(He seats her on one of the benches.)

Mary: Yes.[28] We did talk a lot about our wedding. Elizabeth and I became quite close, Joseph, probably because wonderful things are happening to both of us.[29]

Joseph: Yes! She's expecting a child—

Mary: *(Interrupting.)* Yes, a son!

Joseph: *(Continuing.)* –and at her great age.[30]

Mary: Yes! It's quite a miracle for her and Zechariah! They are known as upright people in the sight of God.[31]

Joseph: *(Pausing, considering, and cocking his head.)* Ah, Mary, you sound so certain that it is a son. You sound as if you know it is![32]

Mary: *(Emphatically and confidently.)* Well, yes, I do. It's all involved in what I have to tell you. Elizabeth told me I had to talk to you.[33]

Joseph: *(Joseph is very pleased that she is here. He obviously enjoys her company and loves her.)* Well, tell me about your stay! You left so suddenly and were there about three months, right?

Mary: *(Mary rises.)* Yes. You see, Joseph, an angel told Zechariah that he and Elizabeth would have a son.[34] The meeting took place when Zechariah was serving in the Temple.[35] Elizabeth and Zechariah are to name the child John.[36]

(She takes off her headdrress/cowl and neatly folds it. She places it on the corner of the work center, stage left. It remains there until Joseph picks it up again at the end of the play.)

Joseph: An angel?[37] *(Laughing and rising.)* Our people have not seen angels since Gabriel interpreted a vision for Daniel.[38] It concerned the end of time. Mmm. Zechariah is quite old, Mary, has he lost his mind? *(Joseph walks stage left toward his other work center.)*

Mary:	*(Laughing and following him.)* No! He hasn't lost his mind, but he has lost something else.
Joseph:	*(Laughing, too.)* Really! What?
Mary:	*(Slowly and looking at Joseph carefully.)* He's lost his speech.
Joseph:	What? His speech? Why?
Mary:	*(Quickly.)* The angel—and it was Gabriel—told Zechariah that he and Elizabeth would have a son in their old age.[39] Zechariah did not believe it, and the angel silenced him.[40]
Joseph:	Amazing!
Mary:	*(Laughing.)* Yes! He's been listening to Elizabeth now for nine months! The angel said he would be silenced until the boy was born.
Joseph:	*(Still laughing.)* Well, good! He used to be so pompous![41] *(He walks stage right toward the other work center.)*
Mary:	He has totally changed. I would say he has thought a lot about his encounter with Gabriel. Elizabeth and I would be working around the house and Zechariah would sit at the table, listen to us, and grunt every now and again. Every time he grunted, Elizabeth would hug and kiss him.
Joseph:	*(Laughing.)* Well, good! But regarding angels, I'm not so sure! I never have had an encounter with an angel! So I'll suspend judgment about Zechariah's mental competency!
Mary:	*(Slowly.)* Mmm. But Joseph, the evidence is there: Elizabeth is pregnant and expecting her child momentarily. Doesn't that verify that Zechariah saw Gabriel?
Joseph:	Well, I don't know. It's all pretty far-fetched to me. *(Gesturing around the shop.)* I deal in realities like hard wood. I know what I make.
Mary:	*(Mary goes toward him. A work center separates them.)* You do such a good job, Joseph; that's one reason I have grown to love you so much. *(Joseph is very pleased. He comes around the work center to her and takes her hands. Mary looks at him intently.)* Joseph, I have something to tell you.

Joseph: *(Enjoying holding her hands.)* Tell me, Mary! But first let me guess! It's about how you'll redecorate my house? *(Joseph gestures around his stone house. Mary laughs shakes her head after each guess.)* No? You're going to ask how I like a leg of lamb cooked?

Mary: *(Laughing.[42])* You like a lot of spices!

Joseph: *(Nodding.)* Right. I know! You're going to talk about the wine for our wedding that your father has been saving!

Mary: *(Laughing but showing some concern.)* No, Joseph, although those are all good guesses! *(She pauses and lifts her head to him and draws back a little.)* Joseph, what I have to tell you is this: I also saw Gabriel.[43]

Joseph: *(Thinking she is joking.[44])* My goodness! It runs in the family! Does everybody on your side see angels?[45]

Mary: *(Seriously but smiling.)* No, not everybody, just the ones Gabriel visits.

Joseph: *(Dropping her hands and stepping back.)* The ones Gabriel visits? *(His voice trails off.)*

Mary: Yes, Joseph. Gabriel visited me.[46] *(Joseph is amazed. He walks around. Mary gives him time. She's stationary.)* He told me things, Joseph, amazing things.

Joseph: *(Seriously. Suddenly knowing he's about to hear something extraordinary.)* What things, Mary?

Mary: He told me things that made me rejoice. I must say this: "From now on all generations will call me blessed! The Mighty One has done great things for me and holy is his name!"[47] Yes, that is what I have been singing now for three months.[48]

Joseph: Well, Mary, tell me what the angel said.

Mary: *(Walking around to give herself time.)* He greeted me by saying I had found favor with God. Oh, first of all he told me not to fear.[49] I guess that was out of courtesy because he startled me; he arrived so suddenly.

Joseph: *(Mystified, running his hand through his hair.)* An angel arrived suddenly. Mmm. What were you doing, Mary?

Mary:	*(With bravado. She is very positive.)* Well, nothing much. Just sort of sitting and sewing.[50] *(She goes to a bench, sits, and pantomimes the encounter.)* I remember dropping my sewing.[51] It was then he told me not to be afraid and that I had found favor with God.
Joseph:	*(Also with bravado. He is very positive. He speedily comes to her at the bench and kneels. He takes her hand.)* Well, of course, you would find favor with God! Everybody knows you are the best young woman in all Nazareth! Everybody respects you.[52]
Mary:	Mmm. Mmm.
Joseph:	*(Confident now and in control.)* Well, what else did the angel say?
Mary:	*(Taking a deep breath and looking at Joseph.)* The angel said this: "You will be with child and give birth to a son and you are to give him the name Jesus."
Joseph:	*(Relieved and pleased. Joseph is choosing to believe her. He rises and walks during these lines as he thinks through what Mary has told him.)* My goodness, Mary! We will have a son! That's wonderful news! It's interesting that we are to name him Jesus! His name means The Lord Saves! What a famous son he will be. Think of it! Our son!
Mary:	Yes, he will be famous, Joseph. *(She looks at him intently.)*
Joseph:	There's more, isn't there, Mary. *(She nods. He senses the soberness of the event.)* Well, tell me.
Mary:	*(She begins to walk quickly. She touches her head and then her belly. She seems to be talking to herself. She ends with a prayer with her hands raised and her eyes toward heaven.)* Elizabeth said to just tell him straight. Oh, God, be my help![53]
Mary:	Let me continue what the angel said. The angel said that the son I will bear, Jesus, will be great and will be called *(She takes a deep breath.)*, will be called the Son of the Most High.[54]
Joseph:	*(Taken aback. Absolutely amazed. He looks around and glances toward the open door. He whispers loudly.)* What? Mary! You are speaking blasphemy!

Mary:	*(Positively. Honestly. Forthrightly.)* No, I am not! I am telling you the truth. I'm telling you what happened. Please believe me, Joseph. *(Pausing, she slowly continues.)* Elizabeth and Zechariah did.
Joseph:	*(He moves away, stays standing, and folds his arms across his chest.)* Continue.
Mary:	*(Understanding the body language.)* The angel kept saying wonderful things about this son, Jesus. He said, "The Lord God will give him the throne of his father David, and he will reign over the house of Jacob forever; his kingdom will never end."
Joseph:	Well, you and I both are from the house and lineage of David.[55] My line comes through his son Solomon and yours through Solomon's brother Nathan, also David's son.[56]
Mary:	Yes, Solomon and Nathan were the sons of David and Bathsheba.
Joseph:	*(Musing. Talking to himself. Walking around. He begins to talk things out slowly.)* So if what you say is true, God is on the move and will restore the Kingdom of Israel once again![57] Oh, Mary, this is wonderful news! And we are to be the parents of the King! *(Joseph muses. His joy is apparent! He walks around shaking his head and lifting his hands in amazement. He is stage right. In jubilation he claps his hands and comes toward Mary. She is center stage. He grabs her around the waist, twirls her, shoulder to shoulder, once or twice. Releases her. He does a grapevine step toward stage left. His hands are in the air. He claps his hands. He twirls by himself once or twice and ends facing the audience. Mary watches, stationary.)*
Joseph:	Oh, Mary! Mary! I believe you! You could not have made me happier! The King of Israel is coming![58] God will restore Israel! God will restore Israel through us![59] *(Joseph continues to be very happy. Mary is very silent. Joseph notices. He lowers his hands and turns to her.)* Mary, there is more, isn't there?
Mary:	Yes. *(She turns to Joseph.)* Joseph, my betrothed, my darling, I must tell you what more the angel said.
Joseph:	*(Smiling and very happy.)* Continue! I believe you! I am excited!

Mary: Joseph, the angel did not mention you.[60] *(Joseph is startled.)*

Joseph: What? I don't understand.

Mary: *(She speaks slowly.)* I asked how I could have a son since I am a virgin.[61]

Joseph: *(Kindly, taking her hands.)* Mary, I have no doubt you are a virgin.[62] I trust you completely. The whole town knows your character. Ah, we will be great parents of the great king!

Mary: Yes. Well, I asked how I could have a son since I am a virgin.[63] The angel answered that the Holy Spirit will come upon me.[64]

Joseph: What? *(Dropping her hands.)* What does that mean? "The Holy Spirit will come upon" you?

Mary: *(Patiently and trying to understand it herself.)* Well, it's hard to explain, but it happened. Let me continue telling you what the angel told me. The angel said, "The Holy Spirit will come upon you, and the power of the Most High will overshadow you. So the holy one to be born will be called the Son of God."

Joseph: *(Puzzled, drawing away.)* What? "The Most High will overshadow you? So the holy one to be born will be called the Son of God."[65] What do these statements mean?

Mary: I will tell you. But let me continue what the angel said. Then the angel immediately told me that my relative Elizabeth was going to have a child in her old age and was in her sixth month. It was as if Elizabeth's pregnancy was to be a sign that everything the angel said to me was true.

Joseph: Well, Elizabeth is pregnant.

Mary: *(Taking a deep breath, walking over to him.)* Joseph, this is what I must tell you. I am pregnant.[66]

Joseph: *(Astonished!)* What?[67] *(Many emotions cross his face. Disbelief. Amazement. Anger, especially anger. He backs away from Mary. He storms around the stage. He rubs his hand through his hair. He returns to Mary.)* Pregnant? You? Who has done this?[68] Who has defiled my betrothed?[69]

Mary: No man has defiled me. No one has raped me. I am still a virgin.[70]

Joseph:	*(Loudly. Beginning to show anger.)* But how can you be pregnant?[71]
Mary:	*(Also loudly.)* It was as the angel said. The Holy Spirit came upon me. The power of the Most High overshadowed me. I am pregnant. I am in my third month. I am a virgin.[72]
Joseph:	*(Stunned.)* That's impossible![73] *(Slowly.)* I, I do not believe you. I cannot believe you.
Mary:	I am pregnant. I am a virgin. I am in my third month.[74]
Joseph:	*(Pleading.)* Mary, Mary! We are pledged to be married! In Israel, that is the same as being married![75] We have not come together—and I was so looking forward to our wedding night when I could make you my own.
Mary:	*(Blushing.)* Yes, yes, I have dreamed of that, too.
Joseph:	*(Angry again. Laughing in a sneering way.)* Yet you are pregnant! You say you are in your third month. You say you are a virgin. A virgin! Ha![76]
Mary:	*(Proudly. Honestly.)* No man has known me. I have been faithful to you, my betrothed.[77] Yes, I am a virgin. Yes, I am pregnant.
Joseph:	*(Almost screaming.)* You lie! What you say is impossible![78]
Mary:	*(Also loudly, but honestly and with confidence.)* No! And no again! Joseph, Zechariah and Elizabeth believe me.[79] *(Desperately.)* Zechariah went to the Isaiah scroll and rolled it out. He pointed to an obscure prophecy from Isaiah and indicated I should share it with you: "Therefore the Lord himself will give you a sign: The virgin will be with child and will give birth to a son, and will call him Immanuel."[80]
Joseph:	*(Musing.)* Immanuel, God with us.[81] *(With derision.)* Ha! How can God be with us when he has dashed my dreams? How can God be with us when you have brought shame to my name and to your family's name? Mary! Mary! You know the law!
Mary:	Yes, every girl in Israel knows the law from Deuteronomy. Every man, too.

Together: *(Turning and facing the audience.)* "If a man is found sleeping with another man's wife, both the man who slept with her and the woman must die. You must purge the evil from Israel."[82]

Joseph: *(Facing Mary.)* There is more law from Deuteronomy. Mary, were you in town when the man defiled you? You could have cried out and screamed for protection.[83]

Mary: I have not been defiled by a man. I have not been defiled in the city. I did not need to cry out.[84]

Joseph: *(Desperately.)* There is still more law from Deuteronomy. Were you defiled in the countryside? I know you love to walk and pick the wildflowers. Did a man meet you in the countryside, in a place far from the town? In a place where no one would hear your cries?[85]

Mary: No. I always go into the countryside with my friends; I am never alone. I was not defiled by a man. I did not need to cry for protection.

Joseph: *(He sits.)* Because we have been pledged in marriage for more than a year, another law in Deuteronomy cannot apply to you.[86] There is no way for the man who defiled you to pay the fifty shekels to your father and marry you, you, the violated one.[87]

Mary: *(She kneels before him and looks up at his face. He turns away.)* I have not been violated. I am a virgin. I am pregnant. *(Brokenly.)* And, and, I love you so very much, Joseph.[88]

Joseph: *(Shouting.)* Stoning, Mary, stoning![89] *(Mary lifts her chin and looks levelly at Joseph. Joseph adopts a pleading attitude.)* Mary, the law for a betrothed woman is the same as that for a married woman. Mary, you are deceived! Mary, admit it to me: You broke the Law! You committed adultery![90]

Mary: No, Joseph. I cannot lie.[91] I am a virgin. No man has come near me. I am pregnant.[92]

Joseph: *(With derision.)* And you are pregnant. Who can possibly believe you? Who can possibly believe your, er, story, your explanation?

Mary: *(Lifting her chin again. Composed. Smiling while remembering a happy memory.)* Elizabeth did without my saying a word.[93]

Joseph: *(A derisive grunt.)* Elizabeth!

Mary: *(Knowing the battle, so to speak, is lost, but still calm, gracious, and loving.)* As soon as I arrived, Elizabeth started talking. Actually she started shouting![94]

Joseph: *(Patronizingly.)* Well, what did she say?

Mary: *(Remembering a good memory, she smiles with fondness.)* Elizabeth said to me, "Blessed are you among women, and blessed is the child you will bear!"[95] Then Elizabeth wondered something very unusual. She said, "Why am I so favored, that the mother of my Lord should come to me?"[96]

Joseph: "The mother of my Lord"? *(Aghast.)* Mary, she is calling you the mother of God![97]

Mary: *(Slowly.)* Yes, I guess she is.[98] I hadn't really thought of it that way. But yes, that is what she was saying.[99] I agree. It is amazing.[100]

Joseph: Mary, everything you say about Elizabeth is against our culture. You are the younger! She is the elder! You should be honoring her![101] Again, you are deceived, deceived!

Mary: *(Sadly because the man she loves does not understand.)* No, I am not deceived. I agree that what I am telling you is hard to understand. Then something funny happened. *(Mary's face softens.)* Elizabeth started holding her belly. She started laughing! There was lots of activity in her belly![102]

Joseph: *(Not understanding.)* How so?

Mary: Elizabeth told me that as soon as I called out her name, the baby in her womb started leaping for joy! She was filled with the Holy Spirit and started prophesying.[103]

Joseph: *(Incredulous.)* Prophesying? No woman has prophesied in Israel since Huldah in good king Josiah's time.[104]

Mary: *(Confidently. Straightening her shoulders and lifting her chin.)* Yes, indeed. Elizabeth prophesied this about me: "Blessed is she who has believed what the Lord has said to her will be accomplished!"[105]

Joseph: It's almost the same as what you said the angel said.

Mary: Yes. The angel greeted me by calling me highly favored. Their similar words and attitude toward me give me courage to go on.

Joseph: *(Suddenly thinking there might be a way out of this dilemma. He loves her and here exhibits a beseeching manner.)* Mary. Mary. Maybe you are not pregnant. I'll give you a chance. Young girls don't have regular cycles. Let's agree to this: We'll wait and see.[106]

Mary: Joseph, I cannot agree to that because I already agreed to something else.

Joseph: *(Sternly.)* What did you agree to, Mary? You know that I as your betrothed am to be consulted on your vows. [107]

Mary: *(Slowly.)* Well, when the angel came to me, he told me what I've told you. I was troubled. I was silent. I kept looking up at him and down at my hands. He gave me time to consider a response. *(Sighing and laughing.)* I felt as if all creation held its breath.

Joseph: *(Slowly.)* Well, what did you say?

Mary: *(Looking at Joseph.)* I told the angel this: "I am the Lord's servant. May it be to me as you have said."[108] Then I curtsied and bowed my head. I don't know why I did that, but I felt as if I were in the presence of royalty. *(Laughs quietly and kindly while Joseph looks on and shakes his head.)*

Joseph: *(Pausing.)* Well, what happened next?

Mary: Then the angel left me, and I decided to go quickly to see Elizabeth.[109] *(They look at each other. Joseph paces. It is evident that he is a man with conflicting emotions. Gradually his face hardens. Mary sees it and raises her chin.)*

Joseph: Mary, I could have you stoned. *(Mary is alarmed but nods her head.)*

Mary: Oh, Joseph, no. Please believe me![110] How can I convince you that I am telling the truth?[111] When I told these things to Zechariah and Elizabeth, Zechariah found another passage in the Isaiah scroll.

Joseph: *(Petulantly.)* Well, what is it?

Mary: *(Quietly, confidently.)* The Lord is speaking. The Lord says, "Behold, I will do a new thing."[112]

Joseph: *(Shaking his head and his hand at her.)* No![113] There is no "new thing"! You have committed adultery against me. I dissolve our marriage contract because of your unfaithfulness. That is my verdict. I will have a divorce decree written privately.[114] You are free to go—*(Derisively.)*—to go back to your lover![115] Leave me. Leave my house![116] You, the one I loved so much! You have made your father's name an abomination in Israel.[117]

Mary: *(Crying.)* Oh, Joseph! Oh, Joseph! No! You are a just man.[118]

Joseph: It is because I am a just man that I cannot marry you.[119] I cannot say the child is mine.[120] *(Derisively. Brokenly. Defiantly.)* The only "new thing" I will believe is if an angel comes to me, too.[121] *(Mary leaves quickly, obviously broken.[122] She exists through the open, imaginary door. She freezes with her back to the audience, upstage stage left. Joseph watches her go and notices that she has left her headdress/cowl. He grabs it, reaches out to the doorway. But she has gone. He holds the garment against him, buries his face in it, and collapses in tears. He freezes. The Announcer enters.)*

Announcer: Luckily, the story does not end that way.[123] Yes, Joseph sets his terms, and God meets them.[124] An angel visits Joseph, too.[125] Listen as Matthew continues the story.[126]

(*The Announcer opens the Bible.*) Matthew 1:20–25: "But after he had considered this, an angel of the Lord appeared to him in a dream and said, 'Joseph son of David, do not be afraid to take Mary home as your wife, because what is conceived in her is from the Holy Spirit.[127] She will give birth to a son, and you are to give him the name Jesus,[128] because he will save his people from their sins.'

All this took place to fulfill what the Lord had said through the prophet: 'The virgin will be with child and will give birth to a son, and they will call him Immanuel—which means, 'God with us.'"

When Joseph woke up, he did what the angel of the Lord had commanded him and took Mary home as his wife.[129] But he had no union with her until she gave birth to a son.[130] And he gave him the name Jesus."[131] (*The Announcer closes the Bible.*)

You know, the Bible in this passage gives another summary of a silence.[132] It does not record in detail the angel's encounter with Joseph in a dream.[133] It does not record Joseph's conversation with Mary. It does not recount when Joseph tells Mary of his own encounter with an angel. It summarizes all these meetings. But the Bible invites us to imagine them.[134]

(*A pantomime begins for Joseph and Mary. The Announcer watches, speaks slowly to the audience, and allows time for the pantomime to take place.*) From the biblical text we see that Joseph must have believed the angel.[135] (*Joseph raises his head, listens, and indicates agreement.*) Joseph must have gone to Mary. (*Joseph gets up, runs through the imaginary door, and walks to Mary. She turns*). He must have told her of the encounter. (*Joseph pantomimes the dream.*)

Joseph must have asked for forgiveness.[136] (*Joseph kneels and looks up at Mary.*) And Mary must have given her forgiveness.[137] (*Mary indicates her forgiveness; she caresses his bowed head. Joseph rises, relieved. Joining hands, they twirl. Mary smiles. They stop. Joseph bows and offers his arm.*[138] *Mary takes it. Together they come through the open door and join the Announcer at center stage.*)

And the story goes on.[139] (*All three bow.*)

QUESTIONS FOR CONSIDERATION AND DISCUSSION

1. What are some new insights this drama gave you about Mary and Joseph?

2. In past productions, members of the audience frequently are in tears. Why do you think this is so?

3. Put yourself in Mary's shoes. What would you have done?

4. Put yourself in Joseph's shoes. What would you have done?

5. Discuss the importance of supernatural elements like dreams and a visit by an angel.

6. Why do Matthew and Luke stress Mary's virginity?

7. Why is her virginity an important doctrine in Christianity?

CHAPTER 4

Astonishment and Joy
Luke 1 as Told from the Perspective of Elizabeth

This chapter, a dramatic, scholarly monologue, examines the events that Luke 1 recounts and retells them from the viewpoint of Elizabeth, the elderly wife of Zechariah, a priest.[140] The play uses a literary methodology and presents an eyewitness account. Luke 1 frames its central events from a female and gynocentric perspective.[141] As a named participant in the infancy narrative in Luke 1, Elizabeth should figure predominantly in scholarly articles and sermons. Surprisingly, she does not. Instead scholarly, lectionary, and congregational attention focuses primarily on Zechariah, Gabriel, and Mary, the chapter's three other speaking characters. Consequently, this play seeks to showcase, honor, and analyze Elizabeth, an overlooked yet pivotal character in Luke's gospel. Via a dramatic monologue, it lets her speak of the astonishing recent events in her life and thereby invites readers and hearers to share her joy, surely a singular theme in Luke's gospel.

SETTING AND PRELIMINARY INSTRUCTIONS

Setting: The scene is the small, stone home of Zechariah and Elizabeth. The stage is bare except for a rustic wooden table, downstage stage right, and a wooden bench, stage left. Elizabeth works between them for her monologue.

The **Announcer** and six other people come on stage. They form a line facing the audience, and all have scripts in uniform black books. Elizabeth also enters and stands immobile upstage left with her back to the audience.

Announcer: Hello. You are about to see and hear a dramatic monologue based on Luke 1.[142] We will first read the chapter as it is rendered in the NIV, the New International Version.

The **Announcer** begins with Luke 1:1–4.

> The other six follow with these passages: Luke 1:5–25; 26–38; 39–45; 46–56; 57–66; and 67–80. When the six have finished, they bow and exit the stage together. The Announcer remains on stage.

Announcer

As you just heard, the chapter's key characters are Zechariah a priest; Gabriel, an angel; Elizabeth, the wife of Zechariah; Mary, the kinswoman of Elizabeth; and John, the infant son of Zechariah and Elizabeth.[143]

We have been invited today to the home of Elizabeth and Zechariah.[144] It is in the hill country of Judea. Imagine[145] with me their small, simple stone house in a small village.[146] It has wooden furniture. (*The Announcer gestures stage left and stage right.*) The view from a window looks out on a pasture where sheep graze.[147] (*The Announcer gestures toward the audience and smiles.*)

The time is around 4 BC. Herod is king in Judea. The hated Romans occupy the land.[148]

A great event has just taken place in their small village. Elizabeth will tell you about it.[149] (*The Announcer goes upstage stage left and holds open an imaginary door. Elizabeth turns and enters. They bow as she comes center stage. The Announcer exits.*)

Elizabeth enters

Elizabeth enters from upstage stage left.[150] *She has just nursed John, her infant son of eight days, and put him down for a nap. A separate room where John sleeps is stage left. She wears a new shawl.*[151] *She is about sixty-eight years old and still lovely and energetic; she bustles. She is full of joy. She has an expressive, mobile face.*

Introduction

(Elizabeth enters smiling. She exudes joy. She has fully recovered from the birth of her son. She greets the members of the audience warmly, confidently. She uses the full stage throughout her monologue.) Hello. I'm Elizabeth.[152] I am so glad you're here! My baby son, John, is asleep. He was born last week and circumcised today. Zechariah, my husband, is in town talking, talking, talking! *(She smiles and shakes her head lovingly.)* Mary, my kinswoman, left two weeks ago. The house is deserted, and I have a chance to tell you a bit about what has happened in our lives.[153]

I'll start with who we are, our background.[154] Then I'll tell you about Zechariah's experience in the Temple nine months ago. I'll talk about our marriage—over the years and what it is now. Mary visited us; you surely want to know about her. And then I'll come around to what happened to-day at the circumcision.[155] It has all been so unexpected![156] I am astonished at the work of the Holy One of Israel. I am full of joy because I and my family figure in his ongoing plan.[157] Oh, and this is my new shawl.[158] Zechariah gave it to me today in honor of our son's birth.[159] *(She touches her shawl to her cheek and smiles; it is a loving gesture.)*

Our Background

(Elizabeth walks and smiles.) I married at age thirteen. That was fifty-five years ago. I married a member of my tribe, the tribe of Levi.[160] *(Proudly.)* I am a descendant of Aaron, the brother of Moses.[161] I married Zechariah, who belongs to the priestly division of Abijah.[162] He was seventeen, and, oh, so handsome! *(She smiles fondly.)*

(Elizabeth addresses the guests in her house and gestures.) We live in the hill country of Judea in a village; in your terms it is about five miles west of Jerusalem.[163] We are people of integrity and some education.[164] We both can read and write. This is very important, and you will see why shortly. Zechariah as a priest reads the scrolls and studies them.[165] We determined immediately in our marriage to walk uprightly in the sight of God and each other. We decided to observe all the Lord's commands and regulations. We have tried with all our heart to please him.[166]

(She chooses her words slowly, carefully, courageously.) I guess any marriage has its hurting point, its tender or sensitive issue. Ours was my barrenness.[167] We prayed. I fasted. We sought the Lord. Month after month.

Year after weary year. No child. Here in Israel, childlessness is considered a curse.[168] *(Slowly, sadly.)* I was blamed.[169] My neighbors talked about me first behind my back and then to my face. Over the years, my friendships dwindled.[170] *(This is obviously very hard to say. Elizabeth cries; the hurt is raw and real.)*

(Elizabeth is very concerned; her mobile face expresses much sorrow. She continues bravely.) I was afraid Zechariah would divorce me. You probably know the story of Hannah. She longed for a child and her husband, Elkanah, took a second wife, Peninnah, in order to have children. Peninnah had many children and made Hannah's life miserable.[171] The Lord heard Hannah's prayer and she gave birth to Samuel. Zechariah never divorced me, and for that I am so grateful. Instead he chose to share my shame. But we could not meet each other's eyes; for years there was silence between us.[172] *(She hangs her head.)*

Zechariah

(Elizabeth seems to shake herself. She smiles and touches the shawl with tenderness.) Now I will tell you a bit about Zechariah.[173] I call him an old coot![174] And he is! *(She laughs gently with kindness; she obviously loves and understands her husband.)* He has a bristly white beard. He has to have the last word! He is always right! Over the years he became more and more precise.

(She pauses and cocks her head.) Well, those are the ways he was. Zechariah, my husband, is much different now. But I get ahead of myself. I've studied my husband for years and tried to please him. He wants his meals on time, and his priestly garments laundered just so! On the one hand, he is scholar and a man of prayer. He loves the Lord, the Holy One of Israel. He believes the prophets; he sings the psalms. Yet, on the other hand he is a man of facts. The facts. The facts! He believes facts. Well, in these last nine months, he has recognized that miracles are facts. *(Elizabeth expresses wonderment; her face lights up.)* Zechariah has changed. But I'll get to that.

The Time in the Temple

(Elizabeth continues. She smiles and expresses excitement.) Now I'll tell you when our lives started to change.[175] Temple assignments are drawn by lots. Zechariah is of the order of Abijah, one of the twenty-four shifts in the

management of the Temple; each has a shift of a week twice a year.[176] We went to Jerusalem together. Zechariah loved his service. He loved praying for Israel. His temperament was such that he took his job very seriously.[177]

He was chosen by lot to administer incense outside the Holy of Holies.[178] It was the honor of a lifetime; Zechariah was very excited. I waited outside with many other worshippers. As the officiating priest, Zechariah's job was to clean the altar of incense and to offer fresh incense.[179]

(Throughout this section, Elizabeth acts out Zechariah's encounter and emotions.) Well, Zechariah was meticulously performing his duties when an angel of the Lord appeared to him standing at the right side of the altar of incense.[180] Zechariah was startled and then afraid.[181] He wrote me this later, because he has been unable to speak. But again, I get ahead of myself. What I am telling you is what he wrote down for me when we came home. He did not share this information with others in our village. We kept it to ourselves. I read it with wonder and awe.

The angel then said to him, "Do not be afraid,[182] Zechariah; your prayer has been heard."[183]

Zechariah wondered what prayer.[184] Which of his many prayers did the angel mean? Then the angel was specific. "Your wife Elizabeth will bear you a son, and you are to give him the name John."[185]

(Elizabeth faces the audience. She laughs and smiles.) I like that part because it mentions me!

(She starts the re-enactment again.) Zechariah gasped. The angel continued. "He will be a joy and delight to you, and many will rejoice because of his birth."[186]

Zechariah gasped again. The angel kept on. "He will be great in the sight of the Lord."[187]

Then the angel gave some requirements about how we are to raise this boy, John. The angel said that "he is never to take wine or other fermented drink."[188]

Zechariah's mouth was open and his eyes were big![189] I think the angel chuckled a bit. *(She laughs, too.)* The angel continued with this news about our son: "He will be filled with the Holy Spirit even from his mother's womb."

And I can tell you that that has happened! *(Facing the audience again, Elizabeth says this with great joy.)*

(Elizabeth emphasizes the words Our son *throughout this section.)* Then the angel concluded about the purpose of our son and the reaction of

some people of Israel. Our son, the angel said, "will bring back many of the people of Israel to the Lord their God." Our son will go before the Lord, in the spirit and power of Elijah.[190] Our son will turn the hearts of the fathers to their children and the disobedient to the wisdom of the righteous. Our son will make ready a people prepared for the Lord.[191]

The news overwhelmed Zechariah. *(She pauses and paces as she acts out Zechariah.)* He paced back and forth in front of the altar of incense. The angel waited patiently. Zechariah undoubtedly pulled his beard, which is what he does when he is thinking through something. *(Elizabeth laughs and allows her guests to laugh, too.)*

(Elizabeth turns stage left.) Zechariah turned to the angel and said, "How can I be sure of this? I am an old man and my wife is well along in years."[192] *(Elizabeth acts out the encounter. She puts her hands on her hips.)*

(Elizabeth faces the audience and becomes herself.) That is not something you say to an angel![193] I could have told him that![194] Zechariah has since learned a hard lesson.[195] The angel took umbrage,[196] *(Elizabeth turns stage right and resumes acting out the encounter.)* The angel said this: "I am Gabriel. I stand in the presence of God, and I have been sent to speak to you and to tell you this good news."[197]

(Elizabeth faces the audience, becoming herself again.) Then the angel decreed a punishment for Zechariah! Zechariah has not been reprimanded for decades! *(Elizabeth resumes the re-enactment.)* The angel said to Zechariah, "You will be silent and not able to speak until the day this happens because you did not believe my words, which will come true at their proper time."[198]

Then the angel left. Zechariah tidied up the area around the altar and came out to see us worshippers. He acted dazed. He could not speak. He looked for me. I pushed forward in the crowd and came to him. He took my hand. Another priest pronounced the blessing.[199] We all knew something profound had happened in the Temple.[200] *(Elizabeth's face shows concern.)*

We walked the distance back to our temporary lodgings in Jerusalem. Zechariah was alternately crying, filled with emotion, trying to talk, remorseful, and skipping! I couldn't believe what I was seeing. My husband was skipping! I prepared his dinner. He went to sleep with a smile on his face.

(She picks up the pace of the story.) His duties at the Temple lasted a few more days. Everybody avoided him because he couldn't speak. As we

walked home from Jerusalem, his confusion seemed to lift. Once we got home, he brought out a writing tablet.

(Elizabeth gets more and more excited, more and more joyful throughout this portion. Her voice gets louder and louder, too. She dances in joy.) He wrote me the angel Gabriel's words. I rejoiced! I believed! They concerned me, too! I became the big noise in our small house. We hugged. We kissed. We prayed together. We thanked the Lord. We were secluded in our house for a second honeymoon period. Our neighbors kept their distance. They thought we were odd before—and now they thought we were really odd! *(She laughs and lets the audience laugh with her.)*

(Slowly.) And I became pregnant.[201] *(Elizabeth is full of wonder and adoration. She faces the audience, tears falling down her face. She squares her shoulders.)*

I hid myself for five complete months in this small house and worshipped the Holy One of Israel.[202] I did not tell anyone of my joy.[203] I did not tell anyone of our miracle. No one except Zechariah knew I was pregnant. Truly, my pregnancy is a miracle, an answer to the prayers of Zechariah in the Temple and our prayers throughout our marriage.[204] My shame is taken away. *(Proudly.)* I am like Sarah—although I am younger than she! I am enjoying my husband again and bouncing a baby boy on my knee! Truly with God nothing is impossible![205] *(Elizabeth pauses in worship, awe, and adoration.)*

Mary's Arrival

(Elizabeth walks back and forth smiling.) One day in my sixth month, I was in my house singing. Zechariah was out shopping for us. I heard my name called by a young woman's voice.[206] Suddenly things started happening all at once.[207] Bear that in mind as I tell you about Mary's arrival.

I was startled. I turned around and saw my kinswoman, Mary.[208] Mary is the daughter of Anna, my mother's sister.[209] Mary is fourteen.[210] I knew she was engaged to be married to Joseph, a carpenter in Nazareth.[211]

She called my name.[212] As soon as she did, the baby in my womb started leaping! What a commotion! I was being strongly kicked! Yet they were happy kicks! *(Elizabeth chuckles.)* Then I felt something entirely new: The Lord came upon me; I was filled with the Holy Spirit![213] Then in a very loud voice that surprised me,[214] I turned to Mary and said, "Blessed are you among women, and blessed is the child you will bear!"[215]

We looked at each other! I was amazed at what I had said, for I had no idea she was pregnant![216] *(Elizabeth pauses, amazed.)* My baby was kicking energetically! Mary's mouth opened. My mouth opened. We reached for each other's hands. I continued to shout.[217]

"But why am I so favored that the mother of my Lord should come to me? As soon as the sound of your greeting reached my ears, the baby in my womb leaped for joy!"

(Elizabeth acts out this encounter, too. She exudes joy, wonder, and laughter.) We looked at each other in astonishment. It was really a meeting of four—our two babies and we two women.[218] We hugged. We kissed. We shouted. We danced. We patted each other's stomachs. We hugged and kissed again.[219] We praised the Lord.[220] *(Elizabeth pauses.)* But the prophetic word was not over.

(Elizabeth kneels suddenly.) I dropped her hands and knelt before her. I, the older, I, the woman of the house, I knelt before a young woman and my guest.[221] Even though all that is against our culture, I would do it again and again.[222]

I looked up at her sweet face and said this prophetic word: "Blessed is she who has believed that what the Lord has said to her will be accomplished!"[223]

Mary nodded. Mary understood. Mary reached out her hand and helped me up. *(Elizabeth rises.)* Mary said later that I greatly encouraged her,[224] for I gave her a prophetic word, a spontaneous witness verifying what had happened to her.[225]

Mary's Visit Lasted almost Three Months

(Elizabeth's face softens. She smiles kindly.) Now I'll tell you about Mary's visit.[226] Oh, what a joyful time it was! She stayed with us almost three months.[227] I believe we gave to her and she gave us so much as well. First, we believed her. We believe she carries the Son of God in her womb. Second, we gave her space to be, to ponder, to consider what to do, to praise God. Third, she could be herself around us. We gave her sanctuary.[228]

(Elizabeth goes to the table and pantomimes this portion.) Zechariah encouraged her greatly. One day he brought home a portion of the scroll of Isaiah and unrolled it on this table. He pointed to some words, indicating they were for Mary. Mary and I leaned down to read them. "Behold, the virgin will be with child and will give birth to a son, and will call him

Immanuel."[229] Yes, Mary is that virgin![230] *(She pauses, walks, and considers her words.)*

(Elizabeth's smile is tender and that of an older woman who knows life.) I would watch her as she sat at the window, the light gently on her face. Mary is hard to describe. She is small. You would not notice her in a crowd.[231] Yet when you look into her eyes, there is peace.[232] I've never seen eyes like hers. Her eyes tell what is in her soul: Peace. It makes her beautiful beyond description. *(She pauses and walks.)*

Mary has several strong characteristics that I observed. First, she sings.[233] Mary composed a song while here.[234] Here are some of its words: "My soul magnifies the Lord, and my spirit has rejoiced in God my Savior. For He has regarded the lowly estate of his maidservant.[235] For behold, from henceforth, all generations will call me blessed. For He who is mighty has done great things for me, and holy is His name."[236]

Mary gave my husband a gift that helped him understand why he was silenced. She told us her story.[237] She told us how Gabriel came to her.[238] Gabriel told her she had found favor with God.[239] She would be with child and give birth to a son and was to give him the name Jesus. He would be great and would be called the Son of the Most High.[240]

Like Zechariah, she paused to consider the angel's words. She asked a technical question. She asked how his words would come to pass because she is a virgin.[241]

Gabriel told her that the Holy Spirit would come upon her and the power of the Most High would overshadow her.[242]

Mary accepted what the angel told her.[243] She said, "Behold, I am the Lord's servant. May it be to me as you have said."[244]

As Mary told us her story, emotions of fear, wonder, joy, and perplexity crossed her face.[245] When she finished, I was thrilled! I reached for her hand. I immediately started talking—but was interrupted by Zechariah's sobs. Amazed, Mary and I looked at Zechariah.

Zechariah was weeping great wrenching sobs. His keening came from his innermost being. It was if a boil had been lanced. Mary and I held hands as he wept. We bowed our heads, knelt, and prayed.

In our presence, Zechariah knelt and repented before God for his unbelief.[246] Because he couldn't speak, we do not know exactly what he said. He wrote this to us later. He bared his heart to the Lord. Mary's story broke him, for he saw before him this small young woman who believed.[247] And he, a priest in Israel, had not believed what Gabriel had said. *(Elizabeth lowers her head.)*

(Elizabeth pauses and smiles in tenderness.) But ever since that moment of repentance, Zechariah has been a changed man. He is kinder to me. His sense of humor has returned. He enjoys my company. He listens to me. He sees me with eyes of love and understanding. Oh, I hug him all the time and pat his boney shoulder as I go about my tasks. Together we praise the Lord. *(Elizabeth pauses, walks, and smiles.)*

Mary left two weeks ago with a group to walk back to Nazareth. I've mentioned Mary's peace and singing ability. Now I'll tell you about her courage.

Mary's courage significantly marks her.[248] She must tell Joseph she is pregnant! Mary's courage amazes me.[249] Zechariah and I pray daily for their meeting to go well. As a betrothed woman, she is treated as if she were a married woman.[250] Her pregnancy puts her in great danger, for according to our law, she could be stoned, strangled, or even burned to death.[251] Joseph is not the father of the child she carries.[252] We pray that Joseph, too, believes her and marries her quickly.[253] *(Elizabeth's face shows concern.)*

After Mary left,[254] Zechariah and I began to sit outside in the evening and watch the stars over Judea. I liked the cold stones on my back. I liked to sit, for the last days of my pregnancy were quite uncomfortable.

Zechariah would hold my hand and pat it kindly. I talked of our son, how great he would be. I am sure he will be like the first prophet, Abraham, or maybe like the greatest prophet, Moses.[255] Zechariah always smiled a little sadly at me as I went on and on, as if he knows something I do not. Maybe he does, for he has studied the scrolls all his life. *(Elizabeth shakes her head and is a bit sad but then recovers and smiles.)* But still, our joy is great and even bursting at this time! We truly have been surprised by joy! We have a baby at our ages! Imagine that![256] Truly, we are smitten parents—astonished and full of joy!

The Circumcision

(Elizabeth, the homemaker and happy mother, bustles about her small house.) Now let me tell you about what happened this morning. My son was born eight days ago. Mine was a difficult pregnancy. I was sick. The birth was difficult. After all, I am sixty-eight years old! Miracles may happen, but they take place in human form and to human beings!

Yet I knew I would live through the birth and that my son would be a viable child. After all, I had the prophetic word! According to the custom of our people, our son was to be circumcised today, named, and dedicated to the Lord. All our neighbors and relatives were with us, for they knew that the Lord had shown great mercy to me.[257] Zechariah gave me this shawl as a special gift. *(She again brings the shawl tenderly to her face.)*

When it came time to name the child, everyone thought the child would be named Zechariah for his father. I said, "No! He is to be called John."[258] There was a big fuss, for we have no relatives of that name.[259]

(Elizabeth, predictably by now, gets louder and louder and happier and happier as she remembers what happened this morning.) A writing tablet was brought for Zechariah. He wrote, "His name is John."[260] Immediately his tongue was loosed and he could speak![261] He started shouting![262] He kissed me. He kissed John. He kissed the rabbi. He kissed all our relatives— even the ones he never liked! I held up the baby. Soon John was being passed around to everybody. He was almost being tossed back and forth! We shouted and praised God, but Zechariah shouted the loudest. He could speak again! Oh, the amazing joy![263] *(She laughs with joy.)*

Then Zechariah started singing! Oh, the dear old coot! He was filled with the Holy Spirit, I could tell because I am, too. He started prophesying. He praised the Lord, the God of Israel for redeeming his people and raising up a horn of salvation for us.[264] He praised God for rescuing us from the hand of our enemies[265] and enabling us to serve him with righteousness and holiness all our days.[266] *(Again she smiles fondly and joyfully.)*

Then he tenderly took young John from my arms and cradled him.[267] He spoke to the baby in this way: "And you, my child, will be called a prophet of the Most High.[268] You will go on before the Lord to prepare the way for him. You will give his people the knowledge of salvation through the forgiveness of their sins.[269] *(Elizabeth pauses in wonder.)*

"The tender mercy of our God has come upon us. The Dayspring from on high has visited us.[270] God will give light to those who sit in darkness and the shadow of death.[271] God will guide our feet into the way of peace."[272]

Well, after that, we hugged and kissed some more. Our guests and neighbors were filled with awe.[273] John got cranky, so I took him and fed him and put him down to sleep. Oh, how I pray that joy will mark my son's life as it has done so far![274] *(Elizabeth quietly rests her cheek on her shawl.)*

Conclusion

(Elizabeth smiles at the audience. She pauses and paces.) Well, what would I like you to know?[275] I believe it is this. What I have spoken to you is true.[276] Mary, of course, was the first to know that Jesus, the son she carries, is the Son of God. *(Proudly.)* But I, Elizabeth, I and the baby son within me were the second and third to recognize that the Son of God is in the womb of Mary.[277] *(Quickly. Emphatically.)* There will be others, many others who will know Jesus as the Son of God.[278] I hope you are one of them.[279] While I knelt before Mary delivering the prophetic word to her, I listened as well. The pronouns were *she* and *her*. "Blessed is *she* who has believed that what the Lord has said to *her* will be accomplished."

(Elizabeth thinks as she walks. She again faces the audience.) Let me teach you. At times the prophetic word is deliberately vague and ambiguous; the word *man* can include *woman* as well.[280] At times the prophetic word is like ripples in a pond and can apply again and again. The pronouns *she* and *her* obviously applied to Mary. I thought later that they could apply to me as well.[281] I have believed the Lord; I, too, have received his favor.[282] What he has said to me has been accomplished. And so I tell you as well, take this word, be you woman or man. It is God's living word.

(Elizabeth puts out her right hand toward women in the audience.) "Blessed is *she* who has believed that what the Lord has said to *her* will be accomplished."

(Elizabeth puts out her left hand toward men in the audience.) "Blessed is *he* who has believed that what the Lord has said to *him* will be accomplished."[283] *(She pauses, smiles, and directs her praise to the Lord.)*

And blessed, blessed, blessed be the Holy One of Israel! *(Her hands are raised in joy and praise.)*

(Her face melts in happiness. She cocks her head stage left. She smiles in joy and lowers her arms.) Ah, do you hear what I hear? I hear John. He's awake and fussy. I must go and nurse the little prophet. Please excuse me. Please come again.[284] *(Elizabeth bobs a curtsy, adjusts her shawl, and exits stage left.)*

QUESTIONS FOR CONSIDERATION AND DISCUSSION

1. Can you relate to Elizabeth's anguish over her barrenness? If you are comfortable sharing, please do.

2. According to Elizabeth, how does her marriage to Zechariah change?

3. Elizabeth and Zechariah are dynamic characters in the sense that they grow during the course of the play. What are some areas of growth that you see?

4. Describe the miracles recounted in the play. Do you believe in miracles? If so, what have been some miracles in your life? If you are comfortable sharing, please do.

5. When this play is presented, men and women in the audience frequently weep. Why is this so, in your opinion?

6. What new insights about the character of God can you share as a result of this play?

7. Why are Elizabeth's blessings on the men and women—"Blessed is *she* who has believed what the Lord has said to *her* will be accomplished," and "Blessed is *he* who has believed what the Lord has said to *him* will be accomplished"—in the audience important today?

8. What other passages of Scripture do you see that are good possibilities for plays and dramatic monologues?

CHAPTER 5

He Is Risen!

A Play Based on Acts 1:1–12

INTRODUCTION

This play was written in response to a request to conduct a worship service for primary school children on Ascension Day, 21 May 2009, a Thursday.[285] The students, ages six to thirteen, attended Potchefstroom Christian School, an English-speaking school in Potchefstroom, South Africa.[286] The worship service was part of an annual outreach of Potchefstroom North congregation, a member of the GKSA (Gereformeerde Kerke in Suid-Afrika), to two local schools.[287] An hour earlier on the same day, children from an Afrikaans-speaking school heard a sermon by Prof. Dr. Ben de Klerk, my colleague in the Faculty of Theology at North-West University in Potchefstroom.[288]

Here's a bit more background. The request came when I was back in Potchefstroom as a visiting scholar with the Faculty of Theology. I had earlier spent two and a half years with the Faculty of Theology—first on a Fulbright Fellowship and then as an Associate Professor for a finite term of eighteen months (July 2002 through December 2004). The invitation to lead a worship service on Ascension Day was initially received with surprise, for it came without prior notice. I wondered what to do, what to speak on. After prayer, I decided to write a play.[289]

I wondered who would be my actors. During the announcements at a mandatory chapel service for theology students and faculty members, I asked for "six strong, broad, energetic, excited, and very handsome men" to be disciples in my new play for children.[290] I got them!

The play was well received by the children.[291] They learned a bit about the book of Acts and its opening story, the Ascension, in a manner faithful to the biblical text and yet one that creatively[292] incorporated contemporary elements.[293] The play keeps the attention of audiences because it is fast-moving and fun.[294]

Text: Acts 1:1–12; one of the disciples reads the text to the audience before the play starts.[295] It is from the NIV. He then goes back through the audience to join the other cast members.

Set: A stage with a chair on stage left and a chair on stage right. If possible, have a PowerPoint slide of the Mount of Olives in the background.[296] A website with a contemporary picture of the Mount of Olives like www.bibleplaces.com can be used.

Props: The disciples wear laminated nametags. So does the SABC EyeWitness News reporter. She carries a hand-held mic which she passes around to the disciples during the play. The characters are in normal clothes, not in period dress.[297]

Scene: The Mount of Olives.

Mannerisms: The disciples exude excitement and good will toward one another. Some rough-housing prevails. They punch and high-five each other. They are regular guys—and very excited about what they have seen! Two can come in and go out on piggy-back, for example. All can move around and change positions on stage. The pace is fast and excited. The disciples have fun! The disciples enter through the audience one way (from the Mount of Olives) and exit at the end of the play also through another part of the audience (on the way to Jerusalem). A possibility for staging is to think in groups of three: Matthew/Thomas/John and Peter/James/Andrew, for example.

Time: Time AD 30. It is forty days after the crucifixion of Jesus; forty days after Passover; and ten days before Pentecost.

Characters: SABC EyeWitness News Reporter. Pretty, professional, not a believer

Disciples: Matthew, a tax collector
Peter, a fisherman
James, a fisherman
Andrew, the brother of Peter, a fisherman
Thomas, a farmer
John, the brother of James, a fisherman[298]

Additional Information: After Acts 1:1–12 is read, the reader, a disciple, closes the Bible and walks back through the audience and joins the other five disciples at the back. The woman who plays the SABC reporter then gives the Introduction. A suggestion is that she dress in a black turtleneck and black trousers. She does not yet wear her nametag.[299] She begins speaking. Her manner is natural, welcoming, and polished. She smiles a lot and has excellent eye contact with the audience. During the Introduction, she walks around the stage with ease and confidence.

Woman/SABC Eyewitness News Reporter: The story you just heard is contained in the book of Acts.[300] In a few minutes you will see a play based on this story.[301] But first I'd like to give you a bit of information about the book of Acts. Its author is Luke. He wrote a kind of history that reads like an adventure story. He wrote to a man named Theophilus. Theophilus was his patron. A patron is like an employer; a patron pays for someone to do something. That meant that Theophilus paid Luke's expenses as Luke traveled around getting accurate information about what had happened concerning Jesus and his disciples. Probably Theophilus was a wealthy Greek who had a lot of knowledge about the Roman world.[302]

The book of Acts is theological history.[303] Theological history means that the book contains stories about real people and the ways God directs their lives. The writer, Luke, was a physician, a doctor. He was a Gentile, not a Jew. The Jews were the people to whom God gave his law. Luke is probably the only Gentile writer in the biblical text. He also wrote the Gospel of Luke. So it is natural to read the two books, Luke and Acts, together. Scholars think the book of Acts was written for many reasons including the following:[304]

- Acts was written to bring together different faith communities and to show them their common heritage of belief in Jesus.

- Acts takes a strong stand against idolatry. Idolatry is the worship of idols. It was prevalent throughout the Roman world.

- Acts defends Christianity. The big word in Latin for *defense* is *apologia*. Acts defends the claims of Jesus and establishes a new religion.

- Acts shows many missionary endeavors and journeys. It establishes a focus of the new church: missions. Missionary work is telling somebody about the love of Jesus and how to become his follower.

The author, Luke, has a talent for writing about people who seem ordinary or insignificant and showing how interesting they are. The book of Acts takes readers all over the known Roman world. There's a lot of adventure in Acts. Acts contains stories about a shipwreck and someone who is bitten by a viper and lives; and stories about a crippled man healed and a dead woman brought back to life.[305] The book is really amazing and unforgettable.[306] It talks about ordinary people who live extraordinary lives as people of faith and believers in Jesus.[307]

Let's look at the themes of the book of Acts in another way.[308] First, the book of Acts is the story of the beginnings of Christianity. Second, it shows that the Good News of being loved by Jesus is for both the Jews and the Gentiles. Both are saved from their sins through his death on the cross. Both Jews and Gentiles can believe on him. Third, the book of Acts talks a lot about right and wrong ways to live.[309] Fourth, it reaffirms that Jesus will come again. It gives people assignments, work to do, until Jesus does come again. Fifth, it affirms that God is still at work in his world and has good purposes for his world.[310]

Now I am going to put on my "imagination hat"; it is right here on this chair. *(She goes to the chair on stage and pantomimes picking up a hat. She can describe it in ways that help the audience visualize it.)* I am going to put it on. *(She pantomimes putting it on,)* You, too, have imagination hats. They are in front of you. Imagination helps us to understand what is happening on the stage. Now I want you to put on your "imagination hats."[311] You can pretend that your hat has flowers on it or is a baseball cap or is whatever you want.[312] *(She guides the members of the audience in putting on hats. She may have to do the motions several times. She smiles throughout as a means of encouragement.)*[313]

Good job! We are going back to the year AD 30. That is about 2000 years ago! A long time ago! You are going to participate as the audience in a play.[314] We're going to a place called Judea; sometimes it is called Israel. It is an occupied nation. That means the people, the Jews, are conquered by the Romans. Roman soldiers are everywhere, and the people have to pay taxes to Rome. Most do not like it! Rome is not popular at all! Almost all the Mediterranean world has been conquered by Rome. The king of Rome is called the Caesar. He is the most powerful person in the world. Many people call Caesar a god.

Right now we are on the Mount of Olives, a big hill about three-quarters of a mile outside Jerusalem.[315] Forty days ago the Romans executed three men they called criminals. Two were robbers.[316] One was Jesus of Nazareth, a man known to everybody in Jerusalem and the surrounding area for his good teaching and his many miracles. For three years he healed many people and sometimes fed thousands.[317] His disciples and those who loved him did not think of him as a criminal, but he died, charged with treason. He said he was a king, but he said his kingdom was not of this world.[318] What could that mean? (*She leaves the question open for the audience to consider.*)

Remember, the execution was forty days ago. Jesus died and was buried.[319] But today, here on the Mount of Olives, his disciples are saying they have seen him! But that is not all! They are also saying that they watched him go up in the sky! Let's find out what they're saying.[320] (She puts on her nametag, SABC Reporter.)

I am now a reporter for SABC and this is EyeWitness News![321] My character is not a believer in Jesus. The character I portray is a television news reporter who asks a lot of questions. SABC stands for South African Broadcasting Corporation. You are the TV audience. This is breaking news![322] The play begins!

(*The disciples enter boisterously.[323] They wave and say hello. They wear nametags. They interact excitedly[324] with the audience as they enter.[325] A feeling of good will prevails.[326]*)

Reporter: I am here on the Mount of Olives with Matthew, Peter, Andrew, James, John, and Thomas. Hello, gentlemen. We can see Jerusalem in the distance.[327] (*She points in a direction through the audience. At the end of the play, the disciples leave in that direction.*)

Reporter: Matthew, will you start telling our viewers what happened, please? You other disciples can say things as well.[328] I know each one of you has something amazing to share![329]

Matthew: Jesus was killed forty days ago. He was crucified on a cross on the execution hill outside Jerusalem called Golgotha.[330]

Andrew: Then he was buried in the tomb of a rich man, Joseph of Arimathea. Roman guards guarded it.[331]

John: He suffered greatly. He died. But there was a resurrection![332] He left the tomb! He's alive! He rose from the dead![333] We've seen him on and off for forty days. *(John joins Peter.)*

Peter: *(With wonder.)* The tomb could not contain him! The Roman guards could not stop him![334] We saw him today go up into heaven![335]

James: Since his resurrection, he has eaten with us many times and performed many signs for us, too.[336] Today he disappeared into a cloud![337]

Thomas: Yes, we have seen him again and again![338] He is Lord and God! He has a body, but it is different from our bodies. Jesus can appear and disappear as he wishes.[339] I even touched him![340]

Matthew: Jesus spent the days after his crucifixion and resurrection teaching us that his suffering, death, and resurrection were in accordance with our Scriptures.[341] Together his life, death, and resurrection, constitute God's mightiest act for the salvation of the world.[342]

Andrew: You know, on a human level, it was so interesting to see Jesus just be a regular guy and eat with us.[343] *(General laughter,)*

Reporter: My goodness! You men are so excited! You've seen a lot! James, tell me and our viewing audience more, please.[344]

James: *(Excitedly.)* Jesus spoke to us about the kingdom of God. The kingdom of God is God's good rule on earth.

Reporter: When will that happen?[345]

James: It has started already—with Jesus! Jesus has been instructing us about the kingdom of God. This was always central to

Jesus' preaching and ministry.[346] (*James and Thomas exchange places.*)

Thomas: (*Amazed and in awe.*) We're a continuation of what Jesus began. Our work as witnesses will continue the work of Jesus.

John: (*Reverently but with excitement.*) We want to tell everybody all that Jesus did and taught from the beginning to the end!

Matthew: Throughout these forty days, Jesus kept on showing himself to us. He kept appearing in our midst when we were gathered together. By this he gave us many, many proofs that he is alive!

John: (*Adamantly but with reverence.*) Death cannot keep him! It seems that he came the most to us when we were praying.

Andrew: (*Smiling and giving a chuckle.*) Yes, prayer seems to draw Jesus. Jesus loved to pray. And he made prayer fun!

James: Let me explain why prayer became fun. We asked Jesus to teach us how to pray. He taught us to talk to the Father, the One who loves us the best.[347]

Peter: That's right. He taught us to say, "Our Father in heaven, hallowed be your name. Your kingdom come, your will be done on earth as it is in heaven."[348]

All: (*The disciples walk around talking to each other and reciting the Lord's Prayer. They change places on stage.*) "Give us today our daily bread. Forgive us our debts as we also have forgiven our debtors. And lead us not into temptation but deliver us from the evil one."

Reporter: (*Amazed.*) That is a beautiful prayer! You must have been praying a lot during these forty days. John, tell us more!

John: (*Quietly. Sadly.*) Yes, we thought Jesus would be dead forever. At first we thought that everything was lost. We wept.[349] We did not realize that the work of God in Jesus goes on! Yes! We have seen the risen Jesus![350] We were so surprised to realize that the work of God continues.[351]

Andrew: We are waiting for something definite, the coming of the Holy Spirit.[352] Right now we don't know what that means. But we're excited! Jesus promised us the Holy Spirit, and Jesus always keeps his promises.

Peter: It's a promise! Right! We don't know what it means to be visited by power from on high! We're curious![353]

Thomas: He gave us some commands.

Reporter: Commands? What did Jesus command, James?

James: He told us not to leave Jerusalem. He told us to wait for the gift the Father had promised. *(The disciples become animated and walk around and change places.)*

Matthew: We believe Jesus meant the gift will be the Holy Spirit. Then Jesus also reminded us that John the Baptist, his cousin, baptized with water. But soon in a few days we will be baptized with the Holy Spirit.[354]

Reporter: *(Genuinely bewildered.)* What does that mean?

All: We don't know! *(They smile and laugh.)*

Peter: *(Confidently.)* But we know it will be good because it comes from Jesus!

Reporter: How will you wait, Andrew?

Andrew: We'll wait together! Everybody will be together! We love each other so much that we cannot be separated![355] There are about one hundred twenty of us—the disciples, the women, and Mary, the mother of Jesus.[356]

Thomas: We will wait praising and praying and thanking God! We will be very active while we wait! The living Jesus shows us the Father's love!

James: We have come through such sorrow, and now we are rejoicing! Jesus is alive! The kingdom of God is here! Jesus is alive! We want the whole world to know the joy we have![357]

Reporter: What is the Holy Spirit? I'm confused, Peter.

Peter: *(Truthfully. Confidently.)* We don't know much about the Holy Spirit. But we're going to find out! I have a feeling the Holy Spirit will dominate our lives and the way we tell the story of Jesus.[358]

Reporter: Please tell our audience more! What happened?

Matthew: *(Chagrined.)* Well, we did ask him a rather stupid question. *(The disciples walk around and change places. Their shoulders slump.)*

Reporter: Matthew, you sound a bit embarrassed. What was it?

Matthew: *(Also chagrined.)* We asked him when he would restore the prominence of Israel in the world and the kingdom of Israel.

James: *(Laughing a bit.)* Yes, Jesus rebuked us, but in a nice way. He is always to the point and gracious. He basically said it was none of our business!

Thomas: *(Explaining the situation.)* You see, we cherish dreams about the glory of our country, Israel. We want Israel to be restored. We want the God of Israel to be worshiped all over the world. But Jesus told us that we were not to know when these things would happen. That's part of waiting. But while we wait, he has given us assignments.

Reporter: *(Bewildered and gesturing widely with her mic.)* How can Israel be restored? After all, Rome is in control and Caesar rules the world. There are Roman soldiers all over the city of Jerusalem. Any rebellion will be met with death. You know that, John.

John: Jesus said it was not for us to know the times and the seasons. I think he meant we were not to expect to see immediately what God's total purpose is.[359] Maybe we can't handle all of that knowledge! *(John says this sadly and pauses.)*

Andrew: The amazing thing is that whenever Jesus gives a rebuke, he gives a new assignment. This new assignment is to work for the kingdom of God on earth.[360]

Peter: Minding your own business turns out to be doing what God tells you to do and letting God do his part! *(The disciples high-five each other and change places on stage. They laugh.)*

Reporter: This is all so exciting! A dead criminal comes back to life! Tell our viewers more about the kingdom of God! What was Jesus' command, John?

John: He gave us the assignment to wait. He told us to wait in Jerusalem until we receive power!

Andrew: You see, we had wanted Israel to be restored to its former glory and to shake off the shackles of Rome. The prophets have decreed the return of the glory of Israel.

Peter: But I guess it will happen later. God probably has something bigger and greater in store.

Andrew: And we're a part of it!

All: Yes! We're part of it! *(The disciples again express great joy with hands raised, back slaps, rough housing. John and Andrew can kneel.)*

Thomas: We can expect God to surprise us! He is full of big surprises! He delights in doing the unexpected.[361]

James: The amazing thing is that what God began continues![362] We are part of it, and it keeps on continuing![363]

Andrew: We're about to tell the story of our friend, God's servant Jesus, to the world![364] But first, we must obey his command to wait in Jerusalem.

Reporter: I can see you are excited. You look like men who are telling the truth. Keep talking! Tell our viewers what happened, Andrew.

Andrew: He told us to wait in Jerusalem. The Holy Spirit will come upon us. *(Pausing. All are quiet as they consider what this might mean.)*

James: *(With wonder.)* We will receive power. We will be his witnesses.

John: *(With louder wonder.)* We will be his witnesses first in Jerusalem, then in all Judea, then in Samaria, and then to the very ends of the earth.[365]

Peter: *(Breaking in, stepping forward, and spreading his hands in a wide gesture.)* Then while Jesus was talking to us, he started to rise in the air!

Reporter: *(Mouth agape, almost dropping her mic.)* Rising in the air! That's amazing! You mean straight up, Peter?

Peter: *(Confidently. Laughing a bit.)* Yes. He kept on going. And we kept on watching him.[366]*(Everybody pauses and laughs.)*

Reporter: *(Amazed.)* How did you feel?

Matthew: *(Truthfully. Slowly.)* We felt a lot of things—fear, awe, confusion. We had never seen anybody go up into the sky before and disappear into the clouds. I felt some grief, too. I felt as if my best friend were leaving me. *(The disciples agree. They walk around in reverence and amazement.)*

Reporter: What does the cloud mean, Thomas?

Thomas: In our Scriptures, God is often in a cloud. He uses it as a covering.[367] *(Thomas says this with reverence.)*

Reporter: There were reports you also saw an angel. What was the angel like?

Thomas: Suddenly two men appeared. Yes. Two. They were in white.[368]

Reporter: *(Amazed.)* What does that mean—that they were dressed in white, James?

James: It is a traditional way to refer to an angel as someone in white.[369] We believe they were angels.

Matthew: Yes, two angels, dressed in white. Angels bring messages from God. Actually, angels are quite common in our Scriptures.[370]

John: But it's always rather a shock to see them! *(The disciples laugh and walk around nodding in agreement.)*

Reporter: Andrew, have you disciples seen angels before?

Andrew: Yes, women in our fellowship saw two angels three days after Jesus' death. We didn't believe them.[371] Now that we've seen them, too, we believe the women. *(The disciples walk around indicating with facial expressions that they should have believed the women immediately.)*

Reporter: *(Nodding her head.)* I'm glad you believe the women! What happened next?

Thomas: There we were, looking up and watching him go up into heaven. We couldn't say anything. It was all so amazing. *(Everybody laughs.)*

Reporter: John, did the men in white say anything? *(Her voice expresses wonder.)*

John: Yes. Again we sort of got rebuked. It's as if we weren't getting it—as if we were not understanding anything. They asked us why we were looking up.[372] *(John laughs and shakes his head.)*

Andrew: We told them we were watching Jesus.

James: They seemed to want us not to waste any time! They told us this Jesus would return in exactly the same way—only coming down. *(James laughs in amazement.)*

Thomas: And we were to do what he told us all to do. So we are going back to Jerusalem rejoicing. We are jumping all over each other with joy. Praising God! We're stopping people on the way and blessing them. We cannot contain our joy—so we have to share it. *(Two disciples can leap frog over two others.)*

Reporter: Maybe I am the one not getting it, not understanding it. This is all very amazing to me. Perhaps it is the same to our listeners. Can you describe it one more time, please? Peter, let's start with you. *(She shakes her head in wonder.)*

Peter: *(In his teaching mode.)* Certainly. Jesus was lifted up into the sky. He departed from us. He was taken away into a cloud.[373] Right before our eyes it happened! The cloud was the heavenly glory of God.[374]

Matthew: The Ascension of Jesus is a guarantee that he will descend again, that he will come again.[375] *(The disciples nod vigorously in agreement.)*

Andrew: Right! If he can go up, he can come down![376] *(Everybody laughs!)*

Matthew: Let us say right now that Jesus is the risen Messiah! He is the Christ, the Anointed one, the chosen Son of the living God. We just saw him go straight up to heaven. He has taken his place at the right hand of God. He is exalted as Lord and King.[377] We worship him. *(The disciples pause in reverence.)*

Thomas: This is the beginning! Our command is to start in Jerusalem, then go to Judea, then go to Samaria, and then to the uttermost ends of the earth. *(The disciples speak hurriedly in this next section.)*

Peter: It will mean a lot of travelling!

John: And adventure! We're so amazed and excited about being part of it!

Matthew: *(Wailing a bit!)* Oh, how will we pay for it?

James: We don't know! But we'll trust and pray and do the task at hand.

Peter: Yes, Jesus has left in body! But he is here in our hearts right now. In each heart![378]

Reporter: In your heart? That's amazing! How do you know that he is in your heart, John? *(She says this slowly with genuine wonder.)*

John: How do we know it? Look at our eyes! He's there! *(She looks into the faces of the disciples. She shakes her head because she does not understand.)*

Reporter: I, I don't understand. There's so much mystery to all this.

John: That's right. There is mystery.[379] But we know enough of God's character to trust him.[380] We disciples certainly know Jesus, and we trust him entirely.

Matthew: The amazing thing is we saw Jesus go up, but I feel him here with me right now. His resurrected body and his spirit mean that he can be present in heaven and here with us on earth.[381]

Reporter: Throughout this interview, I've noticed your joy, and I'm sure our viewers have, too.[382] Can you say in a sentence why you're so joyful?

Matthew: Because he lives! *(Very upbeat and decisive.)*

Thomas: Because he rose from the dead! We saw him ascend into heaven![383]

John: Because he's coming back![384]

Peter: Because he loves me and the whole world!

Andrew: Because he gave us a job to do![385]

James: Because we're part of God's plan![386]

Reporter: All of that is good news! Can you describe this Jesus? Let's start again with you, Matthew.

Matthew: He called himself the good shepherd.[387] *(Very proudly.)*

James: The bread of life; the light of the world.[388]

John: The gate the sheep must enter.[389]

James: The resurrection and the life.[390]

Peter: He said he is the way, the truth, and the life.[391] And Jesus never lies! *(Said with confidence and joy.)*

Andrew: He said he is the true vine. He told us to follow him.[392]

Matthew: We must continue telling the world what God has done and is doing through his servant Jesus.[393]

John: We have the message of salvation in Jesus to proclaim and mighty works to perform in Jesus' name![394]

James: We are the apostles whom Jesus has chosen![395] We will continue to do and to speak what the Lord has begun![396]

Thomas: We are the ones who are sent out! That's what the word *apostle* means. We have something important, very important, to give to others.[397] *(Said confidently and proudly.)*

John: We are so enthusiastic about Jesus![398] He is the Christ![399] God so loved the world that he sacrificed his only son, Jesus. Whoever believes in Jesus will not perish but have eternal life.[400] *(They pause reverently.)*

Reporter: You'll probably encounter opposition![401] The Jewish leaders and Roman officials put Jesus to death. You may also be put to death, Thomas. *(Concerned, warning them.)*

Thomas: Yes, we expect opposition. But we are told to love those who oppose us and to do good to them.[402]

Matthew: We're headed back to Jerusalem. *(The disciples nod to the reporter. They leave the stage and interact with the audience. Two might be piggybacking. Again, they are having fun and expressing their joy.)*

Reporter: Well, thank you, Matthew, Peter, James, John, Andrew, and Thomas. This is SABC EyeWitness News on the Mount of Olives. As you can see, the disciples of Jesus are rejoicing as they go on their way back to Jerusalem. I'm sure we'll hear more of this good news that Jesus is raised from the dead, is alive, and is seated in heaven.[403] They surely will tell others in

Jerusalem.[404] So Jerusalem: Get ready! This is your SABC Eye-Witness News Reporter watching as Jesus' jubilant disciples return to Jerusalem.[405]

(She bows.)

(While there is applause going on, the disciples come back and take their bows with the SABC EyeWitness News Reporter.)[406]

QUESTIONS FOR CONSIDERATION AND DISCUSSION

1. What did you learn from this play?

2. The Gospels and Acts are full of people who are considered credible witnesses. Based on Acts 1:1–12, are these disciples credible witnesses to the life, resurrection, and ascension of Jesus?

3. These disciples convey amazement and excitement about what they have seen. What are other amazing stories in the Bible?

4. What aspects of the play made you pause and think?

5. How is drama one way to convey the message of Jesus?

6. Consider and comment on this thought: Worship is a drama and God is the audience.

7. Describe the humanity of the disciples.

8. What are some "take away" elements of the play for you?

CHAPTER 6

Funny Bone Finds a Home

A Musical Featuring the Body of Christ[407]

INTRODUCTION[408]

This play, a teaching tool, examines the concepts of unity and disunity in the Body of Christ.[409] Based on 1 Cor 12:12–27, the play contains as characters the body parts mentioned by Paul in his instruction on the need for honoring different ministries and functions in the church. Combining humor and song, the play follows in the steps of ancient medieval allegories and illustrates a biblical teaching in a contemporary way.

First Corinthians 12:12–27, a text about the body of Christ, entwines biblical principles and humor. An appropriate response is laughter. Actually, humor may well be a fundamental theme in both testaments.[410] By making characters of the body parts, this play takes Paul literally and carries on his use of imagination. Funny Bone herself is an imaginary character and takes her name from a recognized body part located at the end of the elbow.

This play approaches 1 Corinthians with a light touch,[411] for after all, the letter is addressed to a congregation Paul loves.[412] The musical employs imagination,[413] a God-given gift, for the text (whether read or heard) invites readers and hearers to engage it and to participate in it.[414]

I come to the biblical text from the Reformed tradition. My heritage is the Presbyterian Church, a denomination that combines trained, learned preaching from the clergy and active congregational involvement.[415] Preaching in the Presbyterian tradition emphasizes both order in worship and liberty.[416] It acknowledges the ability and need of the congregation to participate in the service.[417] My training is that of a biblical scholar for a classroom rather than that of a preacher for a pulpit ministry. I serve the academy and church by teaching. I write and publish plays because I find my students learn by doing and memorizing. As a biblical scholar, I seek to present thoroughly researched plays based on sections of scripture in thoroughly engaging ways.[418] This is my sixth such play.[419] I like and employ Brueggemann's insight that a musical like *Funny Bone* can serve as a teaching tool to "*summon and nurture an alternative community with alternative identity, vision, and vocation, preoccupied with praise and obedience toward the God we Christians know fully in Jesus of Nazareth*" (italics, original).[420] The church at Corinth clearly is an alternative community.

This musical uses the standard elements of a play.[421] It also employs a literary methodology and a canonical perspective in examining I Corinthians.[422] *Funny Bone* differs from drama or tragedy. As comedy, it intends that reversals, errors, and our all-too-human "booboos" produce not calamity but prosperity and happiness.[423] I wrote *Funny Bone* with a smile. The play deals kindly with our common human foibles. I also wrote it with a sense of adventure, hope, and freshness. Why? Because, sadly, studies indicate that people today do not trust the old church modes.[424]

The Christian classic *The Humor of Christ* (Trueblood) strongly influences my teaching, thinking, Bible reading, and playwriting. Trueblood believes we fail to see not only the wit and humor of Jesus but also his expectation that we should laugh.[425] I see some of Paul's writings, like this passage from 1 Corinthians, in this vein. We are intended to laugh at the absurdity of nonchalantly not needing a hand (v. 21). Arguably Jesus and Paul could not have influenced people without being enjoyable to be around. I believe each had a delightful sense of humor. Humor, as well as sound teaching, draws people together.

With this in mind, I encourage my students to laugh at a literal interpretation of a big old camel squeezing itself through an itsy, bitsy needle (Matt 19:24); the absurdity of a homeowner putting a lamp under a bed (Mark 4:21);[426] and the bumbling suitor who means well when he likens his sweetheart's hair a flock of goats (Song 6:5). Similarly, Paul's skillful analogy of body parts combines good teaching with humor; it makes me laugh. My musical puts Paul's teaching on stage.[427] While writing this play, I took seriously Trueblood's observation that "any alleged Christianity which fails to express itself in gaiety, at some point, is clearly spurious."[428] Throughout this play's research, writing, and productions, I prayed that it would serve as a teaching tool for the academy and the church. May it strengthen all concerned in their union with Christ. May it engage them in ministry.[429]

Characters: Head, Foot, Ear, Nose, Unpresentable Parts, Hand, Eye, Heart, Piano Player, and Funny Bone. With the exception of the last three, these are recognized members[430] of the Body of Christ as mentioned in 1 Cor 12:12–27.[431] Heart is mentioned in 1 Cor 14:5. Funny Bone is a body part located on the end of the elbow and is associated with mirth and laughter.[432] Probably Foot and Head are played men and Unpresentable Parts and Heart by women.[433] I have written Funny Bone as a young woman, but the part also can be played by a young man. Piano Player has no written speaking lines but is acknowledged by the other actors while on stage. For example, each time a character sings, eye contact can be made with Piano Player. Piano Player also can take part in the times of general outrage and mayhem.

Costumes: The characters wear T-shirts with their names across the front or back, or they dress in a contemporary fashion. If the latter, then Head probably wears a business suit or a fashionable golf outfit.

Foot is in sandals. Unpresentable Parts is in layered tank tops, leggings, and a short skirt.

Funny Bone can be a bit outlandish with a wild tie, khakis, suspenders, and a hat, if played by a man; or be stylish in a fun, contemporary way with a long skirt, big belt, sandals, and bright top with long sleeves if played by a woman.

If T-shirts are chosen, individuality comes from the undershirts, caps, shoes/sandals, and wigs the characters may include.[434]

Set: The setting is a nice but fairly bare room.[435] The stage has an assortment of comfortable chairs. A bar table with bar stools is downstage right in front of a piano. A sofa with pillows is upstage, center stage. Houseplants decorate throughout. A rug is center stage; this is where the huddles take place. A box of tissues is on an end table. The setting could well be the front altar area of a church, for an altar area usually contains levels that permit effective staging.[436]

The characters enter through an aisle in the audience.[437]

Atmosphere: There's general goodwill and general busy talk among the members of the Body of Christ as they enter.[438] They *ad lib* at will.[439] Heart carries a nicely wrapped package which she puts on an end table on stage. Funny Bone nods and smiles but doesn't take part in the banter.[440] Everybody smiles frequently.[441] Eye raises his eyebrows frequently. Until reprimanded, Nose does pick his nose!

Unpresentable Parts: How are you, Foot?[442]

Foot: Great! I'm glad to see you again, Unpresentable Parts.[443]

Hand: Give me five, Foot! *(They slap hands.[444])*

Ear: I've heard good reports about you, Nose.[445]

Nose: Thanks, Ear! It's so good to see everybody again.[446] I'm looking forward to hearing what's been happening to my friends in the Body of Christ.

Head: Right! We've haven't had a meeting for a long, long time!

Eye: We need to get together more often! I've missed seeing each of you![447]

Heart: Eye, what have you been doing? What's the Lord doing through you?

Eye: *(Proudly.)* Well, I was used so greatly recently by the Lord. I want to tell everybody about it![448]

Hand: *(Interrupting.)* So was I! The Lord worked miracles through me! I'm not called Hand for nothing![449]

Head: *(Interrupting with more force.)* What you say reminds me of my own ministry experience, Hand and Eye. Oh, let me tell you about it! I knew just what to do! My study during a sabbatical certainly paid off! I was so very proud.[450]

Ear: *(Said with measured words.)* Well, my recent congregations are measured in acres of people. I preached first in Korea and then in Africa. I had a translator at each service. People listened to me with rapt attention. I was very well received.[451]

Heart: I'm glad, Ear. My speaking engagement went so well that I have three more bookings! *(Heart smiles smugly.)*

Unpresentable Parts: *(Showing some envy.)* My goodness, Heart. You must be earning a lot of money![452]

Foot: I've gone the farthest of all of you since our last meeting. I keep going to remote places. I brought the Gospel to a mountain valley at 10,000 feet. I can't tell you the country because it is officially closed to the Gospel. But I was faithful to give the Good News to all, including the poor.[453]

Nose: *(Kindly, with understanding.)* I'm sure you were, Foot. My fellow members of the Body of Christ, we can continue catching up after our meeting.[454] We must greet Funny Bone! Funny Bone, it's good to see you again. I'm sure you're ready with a joke.[455] *(The men bow.)*

Eye: Yes! Greetings, Funny Bone![456] Let's hear a joke! Funny Bone, bless us with a joke![457]

Funny Bone: *(Laughing.[458])* Well, after listening to all of you, your talk reminded me of something opposite—but humorous—I read recently. Here it is: "The Low Self-Esteem group will meet as usual on Thursday at 7 p.m. Because the church has a wedding that night, the wedding party requests that the Low Self-Esteem group use the back door." *(General laughter.)*[459]

Head: *(Laughing.[460])* Yes, the back door! Thank you, Funny Bone! Well, it's time for the meeting to come to order. Find your places, Body of Christ. As usual, I'll take charge.

Foot: *(Peevishly.)* Why is it always you? Why can't someone else preside?[461]

Head: *(A bit nasty.)* Like you, for instance?[462] You step all over people! Like Heart? A softie on community decisions? *(Head and Foot glare at Head. Heart looks sad, and Foot looks mad.)*

No, no. I'm the best choice. I'm always chosen.

(The other members of the Body of Christ do not look pleased. They scatter around the stage. Funny Bone stands by a bar stool.)

Head: *(Very business-like.)* Yes. Yes. Well, let's get going. I have a golf game to go to! Evangelism on the golf course, you know.

Yes. Yes. *(Looking at Funny Bone.)* Well, this meeting has been called because of you, Funny Bone. Funny Bone wrote me asking for a time to talk to all of us.

Hand: Welcome to you, Funny Bone.

Ear: We're glad you're here. You always make us laugh with your jokes.

Unpresentable Parts: Yes, she does! But they're always nice jokes! Do you have one right now? We seem to have some ruffled feathers and need a little diversion![463]

Funny Bone: *(Laughing.[464])* Sure! I came prepared! I know you! The Body of Christ has plenty of humor because it's full of people![465] This was in a church bulletin: "Because of a conflict, the peacemaking meeting scheduled for today has been cancelled." *(Laughter.)*

And here's a cute story about self-confidence. A student asked his teacher to raise his grade from an A to an A+. The teacher asked why. The little boy flashed a missing-toothed grin and said, "Because that's how good I am!"[466] *(General laughter.[467])*

Heart: Thank you, Funny Bone. Laughter certainly clears the mind—and the air![468] Now tell us why you've called us together.[469]

Nose: Yes! We're all curious!

Funny Bone: Well, it's simple! I love each of you so much! When you ask me, I work with you on assignments from the Lord. I'm a member of the Body of Christ—but sort of on an informal basis.[470] Well, I want to be more involved. I like being with you! I'd like to be formally recognized as a member of the Body of Christ![471] *(The members react with surprise and a stunned silence. For example, Eye raises his eyebrows,; Hand covers her mouth; and Heart puts her hand on her heart.)*

Nose: My goodness! You! You in the Body of Christ and recognized with us![472] That never occurred to me![473]

Ear: Amazing! My goodness! How unusual![474]

Head: We'll have to check the Scriptures!

Funny Bone: Yes! Of course! I want you to search the Scriptures. Let me state my case by singing about it.[475]

Unpresentable Parts: Funny Bone, I'll tell you right now that I want you to be recognized![476]

Funny Bone: Thank you so much, Unpresentable Parts! *(Funny Bone bows and Unpresentable Parts curtseys.)*

Song: **Sung by Funny Bone**
Tune: **"Home on the Range"**[477]
     Oh, give me a home in the Body of Christ
     For I am Funny Bone
     I'll make you laugh with my silly gaffes[478]
     For chuckles add years to your life![479]
     I am Funny Bone
     Stick with me and you'll be tickled![480]
     For smiles and mirth make you many friends—
     And get you out of a pickle![481]

All: *(Clapping enthusiastically.)* Thank you! Well sung! *(Funny Bone laughs with them and bows.[482])*

Head: You state your case well, Funny Bone.[483] Now let us introduce ourselves to you and tell you about our roles in the Body of Christ.[484] The apostle Paul likened the church to a human body with various parts.[485] Paul named each of us here in 1 Corinthians 12 and elsewhere.[486] Our job descriptions are based on Scripture. After we tell you about ourselves, you can see if you really want to join us, and we'll discuss if you really do fit in.[487]

Funny Bone: Great! I'll listen with much interest.[488] *(Funny Bone walks stage right. During the singing, Funny Bone walks naturally all over the stage. Gradually, Funny Bone's face becomes more and more concerned. Throughout the play, she actively listens.[489])*

Ear: *(Sarcastically.)* Well, I guess Head starts![490]

Head: Of course. I'm always the first in any line. Let me introduce myself. *(Head is quite formal and bows profusely. The other characters mimic or guffaw.[491])*

Song: Sung by Head
Tune: Russian Hymn ("God the Omnipotent")[492]

> Greetings to all of you. I am the Head.[493]
> I am not the tail.
> I am always the first.
> You look to me—as well you should—
> For I plan ahead for the common good!
> *(Head bows. There is lukewarm applause. Head continues bowing.)*

Head: *(Misinterpreting the acclaim.)* I'll sing it again! I'm more than ready![494]

Eye: No, no! We get the message![495]

Unpresentable Parts: *(Kindly.)* We all know your work, Head. We appreciate you and thank you.[496]

Foot: I'll go next. I'm more than ready. I'll tell you about myself. Head started. But I'm where the rubber meets the road![497] There's an old saying that an army is only as good as its feet!

Song: Sung by Foot
Tune: "Onward, Christian Soldiers"[498]

> One foot then the other
> Following where he leads
> Faithfully he guides us, meeting all our needs
> Jumping, walking, running—
> Do what 'ere he says—
> Forward, backward, sideways
> Never be dismayed!
> One foot then the other
> Trusting with each step
> Marching behind Jesus,
> Gracious Priest and King[499]

All: Well sung, Foot! We need you in the Body of Christ, Foot! Here! Here!

Nose: Just change your socks more often! *(Agreement and laughter.)*

Unpresentable Parts: And cut your toenails![500] Ugh!

Hand: Hey, Foot! Didn't I see you going into a building that—[501]

Foot: *(Interrupting strongly.)* No, you did not! Let's change the subject![502]

Ear: Come to think of it, I remember hearing something, too. Oh, tell us where you went! We want to know![503]

Nose: Come on, Foot, 'fess up! We know you're prone to wander from time to time.

Foot: *(Folding his arms and walking away.)* I go where I want! I do what I want! I'm not accountable to any of you! I don't have to tell you a thing![504] Humpf! *(General outrage and disagreement come rapidly after Foot's statements.)*

Eye: How arrogant!

Head: Preposterous![505]

Unpresentable Parts: Well, I never!

Heart: Such pride! How could Foot say that!

Nose: What an attitude!

Head: Order, order, everybody! Foot is right! He doesn't have to say where he's been to us, although we would like to know. But Foot needs to remember that our individual reputations as members of the Body of Christ reflect on all of us.[506]

Heart: But it's more important that we remember that whatever we do reflects on our Lord and Savior Jesus Christ. May we seek to honor him.

Ear: What do you say to that, Foot? *(Everybody looks at Foot. He shrugs his shoulders. There's an uneasy standoff between Foot and the other members. Funny Bone, neutral and observant, ponders this.)*

Hand: *(Breaking the uncomfortable silence.)* I think I may have the solution. The Epistle of Jude says this: "Let the Lord rebuke you."[507] Let's just leave the matter of where Foot may have gone and what he may have done with the Lord. Let's trust that the Lord—if necessary!—will discuss the matter with Foot.

Ear: Good idea, Hand.

Nose: Yes, thank you, Hand. *(Turning to Funny Bone.)* Funny Bone, we need another joke![508]

Funny Bone: *(Rising to the occasion.)* Well, let's change the subject. Here's a bit of humor about a first grader who was sent to the principal by her teacher because she disturbed other children. The little girl explained her behavior to the principal this way: "I guess I have restlessness in my blood!"[509] *(General laughter proceeds, but it is a bit uneasy. Things are starting to get edgy.)*

Heart: Thank you, Funny Bone. Your humor helps us, as usual. I'll go next. I'm brief and concise.[510]

Song: Sung by Heart
Tune: "Row, Row, Row your Boat"[511]

Heart, Heart, Heart I am
Beating every day
My mercy, compassion, forgiveness, and love[512]
Come from God above.

Hand: That was so good, Heart, that you need to repeat it. *(Heart does—twice!)*

Heart: Sure thing! Follow me! *(The members of the Body of Christ fall in line behind Heart in a march. Some skip. Some dance. They all sing.[513])*

Song: Sung by Heart and All (repeated twice)
Tune: "Row, Row, Row your Boat"

Heart, Heart, Heart I am
Beating every day
My mercy, compassion, forgiveness and love
Come from God above.[514]

(General laughter and good will come from the members of the Body of Christ.[515] The edginess temporarily abates.)

Unpresentable Parts: *(Showing some jealousy.)* Oh, Heart, everybody loves you. I wish I were like you! Everybody wants to follow you!

Heart: *(Smugly assured of herself.)* Yes, I know I'm loved.

Nose: Thank you, Heart. Unpresentable Parts, you have to sing, too!

Unpresentable Parts: Well, all right! It's the highest form of courage to stand in front of a group! I'm overcoming my glossophobia!

Head: *(Informing everybody.)* Glossophobia—if you don't already know—is the fear of speaking before a group.[516]

Unpresentable Parts: Thank you, Head.

Song: Sung by Unpresentable Parts
Tune: "Tenting Tonight on the Old Camp Ground"[517]

> *(She sings slowly, purposefully.)*
>
> I am well known in the Body of Christ
> As Unpresentable Parts
> Sometimes I embarrass the gently bred
> With my immodesty
> But I don't know what to do, my friends,
> With all my energy
> I need help controlling my hormones
> And must shun immorality!
> Unpresentable Parts! Unpresentable Parts!
> I am my own problem
> Lord, I cry to you! Show me how to serve
> And bless your Holy Name!

Ear: *(Thoughtfully. Thinking aloud.)* God has given us a great gift in our sexuality. Sometimes how we use our sexuality creates problems!

Foot: *(Kindly.)* Thanks, Unpresentable Parts, for talking with us about your struggles.[518] Thank you for letting us hear you bring your need to the Lord.

Heart: *(She takes the wrapped present from the end table.)* Unpresentable Parts, this seems like a good time to give you the present I bought for you.[519] *(Heart hands the box to Unpresentable Parts who is very pleased.[520] She opens it and takes out a lovely shawl that just happens to be match her outfit. She drapes it across her shoulders and the members of the Body of Christ smile and clap.[521])*

Head: *(Taking charge again.)* That was a very nice gesture, Heart.[522] Thank you. Let's move on, everybody. Time is money!

Money is time! Eye, you've been looking mighty smug through all this. What do you have to say for yourself?

Eye: Plenty! I'm ready and sharp! My vision is clear. Call me 20/20!

Song: Sung by Eye
Tune: "Mine Eyes Have Seen the Glory"[523]

> *(Eye begins slowly. As the song progresses, the tempo increases. Eye, quite dramatic by nature, may march around the stage.)*
>
> I am the Eye and function in the Body of Christ
> I spy, I peer, I look, I gaze to see the path ahead
> And I alert you all so that you can be led
> Away from the miry pit![524]
> I am more than essential
> I am quinte- quintessential
> I am more than essential
> I am the Eye! Amen!

Hand: My goodness, Eye. You call yourself more than essential! Probably some of us disagree! You sound full of pride to me![525]

Foot: To me, too!

Eye: Humph! Well, I know my value. Try functioning without me and see how much I'm needed! *(Eye pulls out a blindfold.)*

Here! Let me tie this on you! *(Hand backs away.)* Come here, Foot! You'll fall in a ditch without me! See how far you get in the mountains without me! *(Foot also backs away from being blindfolded.)*

Heart: Careful, Eye. Your attitude sounds over the top![526]

Eye: No, it is not! I know my value! I don't need you![527] *(A general bad feeling prevails against Eye, as it did first against Head and then against Foot.)*

Nose: *(Talking to everybody.)* Hey, let's be civil.[528] We're commanded to act with humility and to esteem others as better than ourselves.[529] Jesus commanded us to love one another as he loves us.[530] We're all acting puffed up.[531] What do you think Jesus thinks of all this?[532] *(In general, the members of the Body of Christ want to continue fighting. They turn their backs on an extended hand from Nose. They shake their heads when he comes to them.)*

Nose: *(Very discouraged.)* All I can do is pray.[533]

Song: Sung by Nose
Tune: "Danny Boy"[534]

> *(Sung slowly as a prayer.)*
>
> Lord Jesus Christ, your body is not unified.[535]
> We fight and hate and show you no respect.
> We tear and wound each other, full of mean intent.
> There is no health among us anymore.[536]
> Lord Jesus, come and turn our Heart again to you.
> Oh, set our Feet along your narrow path
> And may our Hands be lifted high in praise to you[537]
> And may our Eyes behold your lovely, lovely face.
>
> *(Each character turns as his or her name is mentioned. Each appears sad. Nose's song convicts them all of sin.[538])*

Eye: *(Reflectively.)* You're right, Nose. All I want to do is to see the lovely face of Jesus. I'm sorry for my arrogance, Body of Christ.

Foot: *(Admitting guilt.)* Thank you, Nose, for your song. It gives me courage for what I must confess.[539] Yes, I went into a bar. I had too many drinks and did not represent Jesus well because of things I said and did there. I said suggestive words to a woman and got into a fight. The police were called, but luckily I was not arrested. I am ashamed of myself. I did not honor Jesus. I know that my actions also reflect on you, for I am part of the Body of Christ. In addition, my attitude today showed arrogance and pride. *(Foot looks—and is!—contrite and ashamed.)*

Hand: *(Reflectively.)* I think, Foot, I speak for all of us in forgiving you. *(Hand looks around. Members of the Body of Christ nod.)*

But Nose, your song, also spoke to me.[540]

The choice for me is always between doing things for myself or doing things for Jesus. You see, I can make things like a building or an airplane. I can write things like a book or a poem. I can hold a child or shoot a gun. I have such amazing power. But when I lift my hands in praise to Jesus,[541] I surrender my pride. I am asking for his direction. I am praising him.

Heart: (*Nodding.*) Right, Hand. I must guard against deceiving myself. Scripture says this about me: "The heart is deceitful above all things."[542]

(*There's a general quiet for a moment or two. The characters are not so much sad as reflective. This meeting is becoming deeper than they thought. It certainly is raising issues. Funny Bone senses this and moves around the characters giving encouragements like a pat on the shoulder, high-fives, and sideways hugs.*)

Ear: What you say, Nose, has cut me to the quick. I, too, have a confession to make to you, my fellow members in the Body of Christ.[543]

Head: Proceed, Ear.

Song: **Sung by Ear**
Tune: **"I've been Workin' on the Railroad"**[544]
I have been listening to all of you
In this discussion
I have been listening to all of you
And will share my findings.
First, I must confess that
As the Ear, I have sinned
I have liked to "dis' the dirt" on you
Over and over again!
Please forgive
Please forgive
Me for my sin, my sin, my sin!
I repent
I repent[545]
Over and over again!

(*Members of the Body of Christ collectively gasp. Ear hangs his head. A general discussion commences. There is a pause for dialogue, rebuke, repentance, and forgiveness.*)

Head: What did you say about me? I'd like to know.

Foot: You're an eavesdropper! You're a gossip! We should box your ears!

Hand: Or cut them off! (*Heart and Unpresentable Parts gasp.*)

Eye: Libel! I'll slap you with a lawsuit![546]

Foot: A gossip separates close friends.[547] A gossip betrays a confidence.[548]

Unpresentable Parts: You have no right talking in an ugly way about us! How dare you! How dare you spread around what I told you as a secret![549]

(A general commotion occurs. The members of the Body of Christ are outraged!)

Heart: Hey, everybody! Hush and listen to me! *(Everybody calms down a bit and is eventually quiet.)* We have to forgive Ear.

Ear has repented and that means Ear won't "dis' the dirt" on us.[550] We have to forgive Ear.[551] If we don't forgive Ear, our heavenly Father won't forgive us our sins.[552] *(Heart looks around.)*

Hand: Right. When the disciples asked Jesus to teach them how to pray, one of the parts of that famous prayer is "forgive us our sins, for we also forgive everyone who sins against us."[553]

Nose: Jesus told us to forgive seventy times seven times![554]

All: We don't want to. But we have to. *(Pouting.)* OK. We forgive you, Ear.

Ear: *(Very much relieved.)* Thank you, everybody in the Body of Christ. From now on, when I hear something about you, I won't repeat it all over everywhere. I'll discuss it with you privately first. I'll look for the good in each of you and speak well of each of you. I'll pray for you. If you find me in what you think is sin, or if I find you in what I think is sin, let's talk about it privately and see if we can't resolve our issues.[555]

All: Agreed! That's a good idea. That's what Scripture says.

Ear: Thank you. Now I'll finish my song. Yes, I am prone to gossip, but I hate that sin so much that, with the Lord Jesus' help, I'll change! Now I'll tell you what I see in us.

(Ear resumes singing.)

Song:	**Sung by Ear**
Tune:	**"I've been Workin' on the Railroad"**

Now I'll share what I've seen in us
It is not pretty
Be prepared for a rebuking
That just might bring liberty!
Eye, you're quick to see a scandal!
Head, you're always first!
Hand, I've caught you vandalizing[556]
And Heart, your cheatin' hurts![557]
Pride is here, you know
Jealousy also
Arrogance and selfishness, I see!
Pride is here, you know
Jealousy also
Arrogance and selfishness.

(Each named character expresses offense. By the song's end, all the members of the Body of Christ start shouting and fighting. They are mad at Ear!)

Foot:	That was not very nice, Ear![558]
Heart:	And after we forgave you!
Head:	I don't like to be around you, Ear! Actually, I don't like any of you! I'd rather be out playing golf with unbelievers!
Eye:	Nose, stop picking your nose!
All:	Yes! Stop picking your nose! *(Nose is surprised and offended.)*
Hand:	Foot, you smell like a locker room! Wash your feet more often!
All:	Yes! Wash your feet!
Heart:	Pull your dress up to your shoulder, Unpresentable Parts. Use the shawl I gave you![559]
Unpresentable Parts:	Nobody tells me what to do!
Nose:	Head, you're so arrogant and obnoxious!
Head:	I'm gonna punch you in the nose for that, Nose! *(They take up a boxing stand and fisticuffs almost begin.)*
Eye:	Heart, you're full of pride!

Heart: Eye, you're snoopy and rude!

Ear: I agree! Eye, you're arrogant! Conceited!

Unpresentable Parts: Ear, you're narcissistic!

Hand: Foot, you're pushy, pushy!

Foot: Hand, you promote yourself!

Nose: Head, you're untruthful! Boorish!

Heart: Head, you're a gossip! You're a big bully!

(*Other insults volley back and forth. Pillows from the sofa also sally through the air as Piano Player pounds away.*)

Unpresentable Parts: Hand, quit pushing me!

Ear: Foot, you stepped on my toe!

Head: Nose, keep yourself out of my business!

Unpresentable Parts: Hand, stop pinching me! (*She holds out her arm.*)

Eye: Head, you have too many opinions!

Nose: Foot kicked me!

Foot: You deserved it!

Head: How can you judge me when you don't see yourself clearly?

(*General confusion and mayhem abounds. Funny Bone separates the various feuding parties and then stands on a chair and starts to shout. Piano Player crescendos and stops in a loud way.*)

Funny Bone: (*Funny Bone commands order.*) Stop it![560] Stop fighting! Stop biting, kicking, and shoving! Stop it![561] (*Everybody slowly, grudgingly stops.*)

Funny Bone: Hand, keep your hands to yourself. Sit over there. Foot, march to that corner! Head, come down from the clouds. You, Nose, mind your own business and be sure to use a handkerchief! Eye, nobody likes it when you raise your eyebrows. Heart, calm down; remember your blood pressure. Unpresentable Parts, put your shawl around your shoulders. All of you: Stop gossiping! All of you: Stop thinking ugly thoughts about each other.[562]

(Chagrined, they obey. They act contrite as they mill around. There even is some general courtesy. The members of the Body of Christ say things like "You go first. After you. Please sit here. I'm sorry I yelled at you. I didn't really mean what I said." Et cetera.)

Funny Bone: That's better. Everybody sit down. *(Each one finds a spot. All are touchy and don't want much contact with the others.)* Ear, I think you have something more to say.

Ear: Yes, I do. My song really summed us up. I am included in my own song, for I know I am full of jealousy and pride. We have just shown the whole world our arrogant attitude! *(Very sadly.)* Oh, what are we to do?

Unpresentable Parts: *(Very sadly, too.)* Truly, all of us have sinned, and we all fall short of the glory of God.[563] We're all pretty rotten!

Funny Bone: Well, yes, we are. But the purpose of seeing our sin is to become free of it. That's why the Lord Jesus came![564] That's the gospel![565] Jesus seeks to set us free from ourselves, from our sin, and from the power of Satan and the power of Satan's demons.[566] *(After suddenly taking charge and speaking these words, she is hopeful.)*

Head: We surely do tear and rend each other.[567]

Heart: *(Crying and sincerely sad.)* Call me heartbroken!

Nose: *(Rubbing his nose.)* We're wounded! And bloodied![568]

Eye: We don't see anything good about each other.[569]

Foot: We get sick and sore. We do not like or honor the parts who, we think, are weak.[570]

Unpresentable Parts: *(Reflectively.)* I think we really do like each other. Maybe we even do love each other. But the way we act, you'd never know it![571] *(Hand's hand goes up.)*

Funny Bone: I agree! But I also must commend you. Thanks to everybody for stopping your fighting, biting, kicking, shoving, and talking ugly! Hand, would you like to say something?

Hand: Yes, I would! I believe I can add something positive to our discussion.

Song:	**Sung by Hand**
Tune:	**"Sweet Betsy from Pike"**[572]

I am the Hand
And I raise it right now
I stand before you
And give you a bow
Let's all work together
And not pull apart
Paul called us *yokefellows*[573]
We need to start

(Hand dances during the bridge between verses. She puts her hands on her hips and does a polka step.)

To build God's Kingdom
Is our great call[574]
The right hand of fellowship
Binds us all
His wisdom will guide us
His love is the glue
Through times of sunshine
And days when we're blue

All: *(Applause.)* Well done, Hand!

Eye: You've got the right idea!

Hand: Thank you, Body of Christ! Let's listen as Funny Bone teaches us about how we are part of God's Kingdom and how we are to join with God in building it![575]

All: *(Excited!)* Oh, Funny Bone, please teach us![576]

Funny Bone: With pleasure! Let me remind you what the apostle Paul said in 1 Corinthians 12.[577] Let's start with the easy section. The body is made up of many parts. And though you are many parts, you form one body.[578]

Nose: *(Laughing and breaking the tension.)* Yeah. I like being part of the body. I'll even laugh at your silly jokes about me!

Funny Bone: That's the spirit! That's a good attitude, Nose!

Head: We all belong to Christ.

All: Right! Here, here!

Funny Bone: We were all baptized by one Holy Spirit.[579]

All: Right! Here, here! Yes, we were!

Funny Bone: We were all baptized into one body—whether we were slave or free, Jews or Greeks.[580] *(Unpresentable Parts raises her hand.)* Yes, Unpresentable Parts?

Unpresentable Parts: Could we also in this modern age say male and female,[581] employed and unemployed, rich and poor, old and young, black and white, and brown or red or yellow?[582]

Funny Bone: *(Smiling broadly.)* I think we can, Unpresentable Parts. I think you've understood the broader meaning of Paul's words.[583]

Hand: OK. It's obvious and established that the body is not made up of one part but of many parts.[584]

All: That's right. All for one and one for all.[585] *(Laughter and high-fives abound.)*

Foot: I'm getting it, I think. I'm remembering Paul's words.

Hand: We have to be reminded again and again.[586]

Foot: *(Continuing the conversation and turning to Hand.)* Yes! If I as the foot say, "Because I'm not a hand I don't belong to the body," I would not cease to be part of the body.[587]

Hand: Right! We're stuck with you, Foot! We're stuck with each other, actually.[588] *(Hand and Foot go around with locked arms and in lock step.)*

Ear: *(To Eye.)* And if I should say, "Because I'm not an eye I don't belong to the body," yet as the ear, I could not and would not cease to be part of the body.[589]

Eye: Hey! If the whole body were like me—an eye—[590]

Ear: *(Interrupting.)* Then how could we hear? And if the whole body were like me—an ear—[591]

Nose: *(Interrupting and carrying on.)* Where then would the sense of smell be?[592]

Head: *(Kindly.)* Yes, everybody needs a nose.[593]

Nose: Thank you, Head. *(Nose bows. Laughter and goodwill suddenly prevail.*[594]*)*

Heart: That's a good motto!

Funny Bone: *(Laughing, pleased.*[595]*)* Right! Good insights! We can trust that God has arranged us as parts of the body just as he wanted us to be![596]

Eye: I get it! There are many parts but one body. Hand, I need to apologize to you. I certainly said and thought this: "I don't need you!"[597] I was rude and wrong. I'm sorry.[598]

Head: *(Stiffly, and clearing his throat.)* Foot, I likewise owe you an apology, for I commented on your ugly toenails and said I didn't like you or need you![599] But hey, you're changing!

Foot: You're the dude! Hey, I like your haircut!

Funny Bone: *(Laughing.*[600]*)* And Paul goes on. And those parts that are weaker turn out to be indispensible, he says.[601] And those parts we think of as less honorable, we are to treat them with more honor. And those parts we call *unpresentable*, we give even greater honor and make sure to let them have a special modesty.[602]

(All bow. Unpresentable Parts smiles modestly and shows she likes her new shawl. She adjusts it to cover more of her shoulders.)

Unpresentable Parts: I see that God has combined us as members of the Body of Christ and even given special honor, even greater honor, to parts that lacked it.[603]

All: How good and kind is our God![604]

Funny Bone: Yes. That's all true. But, Body of Christ, why is this so? Think about why God does this.

(All the characters walk around talking aloud. The following lines are quickly spoken.)

Eye: Because he wanted to![605]

Foot: Because he's good!

Nose: Because he's just!

Heart: Because he loves us all equally!

Ear: Because it's his plan for the church!

Hand: Because Jesus commanded us to love one another!

Head: Funny Bone wants one reason. Let's get in a huddle, and let's remember what Paul wrote.

(They get in a huddle. Funny Bone smiles and gives them space. Murmurs from the huddle include the following comments that are quickly given.)

Hand: I can't remember.

Nose: I wasn't very good in school about memorizing.

Foot: Isn't it something about unity?

Unpresentable Parts: Hey, I thought it was division.

Eye: That's it! I've got it! I remember! It's so that there's no division![606] We're not supposed to be divided![607] *(As the members break out of the huddle, they are very pleased with themselves.)*

Eye: Let's say it together.

All: So that there's "no division in the body!"[608]

Funny Bone: *(Laughing joyfully.)* Right. Paul writes that there should be no division within the Body of Christ. The goal is equal concern of one for the other.[609]

Foot: Well, since our last meeting I sprained my ankle badly and was on crutches for two weeks.

Hand: And I cut my finger almost to the bone.

Head: My head aches all the time because of all my responsibilities.[610]

Eye: I have eyestrain from studying too much. *(Unpresentable Parts, Heart, and Nose show concern in all this.)*

Unpresentable Parts: *(Sighing.)* If one of you suffers, I suffer.[611]

Nose: So do I! Paul said that, and I agree![612] *(They cry together. Heart brings tissues.)*

Funny Bone: Yes, if one suffers, all suffer. *(Brightly.)* But if one is honored, all are honored, too![613] We all rejoice![614]

Mmm. Let me teach you from Scripture.[615]

Rap: Chanted by Funny Bone (All and Head break in) [616]

(Rap rhythm can be like this: Beat, Beat, Shhhhhhhhhhhhhhh. Or like this:

Beat, Beat, Beat, Beat, Beat Beat Shhhhhhhhh. Or like this:

Beat, Beat, Beat, Beat. This is probably the easiest rhythm. It allows for rests. For example, "Seek to do good" is in three beats plus a rest; "Just as God" has two beats and two beats of rest. The downbeat for the 4/4 beat is on the first word in each line of the rap.

Funny Bone can walk in time, snap her fingers, take the whole stage, dance, et cetera.)

Head: Let's give her a beat. *(Four "snappers" come forward. They can be Hand, Eye, Nose, and Head, for example. They form a "back up" group like "doo-ah" singers following a lead crooner. A simple snapping beat is one, two, three, four. The other characters pretend they're crooning.)*

Funny Bone: Great! I'll give you the tempo! *(She sets the beat she finds comfortable. This beat continues throughout her rap.)*

Funny Bone: *(Rapping to the beat)*
Jesus said it this way[617]
Jesus said it this way
Love one another[618]
Love one another
As I have loved you
As I have loved you.[619]
Paul added this

All: Paul added this

Funny Bone: By love, by love,
By love serve one another[620]

All: By love, by love,
By love serve one another[621]

Funny Bone: Seek to do good
Seek to do good
Especially to those
Especially to those

All: In the Body of Christ
                In the Body of Christ[622]

Funny Bone: Proverbs, James, and Peter
                Proverbs, James, and Peter
                All say this:
                All say this:
                Love covers
                Love covers[623]

All: Well, Funny Bone
                Well, Funny Bone
                What does love cover?
                What does love cover?

Funny Bone: A multitude of sins!
                A multitude of sins!
                Love covers
                Love covers
                A multitude of sins!
                A multitude of sins!

Head: Sum it up, Funny Bone!
                Sum it up, Funny Bone!

Funny Bone: Be kind, to each other
                Compassionate
                Forgiving each person
                Just as God
                Just as God
                Just as God in Christ
                Just as God in Christ
                Has forgiven you
                Has forgiven you

All: "Bee bop, for me and you!
                Bee bop, for me and you!
                Ephesians four, thirty-two
                Ephesians four, thirty-two![624]
                (General applause, laughter.[625] Funny Bone bows.)

Head: Hear, hear! This is all well and good. But Funny Bone, it is now time to consider your request. Body of Christ, this is important! Body of Christ, to the huddle![626]

(Head starts singing and directing. The characters gradually assemble toward the center rug.[627] They huddle.[628] Funny Bone goes to the side respectfully.)

Song: **Sung by Head**
Tune: **"Yankee Doodle Dandy"**[629]

(This song starts with the part of the tune, "Yankee Doodle Dandy," that starts with this line, "Father and I went down to camp.")

(When told by Head, Funny Bone goes upstage on cue with a bow. She prays.)

Hurry up now, Body of Christ
Get into formation
Funny Bone, excuse yourself[630]
And so avoid confusion
Let us all be orderly
Let us all be civil
Let us all debate and see
Meeeeeeeee moderate decisively! *(The members shake their heads at Head's pomposity but follow his directions.)*

Head: Well, what do you think, Body of Christ? Should Funny Bone be recognized?

Ear: She certainly is wise. She straightened us out!

Eye: She's a good teacher. She makes us laugh.[631]

Heart: Did you notice that she was always smiling? Her eyes twinkled even when she fussed at us.[632]

Unpresentable Parts: Because of what she said, I am not jealous of you all anymore, and I am not ashamed of who I am. Even I am needed in the Body of Christ.

Nose: She helped us remember Paul's words. We had forgotten them!

Hand: But admitting Funny Bone has to be based on Scripture, and not just because we like her.

Head: Or she makes us laugh.[633]

Nose: Jesus certainly had a sense of humor.[634] So did Paul.[635]

All: You're right about that![636]

Heart: Well, the reason we're in the Body of Christ is that we're mentioned in Proverbs and Psalms or elsewhere in the Bible.

Foot: Right. There are lots of verses in which I figure prominently. Consider Psalm 1:1: "Blessed is the man who does not walk in the counsel of the wicked." Here's a verse about protection: Psalm 121:3: "He will not let your foot slip."

Hand: I like this one about me. Psalm 47:1: "Clap your hands, all you nations! Shout to God with cries of joy!"

Heart: This is my favorite verse about me. Proverbs 4:23: "Above all, guard your heart, for it is the wellspring of life."

Head: I love this verse about me. David is speaking of the Lord, his shepherd. Psalm 23:5: "You anoint my head with oil."

Eye: In Luke 11:34, Jesus calls me the lamp of the body. Jesus says, "When your eyes are good, your whole body also is full of light."

Unpresentable Parts: A whole book is written about me, or at least it seems to be! The Song of Songs is red hot and ready! Listen to parts of chapter 4. *(She recites or reads. A Bible on a lectern may be part of the stage props. The members of the Body of Christ may sit or stand. They all watch her and pay close attention.)* "How beautiful you are, my darling! Oh, how beautiful! Your eyes behind your veil are doves. Your hair is like a flock of goats descending from Mount Gilead. Your teeth are like a flock of sheep just shorn, coming up from the washing. Each has its twin; not one of them is alone. Your lips are like a scarlet ribbon; your mouth is lovely. Your temples behind your veil are like the halves of a pomegranate. Your neck is like the tower of David, built with elegance; on it hang a thousand shields, all of them shields of warriors. Your two breasts are like two fawns, like twin fawns of a gazelle that browse among the lilies . . .You are altogether beautiful, my darling: there is no flaw in you."[637]

All: *(Applause.)* That was lovely, Unpresentable Parts.

  (She bows.[638])

Ear:	Here's a good verse about me: Isaiah 30:21: "Whether you turn to the right or to the left, your ears will hear a voice behind you saying, 'This is the way, walk in it.'"
Nose:	Scripture often describes sacrifices as sweet savors to the Lord. Here's a description from Genesis 8: "Then Noah built an altar to the Lord and, taking some of all the clean animals and clean birds, he sacrificed burnt offerings on it. The Lord smelled the pleasing aroma."
Head:	But are there Bible verses about Funny Bone or things Funny Bone does?
Hand:	How about this: Laughter is the best medicine.
Head:	That's a good start. But it's practical wisdom. It is not in the Bible. (*Everybody seems a bit discouraged.*)
Heart:	I've got it, Body of Christ! I've got a verse about Funny Bone, about what Funny Bone does. (*Heart whispers the verse in the huddle.*)
Nose:	That's good! Let's all say it. (*They turn from the huddle. Funny Bone looks up from prayer and stands waiting.*)
Eye:	Heart, you've hit a home run!
Head:	(*Shouting.*) Funny Bone, we've decided. Come, join us!
	(*Funny Bone joins the group.*)
Heart:	Funny Bone, on behalf of the Body of Christ, we value you and invite you to fully participate in the Body of Christ as a named member. You belong. You're needed.[639] Here's the verse to prove it. We'll say it together.
All:	"A merry heart doeth good like a medicine," Proverbs 17:22.[640]
	(*General goodwill prevails. The sincerity is in marked contrast to the forced, strained goodwill at the beginning.*)
Ear:	Here's another scripture: Isaiah 61:3: The Lord gives "a crown of beauty instead of ashes, the oil of gladness instead of mourning, and a garment of praise instead of a spirit of despair."
Foot:	And Jesus told his disciples many things on the night he was betrayed. Why did he do this? In John 15, he said this: "I have

told you this so that my joy maybe in you and that your joy may be complete."

Funny Bone: Thank you, Body of Christ! I am thrilled to be part of you! My favorite scripture about me is this from Nehemiah 8:10: "The joy of the Lord is your strength!" (*Authentic goodwill prevails.*[641])

Unpresentable Parts: Well, another song is required, don't you think?[642]

Ear: (*Smiling.*) Most certainly.[643]

(*Everybody groups downstage center stage and starts singing. They pause and bow as their names are mentioned. They may sing it twice.*)

Song: **Sung by All**
Tune: **"All People that on Earth do Dwell: 'Old Hundreth'"**[644]
We are in unity and joy
We honor one another first
We do repent of our ill will
For we obey the Lord Jesus

Of Christ's Body we are Head
Hand, Heart, Eye, Ear, Foot, Nose as well
Do not forget Unpresentable Parts
And Funny Bone joins us, too

(*In the reprise, the cast turns and acknowledges Piano Player before facing the audience with the closing line, "And Funny Bone joins us, too."*)

CONCLUSION

Funny Bone ends with unity within the believing community. Bonhoeffer writes that "Christianity means community through Jesus Christ and in Jesus Christ."[645] He explains that an individual Christian "needs others because of Jesus Christ."[646] *Funny Bone's* cast of ten certainly learns this. The members speak God's word to each other and return to their foundation: The centrality of Christ in their lives.

The play began by showing a misplaced pride and a lack of community commitment. These traits produced disunity, what Bonhoeffer aptly calls "discord between God and man and between man and man."[647] The cast's unity can continue "only by way of Jesus Christ. Only in Jesus Christ are we one, only through him are we bound together," as Bonhoeffer rightly says.[648]

Funny Bone ends, as musicals do, happily. Yet as a realist and cradle Presbyterian, I realize that unity is temporary—even when iced with humor, dance, and song. Bumps in the road—"hiccups," as life's trials are humorously called in South Africa—are normal. However when things go awry, this musical provides a template for public confession and forgiveness, and a model for communal discussion of problems.[649]

QUESTIONS FOR CONSIDERATION AND DISCUSSION

1. How is humor a teaching tool?

2. Did you see yourself in any of the characters in *Funny Bone?* If so, please share.

3. What were some sins that you saw in the Body of Christ?

4. How can we better love and serve each other?

5. If you were asked to be part of this play, which character would you be and why?

6. What to you is the worst sin in the Body of Christ?

7. What new insights did this play give you?

Notes

1. Versions of this play were published twice, first in *Christian Higher Education* 4.1 (2005) 57–69, and next online in the *Society of Biblical Literature, SBL Forum for February/March,* 8 pages (2006). http://www.sbl-site.org/publications/article.aspx?articleId=488.

2. All music is in the public domain.

3. This play has been performed many times. However, reading a play also gives satisfaction. DiYanni puts it this way: "How do we imaginatively reconstruct a play in our minds? Essentially, we translate the script we read into a mental performance that we imagine" (*Literature*, 900).

4. Forde makes this observation: "It is a mistake to believe that there are two different sorts of art: Christian art and everybody else's art. Art is not different in this respect from, say, cooking. Good bread made by a pagan is just as nourishing as good bread made by a Christian. The worth and validity of a piece of art stand separate from the beliefs of its creator. And that is true even when those beliefs are embodied in it. Art is not a matter of content but of form" (*Theatercraft*, 15).

5. Edyvean distinguishes religious drama and its elements from Christian drama. Christian drama combines the following elements:
- The idea that human beings are in some way responsible; they may have freedoms or limits, but they are also held accountable.
- Christian concepts like forgiveness, repentance, atonement, judgment, fellowship, confession, trials, trust, and faith are explored.
- Christian drama emphasizes redemption and hope, no matter how dire the circumstances.
- Love is seen as human love directed horizontally toward others and directed upward toward God. This is in contrast to a worldly idea of love that dotes on self love.
- Symbolism is present.
- Jesus Christ is central. The life of Christ is seen in some way in the characters (Edyvean, *This Dramatic World,* 18–19).

This play is Christian drama, according to Edyvean's definition.

6. David Brown, a strong advocate of combining imagination and Christianity, thinks that imagination and faithful exegesis help explain difficult miracles or difficult moral

lessons, as in the case of Elijah on Mount Carmel and his slaughter of the false prophets (1 Kings 18; D. Brown, *God and Mystery in Words*, 177–78).

That principle holds for this play. For example, this play invites the audience to imagine a carpenter's shop with a dirt floor and scant furnishing and what Mary and Joseph look like. A reader does these things quite naturally when reading a text. Some would call this play a bibliodrama. Bibliodrama allows passionate, literate teachers of the Bible to make the Bible come alive to a modern audience whose members combine scholarship, book knowledge, and street smarts (Pitzele, *Scripture Windows*, 13).

However, Pitzele sees the Bible as a living myth. I see it and its characters as real. We agree, however, that the biblical text is "relevant, disturbing, and still capable of taking our breath away" (ibid.). Bibliodrama begins with the ability to read the biblical text creatively (ibid., 26). Although starting with commentaries, the interaction moves on to the stage where "the text is given a voice and answers me back," he (ibid., 28) writes.

7. The stage is minimal. The blocking, the movements of the actors on the stage (see DiYanni, *Literature*, 929), weaves in and around Joseph's two work stations and the wooden chairs in stage center.

8. As I wrote this play, I remembered insights and definitions given by Quash: "Drama displays human actions and temporal events in specific contexts. Theodramatics concerns itself with *human actions* (people), *temporal events* (time), and their *specific contexts* (places) *in relation to God's purpose*" (*Theology and the Drama of History*, 3–4; italics original).

The central idea of a story "reveals the author's point of view on some aspect of life" (Lostracco and Wilkerson, *Analyzing Short Stories*, 1). My academic work has been largely on obscure portions of scripture and often on silent and unnamed women (see Branch, *Jeroboam's Wife*, 2010). I investigate silences in the biblical text instead of reading quickly over them. This play presents one such time of reflection and pause.

The setting supports the central idea—that Mary told Joseph she was pregnant—by having the meeting take place in the home/workshop of Joseph (see Lostracco and Wilkerson, *Analyzing Short Stories*, 32).

9. A conversation between Mary and Joseph, when she tells him of her pregnancy, must have taken place in some manner, because Joseph decides to divorce her. In deciding to write a play about this conversation, I realized that drama has advantages over succinct prose in the following ways (cf. Clark et al., *Childhood Education in the Church*, 545–46):

- A story often becomes real and alive with enactment.
- A drama on the stage conveys honest emotions and feelings; a reader may miss these feelings with just a casual read.
- A drama provides a teaching venue and a learning venue quite different from a classroom; a drama promotes friendships on levels different from those in a classroom.
- Becoming an actor in a play enables a person to think outside himself or herself.
- Taking part in a drama allows an actor, via imagination, to gain insights into the thinking and actions of another person.

10. The accounts of Matthew and Luke differ in that Matthew stresses Joseph, "whose dreams and actions stitch the narrative together," while Luke's gospel "centers on Mary

and parallels the births of Jesus and John the Baptist" (Strauss, *Four Portraits, One Jesus,* 220). Both gospels, however, focus on themes of fulfillment and promise, on Jesus as the descendant of David and the one born to be king, and on the coming of Jesus as the fulfillment of the hopes of the Jews (ibid., 220).

11. The NIV text is used in this play.

The charge that the birth of Jesus in the way it came about is a myth or simply Matthew's imagination is refuted because similar details are recorded in a different account in Luke; furthermore, the tone of both Matthew and Luke is different from the tone of pagan stories that recount when the gods had intercourse with women (see France, *Matthew,* 76).

12. Hagner notices the tension in verse 19 and suggests it be translated "*although* being righteous . . . and *yet* not willing to make an example of her" (*Matthew 1–13,* 18; italics original).

13. The word *quietly* puzzles scholars because divorce had to have witnesses and Mary's pregnancy eventually and quickly would become well known; furthermore, it would be assumed that her divorce was because of her adultery and the evidence of her adultery was the child (see R. E. Brown, *Birth of the Messiah,* 128). Joseph's decision to divorce Mary quietly may indicate a decision to divorce her leniently (ibid.).

Decades later Jesus addresses the concept of divorce (Matt 19:1–12) and specifically the views of Hillel and Shammai who disputed Deut 24:1–4. Shammai interpreted the "something indecent" portion of Deut 24 as marital unfaithfulness, and Jesus upheld this view. Hillel interpreted the Deuteronomy text to mean that a man may divorce his wife for any infringement of his likes and dislikes—even if she burned the soup (see *NIV Study Bible,* 1466n)! Consequently, many Jewish women must have lived in fear and uncertainty, for divorce may have meant a life of hardship, starvation, and/or prostitution. Perhaps remembering his mother's predicament, Jesus opted for Shammai's version yet added that God's original plan was a lifelong union of one flesh between a man and a woman. Joseph, who became Jesus' legal father, also chooses Shammai's view and decides to divorce Mary because of her perceived marital unfaithfulness.

14. The Announcer invites the audience to imagine a small stone house. Both drama and religion engage the imagination and the dramatic instinct innate in people (see Ehrensperger, *Religious Drama,* 100).

15. The story begins. The details of the action, the structure of the dialogue, and the various incidents form what is called the plot of a play (DiYanni, *Literature,* 920). This is a short play because "a good plot will also be economical" (ibid.). Few scholars write on how Joseph learned of Mary's pregnancy. Bailey is an exception (*Jesus through Middle Eastern Eyes*).

16. Bailey pauses to consider Joseph's reactions as to when he learned of Mary's pregnancy. He sees Matthew's editorial comment—"being a just man" (Matt 1:19)—as meaning that Joseph decided to break the law of Moses and divorce his betrothed "quietly rather than exposing her" (*Jesus through Middle Eastern Eyes,* 43). Bailey considers this a bold act because it goes beyond the ethical expectations normally followed by a person facing his circumstances. Bailey speculates that Joseph followed the mode of Isaiah's suffering servant (Isa 42:1–6), who chooses not to break a bruised reed or quench a dimly burning wick (ibid., 44).

17. Mary's exceptional life entwines emphases on motherhood and the bridal state. Furthermore, she is an "answering woman" because of her response to Gabriel (Von Balthasar, *Theo-Drama,* 3:293, 294).

18. The characters in a play may remind us of ourselves or we may see them as different from us. They may appeal to us or we may not like them (see DiYanni, *Literature,* 922). Mary and Joseph are both major characters because the action revolves around them, and they are both dynamic characters because each grows and changes during the course of the play (ibid., 923).

Truly, "character is the companion of plot" because the actions of the characters propel the plot (ibid., 924).

19. According to tradition, Elizabeth and Zechariah lived in Ein Karem, a village about five miles west of Jerusalem and eighty miles from Nazareth (Holy Apostles Convent, *Life of the Virgin Mary,* 119).

20. Mary did not travel to Elizabeth "in haste" (*cum festinatione*) but in a serious mood of mind (*meta spoude*) (Hospodar, "*Meta spoudes* in Luke 1:39," 18).

21. Themes common in an account of a super-hero's birth are the barrenness of one mother and the unmarried social status of the other mother (Brenner, "Female Social Behaviour," 269). Significantly, there is a lack of rivalry—on issues like status, beauty, ambition, age—between Elizabeth and Mary. Instead, the women are mutually supportive and share the commonality of faith. The good will Mary and Elizabeth enjoy sets the tone for the relationship of their sons by eliminating the possibility of power struggles between them in the future (ibid., 270).

22. Mary has thought through what she must tell Joseph. She begins with her stay with her relatives, Elizabeth and Zechariah. This, however, is what is technically called a subtext (DiYanni, *Literature,* 928). After telling the good news of Elizabeth's pregnancy first, Mary will eventually tell her own good news to Joseph.

23. This play is told from the dramatic point of view through the words and actions of the players (Lostracco and Wilkerson, *Analyzing Short Stories,* 28). The actors' unrevealed thoughts and feelings are interpreted by their words and actions.

24. I have endeavored throughout the play to indicate the tone via italics, stage directions, diction, and various figures of speech and thought (Greenblatt, *Norton Anthology of English Literature,* A56–A60).

25. As Mary tells Joseph about her trip and the amazing things that have happened to her, she is not only someone who speaks for herself but also is the subject of the discussion. See Greenblatt for a fascinating essay on how women defended themselves in prose and verse against written attacks from men—and also leveled a few volleys themselves (ibid., 2589–90)!

26. The betrothal period probably has been about a year. The betrothal, because of the poverty of Joseph and Mary, probably entailed the simplest of dowries (Holy Apostles Convent, *Life of the Virgin Mary,* 69).

27. There were three steps in a Jewish marriage: The engagement (perhaps even taking place when the couple were children); betrothal; and the marriage proper (which took place at the end of the year of betrothal) (Barclay, *Gospel of Matthew,* 9). Significantly, a girl could choose not to enter into a betrothal; if she did become betrothed,

however, the betrothal was "absolutely binding" and during that year the couple was known as husband and wife, although they as yet had no marital rights. The betrothal could be ended only with a divorce.

Here is more on Jewish marriage traditions: The man, the betrothed, was the husband but the woman, the bride, remained in her father's home (France, *Matthew*, 77). When the betrothal time ended, the man took the bride to his home in a public ceremony; it was then that they could come together and enjoy sexual intercourse (ibid.).

28. Mary, throughout this conversation with Joseph, displays an underlying sense of joy, an emotion consistent with the material contained in Luke 1 (see Craddock, *Luke*, 25–33).

29. One of the main sources of pleasure in a play is its surprises (DiYanni, *Literature*, 921). In this play, the audience and Mary know more than Joseph knows. Joseph expresses many aspects of surprise throughout the drama.

30. Although Luke 1:6–7 emphasizes the couple's upright character, it also stresses their outstanding humiliation and outstanding need: They were childless! Childlessness was a valid reason for divorce—and even for excommunication. The rabbis said that seven kinds of people were excommunicated from God; the first two leading the list were as follows: "A Jew who has no wife or a Jew who has a wife and who has no child" (Barclay, *Gospel of Luke*, 4).

Barrenness is the essential social fact about Elizabeth and her great, ongoing disgrace (Bauckham, *Gospel Women*, 72).

31. Luke 1:5–7. Luke's introduction of Zechariah and Elizabeth as pious, law-abiding saints shows that his narrative emphasizes righteous foundations (see Bock, *Luke*, 35).

32. The stories of the births of John and Jesus abound with miracles. Indeed, the Gospel of Matthew presents the situations surrounding Jesus' birth in Bethlehem as filled with intrigue (see Burge et al., *New Testament in Antiquity*, 169).

33. Mary was fortunate indeed to have the guidance and confidence of Elizabeth, an older woman. Quite likely, Mary sought her counsel on how to tell her betrothed, Joseph, about her situation, which definitely affects him, and that she is indeed a virgin and yet pregnant.

Drane discusses the difficulties modern readers have with the concept of a virgin birth. "To be a virgin and pregnant is a contradiction in terms," he begins, and that concept was "quite unacceptable in any form to orthodox Jews" (*Introducing the New Testament*, 55, 57). Matthew seems to draw from the LXX version of Isaiah, which translates 7:14 as *virgin* while in the Hebrew text the term may refer to a *young woman* (ibid., 56–57). Both Luke and Matthew present the material about Jesus' birth in the same way that they present other material about Jesus: Straightforwardly and without elaboration.

34. Angelic visitations announcing births are common throughout the Old Testament; see Gen 16:10–11; 17:15–19; 18:10–15; 25:23; Judg 13:3–21 (Bock, *Luke*, 36).

35. Zechariah, who belonged to the priestly order of Abijah, was chosen by lot to minister to the Lord in the temple and burn incense; while about his duties, an angel of the Lord appeared to him and stood at the right side of the altar of incense (Luke 1:5, 8–9, 11). The division of Abijah was one of twenty-four divisions that served in the temple twice a year and for a week at a time (Gundry, *A Survey of the New Testament*, 217).

36. The child John will become more than a prophet because he fulfills "the prophetic hope of Mal 4:5–6 that Elijah would return before the day of the Lord"; see also Mal 3:1; Luke 7:26; and Matt 17:10–13) (see Burge et al., *New Testament in Antiquity*, 200).

37. Repetition, a tool in drama and in the biblical text, invites the audience to pause and consider the meaning and emphasis of the words or phrase (DiYanni, *Literature*, 922).

38. The major message of Gabriel's visit to Zechariah and to Luke's readers "is that God will do what he promises in his own way" (Bock, *Luke*, 37).

39. Elizabeth and Zechariah's son John, when he grows up, will redirect those responding to his message toward a new walk with God (Bock, *Luke*, 37).

40. Craddock, *Luke*, 26.

41. The play notes Mary's affection for Elizabeth and Zechariah. It seems the miracle of Elizabeth's pregnancy mellowed the elderly priest, for "Luke introduces Zechariah as something of an old grump" (Branch, "Luke 1:68–79," 35).

42. Laughter is an important part of theatre. It is an act of reflection and occurs spontaneously. It comments on something or returns something in a tit-for-tat fashion. It may even punish a recognizable human failing. To hit the mark, to make us laugh, the comment does not necessarily have to be kind-hearted (Bergson, *Laughter*, 197, 198).

43. One tradition is that the Annunciation occurred when Joseph was absent from his home and working his trade as a builder (Holy Apostles Convent, *Life of the Virgin Mary*, 71). Yet another tradition is that Mary lived in the home of Joseph and that he was elderly (ibid., 78).

44. In the theatre, a coincidence that keeps happening becomes a repetition and leads to laughter (see Bergson, *Laughter*, 90).

45. In Matthew, Joseph receives an angelic announcement; in Luke, Mary receives the angelic announcement (Spivey et al., *Anatomy of the New Testament*, 127).

46. Mary was not looking for God, but the angel Gabriel was sent to her (Talbert, "Luke 1:26–31," 289).

47. Mary's statements that all generations shall call her blessed and that he who is mighty has done great things for her reflect not pride or vainglory. Remember this: She earlier had called herself the handmaid of the Lord (Luke 1:48–49, 38) (Holy Apostles Convent, *Life of the Virgin Mary*, 128).
   Mary links what is happening to her with the history of God's workings with Israel when she sings, "The Mighty One has done great things for me" (O'Day, "Singing Woman's Song," 208).
   In the Gospel of Luke, Mary is a spirit-filled singer (Strauss, *Four Portraits, One Jesus*, 265) as this play emphasizes. This play does not contain the song of Zechariah which comes after the circumcision of John and after Mary leaves the home of Zechariah and Elizabeth; it is outside the scope of this play.

48. Praise acknowledges God's goodness and God's actions and brings attention to God (Bock, *Luke*, 45).
   Mary's hymn or canticle bears similarities to the hymns of praise in the psalms, specifically Psalms 33, 47, 48, 117 and 135 (Fitzmyer, *Luke I–IX*, 359). Luke 1:49, "he has

done great things for me," reflects Deut 10:21 (ibid., 367).

Mary's song notes not the high status of David's royalty "but the low status of David's humble origins" (Bauckham, *Gospel Women,* 73). Mary's social status is consistent with the kind of Messiah she carries: This Messiah comes from "lowly origins in order to exalt the lowly and to abase the haughty" (ibid., 74).

49. Conrad explores the relationship between the words *fear not* and *behold.* "Fear not!" is a common command when a heavenly visitor interrupts an earthly scene. Frequently such an encounter is introduced in the Old Testament with the word *Behold! (hinneh).* Behold is a textual marker, a word indicating special emphasis and alerting the hearer/reader that something of note is about to be spoken or take place. The Greek equivalent for *behold* is *idou* (Conrad, "Annunciation of Birth," 660–63).

The angel greets Mary with "Do not be afraid" (*me phobou*), Mary." *Behold* is omitted. The angel appears to Joseph in a dream also with behold (*idou*). "Fear not" in the New Testament "seeks to eliminate the fear aroused not only by the appearance of the numinous but also by other circumstances associated with the announcement of the birth of a son" (ibid., 661).

50. In contrast to the electricity associated with Zechariah's encounter with Gabriel, a simple calmness dominates the angel's assigned visit to Mary (see Bock, *Luke,* 39).

51. Commenting on Gabriel's sudden appearance, Gomes thinks Gabriel "has a lot to answer for" because he "interrupts what we might imagine to be the ordinary routine of the life of this young woman who is about to be married" (*Sermons,* 10).

52. The legends about Mary including her delayed birth, her holiness, her childhood, and her participation with other virgins in making the veil of the Temple are not mentioned in this drama, but for a fascinating account of them read *The Life of the Virgin Mary, the Theotokos,* 1–73.

53. What Mary says here, a prayer and a remembrance, is an aside (DiYanni, *Literature,* 925).

This play was written with this concept in mind: Mary is living out theology as it develops; so is Joseph. They are human beings who are being remarkably used by God. Theology encourages its followers to learn from others. Steurernagel learns from Mary, as do I. For him, "The theologian Mary walks around showing off her pregnant womb to help us understand that theology becomes mature in the active expectancy of the fulfillment of God's actions. It's theology with the gesture of vocation, pointing towards an obedient discipleship" ("Doing Theology with an Eye on Mary," 104).

54. Matthew's birth narrative presents the theme that this child, Jesus, is the promised Messiah and will bring salvation to his people (Strauss, *Four Portraits, One Jesus,* 224). Matt 1:16–25 highlights these facts: Jesus is born into the household of Joseph, a descendent of David (Matt 1:16, 20); Bethlehem is the prophesied birthplace of the upcoming Davidic king (Matt 1:23; Mic 5:2); the baby's name, Jesus, *Yeshua,* means Yahweh Saves (Matt 1:21); the virgin birth confirms the prophetic word in Isaiah that Immanual, God with us, will be among his people (Matt 1:22–23; ibid.).

55. Jesus' genealogy in Matthew contains five women—Tamar, Rahab, Ruth, the wife of Uriah the Hittite, and Mary—perhaps setting the tone for the "possibility of the unexpected" in Matthew (Spivey et al., *Anatomy of the New Testament,* 92). The Christ presented in Matthew "may not correspond to the image of the Messiah for whom Israel

was waiting" (ibid.).

56. Matthew 1:1–17 shows the line of Jesus starting with Abraham and ending this way: "and Jacob the father of Joseph, the husband of Mary, of whom was born Jesus, who is called Christ" (v. 16). Luke 3:23–37 begins this way: "Now Jesus himself was about thirty years old when he began his ministry. He was the son, so it was thought, of Joseph, the son of Heli" (v. 23). 2 Chr 3:1–16 gives the line of David. Verse 5 is noteworthy for this play: "And these were the children born to (David) there: Shammua, Shobab, Nathan and Solomon. These four were by Bathsheba daughter of Amiel."

The genealogies in Luke and Matthew link Jesus to David's line (Strauss, *Four Portraits, One Jesus*, 414). Matthew's genealogy starts at Abraham and ends with Jesus. Luke's goes in reverse: linking Jesus back to Adam. Here are some differences between the two genealogy accounts. Luke's list is the longer with forty names between David and Joseph; Matthew's list contains twenty-six names. A reason the two differ could be that while both relate to Joseph, Matthew presents the kingly, royal line and Luke gives Joseph's actual forbearers (ibid.).

57. Joseph is correct: God is on the move again in ways and patterns familiar to those who know the history of Israel. Here are some examples: The casting of lots for the determination of Zechariah's time in the Temple; a heavenly messenger coming to an old man and later to a maiden; a childless, elderly couple conceiving a son; a delayed child marked as a child of promise (Craddock, *Luke*, 26).

58. The child Mary carries "is nothing less than the fulfillment of God's design, for a prophet had spoken generations ago that 'a virgin will conceive and give birth to a son, and they will call him Immanuel'" (Isa 7:14) (Burge et al., *New Testament in Antiquity*, 169).

59. Respect and awe for God's plan of salvation are factors in Matthew's description of Joseph's characteristic of uprightness or justice (R. E. Brown, *Birth of the Messiah*, 126).

60. France also notices the omission of mention of Joseph. He puts it this way: "That Jesus was conceived by a virgin mother without the agency of Joseph is clearly stated throughout this section" (*Matthew*, 76).

61. Ceroke sees Mary's question as indicating she already had thought about virginity during marriage; he argues, cautiously, that she was psychologically prepared for a lifetime of virginity ("Luke 1:34 and Mary's Virginity," 342).

62. The biblical narrative mentions Mary's virginity twice—once by the narrator and then by Mary herself—because of its importance; it is the singular descriptive element about her (Luke 1:27, 34). Consequently, this play stresses her virginity. Both Luke and Matthew are more interested in a virginal conception rather than a virginal birth (Spivey et al., *Anatomy of the New Testament*, 127).

63. Smith sees Mary's question, "How will this be, since I am a virgin?" (Luke 1:34), as still very much our question, too, when we think about Jesus and the promise to mankind that Jesus' story presents (Smith, "Exposition of Luke 1:26–38," 417).

Mary's question shows wisdom and prudence; she wants to know how what the angel said is possible (Holy Apostles Convent, *Life of the Virgin Mary*, 101). Because her virginity is emphasized in both Luke and Matthew, it is clear she conceives not by a man, but by the overshadowing of the Holy Spirit (Globe, "Some Doctrinal Variants in Matthew 1 and Luke 2," 54).

64. Mary's account differs markedly from pagan god/man birth stories. Mary's account of what happened to her, better termed a virginal conception rather than a virgin birth, stresses the miraculous. There is no hint of "a sexual union between Mary and the Holy Spirit" (Strauss, *Four Portraits, One Jesus*, 415).

65. In the Luke account, the phrase Son of God that applies to Mary's child is linked as well with Adam (Luke 3:38) (Burge et al., *New Testament in Antiquity*, 200).

66. Regarding the angel's visit, "it is not an easy thing to be confronted with a message from God" (Gomes, *Sermons*, 10). Indeed, neither is it an easy thing to say yes to God. Those who say yes to God—Moses, Abraham, Isaiah, Jeremiah and now Mary—find themselves annoyed "not so much at their own unworthiness for such a high calling, for that would come later, but annoyed at the more practical level of inconvenience" (ibid.). Truly, as this play illustrates, Mary's pregnancy is at times very inconvenient!

67. The *Protoevangelion* recounts Joseph's distress, his view that she had been seduced, Mary's tears, and his confrontational manner toward her (see Holy Apostles Convent, *Life of the Virgin Mary*, 134–35; see *Protoevangelion*, 30.)

68. Matthew's account of Jesus' birth shows Joseph's embarrassment at the prospect of the birth of Jesus before his marriage with Mary is consummated (Spivey et al., *Anatomy of the New Testament*, 90).

69. A polemic against Christianity by Celsus written in the late second century AD bears interest. Among other things, Celsus claims that a Roman soldier named Pantera or Panthera impregnated Mary. Later rabbinic literature also includes this story (Tosefta *Hullin* 2.22–24; Evans, *Fabricating Jesus*, 217–18).

70. R. E. Brown's explanation of her virginity, though dated, is still outstanding. I quote it in full. "There is never a suggestion in Matthew or in Luke that the Holy Spirit is the male element in a union with Mary, supplying the husband's role in begetting. Not only is the Holy Spirit not male (feminine in Hebrew; neuter in Greek), but also the manner of begetting is implicitly creative rather than sexual" (R. E. Brown, *Birth of the Messiah*, 124).

71. Bailey picks up, as I do, on Joseph's anger, although Bailey calls it Joseph's fuming. He sees the passage, as do I, as showing that Joseph is extremely upset over Mary's condition. It disrupts his life. It shames him. The root of the Greek word for "he considered" (Matt 1:20) (*enthymeomai*) is *thymos*, wrath (see Bailey, *Jesus through Middle Eastern Eyes*, 44–66). Indeed, Matthew uses it shortly thereafter to describe the rage of Herod upon discovering the wise men had tricked him by leaving Bethlehem without reporting to him where the child lived (Matt 2:16).

72. Mary here shows both her complexity and the complex situation she faces (see Lostracco and Wilkerson, *Analyzing Short Stories*, 13).

73. A church tradition is that Joseph asks Mary the same question that God earlier had asked Eve, "Why hast thou done this?" (Gen 3:13) (Holy Apostles Convent, *Life of the Virgin Mary*, 134–35).

74. There is a theological significance in the virginal conception. Strauss discusses the theological significance of the virginal conception this way:
"Some have argued it was necessary to protect Jesus' sinless nature, but the narratives themselves do not indicate this purpose. The Messiah could have entered human life free

from sin with or without a virginal conception. Nor is Scripture explicit on the details of the conception. Did God create the sperm for Mary's egg? Did he create a fertilized embryo? This latter question raises questions about how Jesus could have been fully human if he had no physical connection to Mary or Joseph. The former raises the question of how Jesus could have avoided Mary's sinful nature. The Roman Catholic answer is the immaculate conception, whereby Mary herself was born free from sin. But this doctrine has no basis in Scripture. In the final analysis, the details remain a mystery. What is certain from the text is that the conception of Jesus was a supernatural act of God, confirming that God himself was about to accomplish the salvation which no human being could achieve" (*Four Portraits, One Jesus*, 415).

I do not believe that Mary was sinless. This play presents her as a strong, normal young woman. I certainly agree that mystery abounds in the infancy narratives. However, the stories in Luke and Matthew give us enough on which to base our faith. Indeed, it is a firm foundation. We know enough to trust the Lord. Deuteronomy 29:29 says this: "The secret things belong to the Lord our God, but the things revealed belong to us and to our children forever, that we may follow all the words of this law."

75. Some may be offended that Joseph could regard Mary as an adulteress; "but among first-century Christians of Jewish origin this would in no way distract from his upright character" (R. E. Brown, *Birth of the Messiah*, 127–28).

76. Joseph immediately assumes she has been unfaithful (ibid., 127). Nothing Mary says from here on changes his view.

After Joseph decides to divorce Mary because of her perceived unfaithfulness, an unspecified length of time occurs. The Bible does not state how long—a day, a week, an evening, an hour?—it is until an angel of the Lord also appears to Joseph and addresses Joseph's assumption of Mary's unfaithfulness. The angel commands Joseph not to fear to take Mary as his wife into his home. The angel's statement makes it clear that Mary has not broken the law and become an adulteress (ibid.). The angel of the Lord puts to rest Joseph's concern that Mary broke the law (Matt 1:20–21).

77. The betrothal meant that the couple was treated as married; however, there had not been a consummation. Consequently, matters of inheritance, death, adultery and divorce were handled according to the law. The betrothal, as with a marriage, could not be dissolved except by divorce (Holy Apostles Convent, *Life of the Virgin Mary*, 69).

78. Othello, likewise, does not believe Desdemona's story or that she is innocent. He calls her foul and claims her chastity is cold (Shakespeare, *Tragedy of Othello,* IV, Scene III:197, 272–273).

79. Zechariah and Elizabeth represent the best of Israel; they show that true piety, based not on meticulous legalism but on practiced prayer, existed in Israel (Dean, *Luke,* 20).

80. Isa 7:14. Matthew's choice of *virgin* shows he follows the Greek text and not the Hebrew (Murphy, *An Introduction to Jesus and the Gospels,* 145).

81. The child Mary carries "is nothing less than the fulfillment of God's design, for a prophet had spoken generations ago that 'a virgin will conceive and give birth to a son, and they will call him Immanuel'" (Burge et al., *New Testament in Antiquity,* 169).

82. Deut 22:22.

83. Joseph is trying to find a way out of the dilemma of Mary's pregnancy. He here mentions Deut 22:23–24: "If a man happens to meet in a town a virgin pledged to be married and he sleeps with her, you shall take both of them to the gate of that town and stone them to death—the girl because she was in a town and did not scream for help, and the man because he violated another man's wife. You must purge the evil from among you."

The biblical text hints at the thoughts Joseph may be thinking because it calls him a just man. Concealing an act of fornication or adultery makes one complicit in breaking the law. Joseph did not believe that he ethically could conceal what he had determined was Mary's sin of adultery (see Holy Apostles Convent, *Life of the Virgin Mary*, 138).

84. Mary sticks to her story; Mary sticks to the truth about what happened to her. Joseph does not believe her. It is hoped that the audience at this time begins to see the polarization of the two sides and to sympathize with both parties. A critical feature of drama is its mimetic nature; drama is interactive (see DiYanni, *Literature*, 900).

85. Here Joseph brings up Deut 22:25: "But if out in the country a man happens to meet a girl pledged to be married and rapes her, only the man who has done this shall die. Do nothing to the girl; she has committed no sin deserving of death. This case is like that of someone who attacks and murders his neighbor, for the man found the girl out in the country, and though the betrothed girl screamed, there was no one to rescue her."

86. Evidently, "if Joseph wished to end the betrothal, he could do so in no other way than by divorce; and in that year of betrothal Mary was legally known as his wife" (Barclay, *Gospel of Matthew*, 9).

87. Joseph also knows this law, Deut 22:28–29: "If a man happens to meet a virgin who is not pledged to be married and rapes her and they are discovered, he shall pay the girl's father fifty shekels of silver. He must marry the girl, for he has violated her. He can never divorce her as long as he lives."

The custom was that an engagement consisted of a formal and witnessed agreement to marry and the payment of the bride price to the father of the bride; the marriage and its celebration and its consummation took place a year later (see Burge et al., *New Testament in Antiquity*, 200).

88. With this statement, Mary shows that part of the drama in this play involves practical theology. In technical terms, it is action-reflection and theory-praxis (see Stevenson-Moessner, *Prelude to Practical Theology*, 59). Part of the drama, involving the necessity of Mary's action of telling Joseph she is pregnant, is the examination of the personal cost and even life-threatening cost to Mary. There often can be a "personal price of praxis," Stevenson-Moessner says (ibid., 59), as was the case for Elizabeth Cady Stanton, an abolitionist; Dietrich Bonhoeffer, a theologian; and Jeannete Noel, a woman involved with the *Catholic Worker* newspaper.

89. Lostracco and Wilkerson note that "what characters say is often more revealing than their actions; however, in order to draw valid conclusions about a character's personality, the reader must consider the character's words in relation to the character's mood, the situation the character is in, the character's relationship to others in the story, and whether or not the character's behavior is consistent with the words" (*Analyzing Short Stories*, 17). Joseph's words and actions clearly show a man distraught, disappointed, and very angry.

90. However, the Law has not been broken because she conceived through the agency of the Holy Spirit; therefore, her virginity remains (see R. E. Brown, *Birth of the Messiah*, 127).

91. Throughout the encounter with Joseph, difficult as it is, Mary conducts herself with poise and courage. She does not lie.

According to O'Day, "Mary speaks of herself in the same way as she speaks of those whom God exalts at the expense of the mighty. God did not choose a woman of wealth and standing to give birth to the savior of Israel, but a woman of low degree, a woman who stands with those who are poor, afflicted and oppressed," ("Singing Woman's Song," 207).

92. A view that has wide credence in Catholic theology is that Mary preferred virginity even after marriage (Ceroke, "Luke 1:34 and Mary's Virginity," 329). Perhaps Joseph later agreed, even after their official marriage; Mary may have resisted conjugal relations because of spiritual motives (ibid., 342). "There is a natural mystery in many human decisions, and in particular those regarding state of life," Ceroke concludes (ibid.).

It seems to me that the biblical text gives scant support to Ceroke's view. For example, Mark 3:31–35 talks about Jesus' mother and brothers joining a crowd outside a place where he was teaching (see also Matt 12:46–50 and Luke 8:19–21). Evidently, in Catholic Church teaching, vowed virginity was "not a genuine patristic teaching before" Augustine's time and the scholastics later formalized it (Faley, "Review of J. F. Craghan," 437). If one holds with Mary's perpetual and intentional virginity, one must see it as total dedication to the will of God (ibid., 438).

93. While characteristics like *blameless* and *upright* describe Zechariah and Elizabeth, the designation *virgin* describes Mary. Mary becomes the first model disciple in the new order. Luke 1 shows her as calm, obedient, full of worship, courageous, willing to take God at his word, willing to experience the unknown, willing to believe past her natural understanding, and even a good songwriter! Likewise, Elizabeth is a model of how to react. Believing and joyful, she is an "amazed saint" (Bock, *Luke*, 43).

It would seem that Elizabeth's filling by the Holy Spirit prepared and enabled her to understand Mary's new condition before Mary told her about it. This is significant, because it enabled Elizabeth to believe the fact that Mary was pregnant with the Son of God and enabled Mary to share the details of how this came to pass.

94. Elizabeth speaks as a prophet (Dean, *Luke*, 23).

95. Elizabeth gives a blessing and a beatitude over her young kinswoman; first, Mary is blest *(eulogeme)* among women because of whom she carries in her womb, and second, she is blessed *(makaria)* because of her faith (see Fitzmyer, *Luke I–IX*, 358).

Regarding Luke 1:39–45, my view is summarized nicely this way: "Mary was a recipient of grace, not a source of grace. Her blessedness was the blessedness of one who became a willing channel of divine blessings to others" (Dean, *Luke*, 23–24).

96. Luke 1:42–43.

97. Some view the doctrine that Mary is the Mother of God as the most important truth about Mary, a truth supported by scripture, tradition, and the teaching and authority of the Roman Catholic and Orthodox churches (see Holy Apostles Convent, *Life of the Virgin Mary*, 123–24).

98. Luke's account of Mary's visit to Elizabeth serves to distinguish the roles of the

sons the two pregnant women bear. John will be a prophet to the Most High (Luke1:76) and Mary's son Jesus will be the Son of the Most High (Luke 1:32). See Strauss (*Four Portraits, One Jesus,* 264–65) for an excellent and succinct explanation of the different roles, functions, and ranks of these two baby boys.

99. The concept of *theotokos* (literally *God-bearer*) is not to give glory to the mother "but to guarantee that the life of Jesus was from its inception due to God's act" (Talbert, "Luke 1:26–31," 291). Mary, both in her call from God and in her response to that call, "becomes the mother not only of Jesus but of our vocation, and of our calling as well. She shows us that it is possible for us to be gifted ones with her, the bearers of Christ in our world" (Gomes, *Sermons,* 15)

100. Theology is learned on the knife edge of life. Theology must kneel at the cross, face death, wait for resurrection, and adjust to a new season in God's salvific plan. Decades later Mary stood by at the foot of the cross (Steuernagel, "Doing Theology with an Eye on Mary," 110).

101. Actually, Elizabeth correctly honored Mary because the son Mary was carrying outranked the son in Elizabeth's womb. The meeting of these four—the two mothers and their two sons—produces "a new tradition of a super-hero's birth" (Brenner, "Female Social Behavior,"269).

102. Luke 1:44. The leaping of the baby John is a prophetic action and intended as a recognition by him of his relation to Jesus" (Fitzmyer, *Luke I–IX,* 357, 363). Luke seems to intend a parallel with the matriarch Rebecca. The LXX recounts Gen 25:22, a similar in-the-womb moment, and notes Rebecca's twins leaped (*eskirton*) (ibid., 363).

The two sons in this part of the story, John and Jesus, meet in the wombs of their mothers. They are coming, by God's mercy, into history. Decades later, one proclaims the upcoming salvation, and One not only is that salvation but also takes people into that salvation (see Bock, *Luke,* 53).

103. Luke 1:41–45. The Holy Spirit works in families. Elizabeth first was filled with the Holy Spirit and then her husband Zechariah was likewise filled (Luke 1:41, 67). Luke makes it clear that the words and views first of Elizabeth and then later in the chapter of Zechariah "are not simply their own; they sing and prophesy about their son and Jesus in speech inspired by the Holy Spirit" (Craddock, *Luke,* 32).

104. 2 Kgs 22; 2 Chr 34:14–28.

105. Luke 1:45. "Blessed is she who has believed" gives the essence of a proper response to God: trust that what God says is true and live joyfully in light of that truth (see Bock, *Luke,* 44).

Landry uses an interesting verb, *congratulates,* as he sums up the meeting between the kinswomen. Elizabeth's speech "congratulates Mary for believing that there would be a fulfillment of what was spoken to her from the Lord" (Landry, "Narrative Logic in the Annunciation to Mary (Luke 1:26–38)," 78–79). The scene certainly carries tones of exuberance, celebration, joy, anticipation, loudness, and singing!

106. Joseph tries yet another way to work out the conflict that Mary's words bring (see Lostracco and Wilkerson, *Analyzing Short Stories,* 21).

107. Here Joseph starts citing the laws regarding vows in Num 30:1–9. The vows of an unmarried woman living with her father and under his care can be overruled by her

father (Num 30:3–5). A married woman can be released from rash vows if her husband nullifies them (Num 30:6–8). The vows of a widow or divorced woman are her own (Num 30:9). Joseph here rightly asserts that according to the law he can nullify Mary's rash vow because he is her betrothed.

108. Mary's response to Gabriel shows the kind of character that gives the image of the heavenly life (see Holy Apostles Convent, *Life of the Virgin Mary*, 79).

109. Mary immediately exhibits faith in three ways. She believes the angel's words; willingly lets God use her; and hurries to visit another, Elizabeth, who also is being used amazingly by God (see Bock, *Luke*, 44).

Scholars wonder about Luke's (1:39) comment, "Mary set out and went in haste." Perhaps her haste reflects more an eagerness and not an anxiety (see Fitzmyer, *Luke I–IX*, 362). I see the phrase "in haste" (*meta spoudes*) as rightly suggesting a normal, proper, and very human reaction to the angel's good news!

The distance could have been as much as eighty miles, might have taken at least four days, and perhaps was done alone (Cooper, "Luke 1:39–45 (46–55)," 95). The text remains silent on these details.

110. Saint Germanos recounts Mary's anguish and her pleading with her betrothed: "Be penitent, O Joseph! Do not drive me in secret from thy home! I am now in a strange place, and am not accustomed to it. I know neither right from left, and I do not know with whom I might find refuge" (Holy Apostles Convent, *Life of the Virgin Mary*, 136–37; *Sermon to the Theotokos*, PG 98)

111. Drama seeks to persuade. It is a vehicle for persuasion (DiYanni, *Literature*, 899). Mary seeks here to persuade Joseph that she is telling the truth.

112. Isa 43:19.

113. "The Cherry Tree Carol," a traditional English carol, picks up on Joseph's anger and his sharpness toward Mary, aspects mirrored in this drama. It also emphasizes a tradition that Joseph was an old man when he married Mary ("The Cherry Tree Carol." In *New Oxford Book of Carols*, 440–43 [#128]).My drama, however, puts the couple at about the same age.

"The Cherry Tree Carol"

When Joseph was an old man, an old man was he,
He married Virgin Mary the Queen of Galilee.
He married Virgin Mary the Queen of Galilee.

Joseph and Mary walked out through an orchard wood,
There were cherries, there were berries, red as any blood.
There were cherries, there were berries, red as any blood.

Then Mary said to Joseph all in a voice so mild:
"Joseph, pick for me some cherries, for I am now with child."
"Joseph, pick for me some cherries, for I am now with child."

Then Joseph spoke up sharply, and angry words said he.
"Let the father of the baby gather cherries up for thee!"
"Let the father of the baby gather cherries up for thee!"

Then up spoke baby Jesus, He spoke up from the womb,

"Let the tallest tree bend over and give my mother some."
"Let the tallest tree bend over and give my mother some."

Then the tallest tree bent over, and into Mary's hand,
And she said, "Now see here, Joseph, I've cherries by command."
And she said, "Now see here, Joseph, I've cherries by command."

When Joseph was an old man, an old man was he,
He married Virgin Mary the Queen of Galilee.
He married Virgin Mary the Queen of Galilee.

114. A private divorce before two witnesses is possible (*m. Sotah* 1:1, 5; France, *Matthew*, 77). A betrothal could only be broken via the formal process of divorce (*m. Ketub.* 1:2; 4:2; Hagner, *Matthew 1–13*, 17).

A divorce means that the relationship ends. It is a kind of death. Death stands, unuttered, behind every play, Often it becomes a play's specific subject matter and not only in a tragedy (see von Balthasar, *Theo-Drama,* 1:369).

115. The Patriarch of Constantinople, Saint Germanos (c. 635–733), in a sermon on the Annunciation emphasizes Joseph's repulsion at Mary's pregnancy and his order that she leave his home straightaway and go to the home of her lover (Holy Apostles Convent, *Life of the Virgin Mary,* 136; *Sermon to the Theotokos,* PG 98).

116. The theme of the play follows with Mary's cry. Joseph, because he is a just man, cannot say the child is his. The point of the play (see DiYanni, *Literature,* 934) is that he does not believe Mary's story; he must have a supernatural confirmation. The Matthew infancy narrative presents the dilemma as how shameful it appeared to Joseph. The shame is contained in Matt 1:18 (Bock, *Luke,* 64). However, *before* they came together, she was pregnant through the Holy Spirit. It is virtually required "that he look for a more faithful potential wife" (ibid., 64). The fact that Joseph determines to divorce her quietly tells "us something of the character of Joseph" and is "part of the Matthean narrative portrayal of him" (ibid.).

However, I wonder how 'quietly' a divorce could be. Who would marry her? Where would she go? Would her parents take her back into their home? How would she care for the child? Quite likely, Mary wondered these and other things when Joseph told her he would divorce her. The Bible records no angelic visitation to Mary to comfort her, no hugs from Elizabeth and Zechariah who are miles away, and no friends to whom Mary could go or in whom she could confide. The Bible shows another of its consistent silences from God in times of acute distress. However, it seems that the Bible does offer some comfort. God had already spoken to Mary. God had said enough through his trusted representatives, Gabriel and Elizabeth. Mary already had the sure prophetic word. Despite her current circumstances—Joseph's choice not to believe her and his decision to divorce her and the subsequent life-threatening prospects that might bring—the command and promise of Gabriel hold true: "Do not be afraid, Mary, for you have found favor with God" (Luke 1:30).

William Blake, the English mystic, poet and artist, held a different view. He interpreted Matthew 1 as showing that Jesus was related to Joseph in spirit and quite possibly in the flesh (Phipps, "Blake on Joseph's Dilemma," 178). For Blake, if Jesus were indeed Joseph's blood son, "he could be acclaimed the God-man regardless of his physical mode of generation" (ibid.). However, this view seems to me to contradict the statements in

Luke 1 and Matthew 1 about the divine nature of Jesus' conception in Mary's womb.

117. Although Joseph chooses to divorce her, the words of the angel remain true: Mary has found favor with God, she is full of grace and filled with favor from God "because she is chosen by the will of God," and God has conferred upon her—despite Joseph's views—"grace sufficient for her new task" (Gomes, *Sermons*, 11).

118. Obedience to the law is a key component of Joseph's uprightness (R. E. Brown, *Birth of the Messiah*, 127). A just man means that Joseph is law-abiding (France, *Matthew*, 77).

A severe legal system demanded that a young woman found not to be a virgin by her husband would be stoned; but a less severe legal system demanded that you "purge the evil from the midst of you" by divorce (R. E. Brown, *Birth of the Messiah*, 127). Therefore, Joseph's action of choosing divorce showed he was not only just but also merciful (ibid.).

119. The medieval pageant play *The Annunciation* portrays Joseph as an elderly man who refuses to believe Mary's story. Joseph thinks she's played him the fool. Knowing the child is not his Joseph says,

"Forsooth, this child, dame, is not mine.
Alas, that ever with mine eyene
I should see this sight!
Tell me, woman, whose is this child?" (lines 114–116)

Accusing her of beguiling him by saying the child is his (as have many other women in similar circumstances), Joseph says,

"But, in faith, Mary, thou art in sin,
So much as I have cherished thee, dame, and all thy kin,
Behind my back to serve me thus." (lines 130–133)

Joseph then lies down to rest. An angel visits him, commanding him to arise and take Mary home again. He is to comfort her because she is clean and has conceived the Second Person of the Trinity. Joseph goes to Mary in haste, kneels before her, and asks her forgiveness. He says,

"Ah, Mary, Mary, I kneel full low;
Forgive me, sweet wife, here in this land.
Mercy, Mary, for now I know
Of your good governance and how it doth stand." (lines 155–159)

Mary replies,

"Now, that Lord in heaven, sir, he you forgive;
And I do forgive you in his name
For evermore." (lines 165–166) (See Cawley, *Everyman and Medieval Miracle Plays*, 74–76).

Joseph's doubt is a familiar theme in English pageantry and drama. A theme like Joseph's doubts and his troubles with Mary occurs regularly in English drama cycles (ibid., 69).

120. This is the theme of the play: Joseph, because he is a just man, cannot say the child is his. The point of the play is that he does not believe Mary's story and must have a supernatural confirmation (see DiYanni, *Literature*, 934).

Joseph faces shame (see Bock, *Luke*, 64). The shame of Mary's confessed pregnancy means, to Joseph, that she has had sexual relations with another man. Matthew 1:18 words it this way: "(B)ut *before* they came together, she was found to be with child through the Holy Spirit" (italics added). Because the culture weighs heavily on shame and honor, it is virtually required that Joseph look for a more faithful potential wife (Bock, *Luke*, 64). The fact that Joseph determines to divorce her quietly tells "us something of the character of Joseph and is part of the Matthean narrative portrayal of him" (ibid.).

121. This play purposefully portrays Joseph as angry. He expresses his feelings of betrayal and loathing. Mary's declaration seemingly shatters his dreams. Bailey ventures—no, asserts!—that a better translation of Matt 1:20, "He considered," is "while he *fumed* over this matter" (italics original) (Bailey, *Jesus through Middle Eastern Eyes*, 46). A significant attribute of Joseph is that he is able "to reprocess his anger into grace" (ibid. 47).

122. The tone of a play or story reveals an author's attitude toward the subject (Lostracco and Wilkerson, *Analyzing Short Stories*, 49). The tone of this play throughout has been favorable to Mary. Consider now what she faces. Yes, she has the splendid promises of God; yes, she carries the Son of God within her. But she has no protection of name or provision from her betrothed. And she has been told she will be divorced. Truly, it must have been a terrible time in her life.

123. As Bock says, "Joseph's plans are stopped by a dream. This is one of several such direct interventions in these two chapters (2:12, 19, 22). God is at work in these events to lead and to guide" (*Luke*, 64).

Dreams are a consistent and striking feature of the infancy narratives (France, *Matthew*, 78). Joseph has many (Matt 1:20–21; 2:13, 19–21). The magi are warned not to return to Herod (Matt 1:12).

Since the audience sees and knows more than the characters on the stage (Ehrensperger, *Religious Drama*, 32), what may be happening on the stage may not necessarily be a tragedy or inevitably be sad.

124. Theology may begin with unexpected encounters, encounters set in the messy confines of day-to-day lives (Steuernagel, "Doing Theology with an Eye on Mary," 103). Joseph's encounter with an angel in a dream changes his theology!

125. The angel's visit in a dream provides Joseph with evidence of Mary's veracity; indeed the visit addresses Joseph's anguish. "This afforded him an unquestionable sign and convincing proof that the angel came from God, because it belongs to Him alone to know the secrets of the heart" (Holy Apostles Convent, *Life of the Virgin Mary*, 141).

126. The Announcer is what is called a static character because he remains the same (Lostracco and Wilkerson, *Analyzing Short Stories*, 14).

127. Gundry emphasizes the importance of this passage: "As a result and because of Joseph's descent from David, Jesus is born into a Davidic family and considered legally qualified to inherit David's throne. Joseph's naming Jesus indicates an acceptance of Jesus as his legal son" (Gundry, Ibid., 170).

128. Hare writes that "Joseph's role was simply to acknowledge this part of the miracle by naming the child" (Hare, *Matthew*, 12).

129. The legal Davidic lineage of Jesus is established when Joseph takes Mary into his

house (Matt 1:20) (France, *Matthew*, 77).

In the Gospel of Matthew, Jesus must be recognized as the son of Joseph "because only so was he an authentic descendant of David" (Hare, *Matthew*, 11). In addition, "for Matthew, God's miraculous action in causing the pregnancy *included* the miraculous incorporation of the child into Joseph's family" (italics original) (ibid.).

130. Citing the verse, "And Joseph knew her not" (Matt 1:25), Saint Ephraim is among those favoring the perpetual virginity of Mary and her abstention from marital relations; others include Basil, John Chrysostom, and Jerome. According to this view, Joseph cared for her all her life and the children associated with his household are his children from an earlier marriage (see Holy Apostles Convent, *Life of the Virgin Mary*, 148–49).

However, concerning Matt 1:24–25, France believes that the Greek phrase *not until* normally suggests "that intercourse did not take place until" after Jesus' birth (*Matthew*, 80). Therefore, when Matthew later talks about Jesus' brothers (12:46), they are the children born subsequently to the new family of Joseph and Mary. "There is no biblical warrant for the tradition of the 'perpetual virginity' of Mary," France concludes (ibid.).

131. Birth announcements are standard in the biblical text. See Gen 18:10; Judg 13:3; Luke 1:13. The birth announcement to Joseph, evidently something he needed for him to believe, commends Joseph by addressing him as a descendant (indeed a son!) of David and addressing his fears of taking Mary home with him (Matt 1:20). The angel of the Lord confirms Mary's amazing testimony that the child to be born of her is from the Holy Spirit. The Matthew account adds these words: "He will save his people from their sins" (1:21).

132. Saint Germanos agrees with the timeframe given in this play. Everything occurred very quickly. Within a day Joseph changed his views. The verification he needs comes in a dream from an angel. Joseph immediately repents, goes to Mary, and even bows before her (Holy Apostles Convent, *Life of the Virgin Mary*, 142). Saint Germanos in his homily renders Joseph as saying, "Yesterday I had false suspicions and brought censure upon thy beauty and goodness. But today, having received a word from above, I apologize, and venerate thy magnanimity and bless thy name!" (Holy Apostles Convent, *Life of the Virgin Mary*, 142; Saint Germanos, Patriarch of Constantinople, *Sermon on the Annunciation of the Most Holy Theotokos* [in Greek], PG 98).

133. Joseph indeed has other dreams that Matthew recounts. They propel the plot forward and confirm that God is in charge and actively protects the child and Joseph and Mary. In addition to Joseph's first encounter with an angel mentioned here (Matt 1:20–21), Joseph has three more dreams: A dream guides him to escape with his family to Egypt (2:13); to return to Israel after Herod's death (2:20); and to settle in Nazareth (2:22). The Magi, the wise men from the East, also are warned by an angel in a dream not to return to Herod (2:12). The angel of the Lord is not named in Matthew; Luke names the angel visiting Zechariah in the Temple and Mary three months later as Gabriel (Luke 1).

134. This play utilizes imagination within the framework supplied by the biblical text. The active imagination of a person (at any age) provides a great tool for training in the faith (see Stonehouse, *Joining Children on the Spiritual Journey*, 158).

135. Please note that the angel is unnamed. Perhaps it was Gabriel, perhaps not.

136. Joseph risks scandal by marrying Mary. Yet he chooses to marry her. Why?

Because he has heard from an angel himself and decided that he can honorably marry this pregnant woman—despite appearances and possible gossip (see Strauss, *Four Portraits, One Jesus,* 225). Matthew closes this part of his gospel by affirming Joseph's obedience (Bock, *Jesus according to Scripture,* 65).

137. Throughout the ages, Mary has been portrayed as gracious. Von Balthasar offers two comments on her importance. Mary's role in the Church can be seen in fruitfulness and as the mother of all believers (see von Balthasar, *Theo-Drama,* 5:465). Likewise, Mary serves as the bridge, the transition, between the Old and New Covenants (see ibid., 466).

138. The angel's visit confirms that Mary is not guilty of sin and therefore frees Joseph to marry her (Hagner, *Matthew 1–13,* 18). Joseph's obedience to the angel's directives in marrying Mary and in naming Jesus indicates "his formal adoption of Jesus and hence the establishment of his Davidic lineage" (ibid., 21).

139. The upcoming marriage of Joseph and Mary takes away any taint of illegitimacy, for an illegitimate child could not enter into the assembly of the Lord (Deut 23:2). Significantly, the scribes and Pharisees, Jesus' later enemies, never taunted him about being born out of wedlock or that his mother played the harlot in Israel.

However, yet another tradition is that both Mary and Joseph had to drink the waters of conviction (Num 5:11–30) to verify that the child Mary carried had not been conceived in adultery or out of wedlock. Both took the waters, both went separately into the hill country for the appointed time, and both returned! The priest who administered the test said, "If the Lord God did not make manifest your sin, neither will I judge you" (see Holy Apostles Convent, *Life of the Virgin Mary,* 145–47).

Experiencing all aspects of a play—its writing, rehearsals, performances, and reception—engages the imagination, the will, and the direction of a life (see Forde, *Theatercraft,* 4).

140. A version of this play was published. Branch, "Astonishment and Joy."

141. Bauckham calls Luke 1:5–80 "a gynocentric text" (*Gospel Women,* 47). The infancy narrative in Luke sets the stage for everything else that follows in the gospel (Murphy, *An Introduction to Jesus and the Gospels,* 197).

Bauckham, writing about the interaction of Mary and Elizabeth, says that it "is undoubtedly *as* the mothers of their unborn sons that they are of central importance in Luke's narrative, but it is from their female perspectives that we view the central events of the narrative" (*Gospel Women,* 51; italics original). However, Bauckham in his chapter on Elizabeth and Mary, gives scant analysis to Elizabeth and concentrates on Mary (ibid., 47–76).

142. Like 1 Samuel 1, Luke 1 contains the perspective of women.

"Astonishment and Joy: Luke 1 as Told from the Perspective of Elizabeth" is creative, religious drama. Creative religious drama can become an effective tool "that just might open the door to new interest in the great biblical truths" (Barragar, *Spiritual Growth through Creative Drama for Children and Youth,* 20). Creative drama as defined by the Children's Theatre Association of America is "an improvisational, nonexhibitional, process-centered form of drama in which participants are guided by a leader to imagine, enact, and reflect upon human experience" (Barragar, *Spiritual Growth,* 16; quoting from "Redefining Creative Dramatics: A CTAA Project," August 17, 1977, paper from the Redefinitions Committee of the Children's Theatre Association of America).

Lostracco and Wilkerson (*Analyzing Short Stories*, iii–vi) note that the main elements of a story are the central idea, character, conflict, point of view, setting, language, and tone.

143. Elizabeth and Mary are the principal persons in Luke 1. Although the chapter begins and ends with Zechariah, he is mute through a loss of speech during its middle portions; this gives his wife Elizabeth a chance to occupy center stage (Martin, "Luke 1:39–47," 394).

144. This monologue is a religious drama. Drama in general may persuade or provoke even while it entertains. Yes, drama may present a portrayal of a slice of life in a timeframe, but also "it offers provocative ideas about the life it portrays, and it provides an imaginative extension of its possibilities" (DiYanni, *Literature*, 901).

Religious drama often investigates these elements (Edyvean, *This Dramatic World*, 17):

- the human condition
- a character's spiritual condition, self-examination, and feelings
- the divine–man relationship
- the meaning of an experience
- the limits of human power

145. Imagination is a marvelous teaching tool and useful for training adults and children in the faith (see Stonehouse, *Joining Children on the Spiritual Journey*, 158).

Loader (*New Testament with Imagination*, ix–x) draws on imagination, a principal component of all drama, in his short book highlighting the lives (and writings) of significant characters in the New Testament: Jesus, Paul, and John. Throughout the book, he engages senses like smell and sound and brings up economic factors like unemployment, slavery, and the fragility of life. He reminds readers of the importance of the seasons and the disparity between the rich and poor and the different perspectives of youth and age. He sees each chapter as "an exercise in imagination" and states that a goal for each is "to imagine our way into" their context (ibid., x).

Loader's work has proved insightful for my biblical plays, and I thank him.

What I particularly like about Loader's work overall is how he uses sources, facts, and scholarly work and manages to invite us back into the biblical world as participants.

146. The setting is where the events of the drama take place (Lostracco and Wilkerson, *Analyzing Short Stories*, 31).

147. This short description, sketched in a few words with a language paintbrush, creates a mental image, a sensory impression, in the minds of readers and hearers (ibid., 37).

148. Zechariah, Elizabeth, and their son John link the Old Testament period to God's new work in the New Testament times; see Geldenhuys, *Gospel of Luke*, 60.

149. Luke's narrative holds a three-fold power, according to Kuist ("Sources of Power in the Nativity Hymns," 289): "The power to attract and to hold the reverent attention of young and old; the power to communicate such significant creative impulses to Christian art and music; (and) the power to sustain and to out-live such acute and protracted historical criticism."

150. Elizabeth is the monologue's major character. Not only is she crucial to the re-telling of Luke 1, but also the story revolves around what she says and does (Lostracco and Wilkerson, *Analyzing Short Stories*, 13). She is a dynamic character, rather than a

flat character, for the following reasons: She grows and changes during the story; she expresses many emotions; and we in the audience get to know her (ibid., 15).

151. Elizabeth wears rustic clothes—probably a loose dress or long skirt, an over blouse, and cloth belt. She wears sandals. She lovingly touches her new shawl throughout the monologue. It is beautiful.

152. Luke 1 gives textual importance to women. Martin noting the "feminine character of the symbols" in the chapter, acknowledges as well "the almost universal neglect of these feminine symbols by Protestant male interpreters" ("Luke 1:39–47," 395).

Indeed an impetus in my researching the character of Elizabeth and in writing this monologue about her is that I have never heard a sermon on her life. Therefore I seek, in this monologue, to honor her contribution to the biblical text. The "tone" in this monologue, to use the term favored by Lostracco and Wilkerson (*Analyzing Short Stories*, 49), is multifaceted. I like her very much. I also respect and admire her. I understand her ache in longing for a child and her joy in giving her husband a son. To me, Luke 1 presents her with much kindness and sensitivity as someone used in a prominent way by God—and as someone delightfully amazed about being used!

153. In this monologue, the narration is in the first person. Elizabeth uses pronouns like *I* and *me*. In literary language, this is called a first person point of view (ibid., 25).

154. The group of people in the birth stories of John and Jesus—Zechariah, Elizabeth, Mary, Joseph, Anna, Simeon, the shepherds, and the Magi—exhibit character traits called righteousness and faith. They are practical people of prayer; and prayer involves intercession, listening, long waits, discerning God's voice, and action. They are not powerful or famous people and, with the exception of the Magi, are not wealthy (Dean, *Luke*, 22).

Elizabeth's monologue details a sequence of events; this sequence forms the plot of the drama (Lostracco and Wilkerson, *Analyzing Short Stories*, 19).

155. Luke's soteriology, as expressed in the infancy narratives of John and Jesus, differs from that of other New Testament writers who emphasize expiation and the transcendence of God, maintains Karris ("Luke's Soteriology of With-ness," 352). For example, in Paul's soteriology, a transcendent God cleanses away sin via the blood of Jesus (Rom 3:24–25). Luke, in contrast, presents an imminent God who is present during life—from birth, through sin, and then in death. This "with-ness," Karris argues, designed to appeal to Theophilus and subsequent readers, shows that God meets us on a deep level and saves us in Jesus (ibid., 352).

156. See Wright, *Luke for Everyone*, 7.

157. Scholars, among them William Barclay, note the prevalence of joy in Luke 1 (*Gospel of Luke*, 8); great joy is proportional to a great task, Barclay adds (ibid., 9).

158. Luke does not mention that Zechariah gives Elizabeth a shawl. I, as a writer, inserted that for several reasons. First, it gives Elizabeth a prop that helps the audience imagine her character. Second, husbands throughout history have given their wives presents at the births of children. My imaginative elaboration, by including a shawl, follows the Jewish tradition of Midrash. Midrash has been called creative exegesis because it combines wordplay, storytelling skill, and interpretation; these elements, when they come together, "liberate pleasure, creativity, and knowledge" (Marx, *Shakespeare and the Bible*, 16).

159. Luke 1 brims with human elements: The longing for a child, doubt, joy, faith, unbelief, friendship, praise, and danger. It combines the human and the divine and presents them not as an oxymoron,for indeed, the text accepts the miraculous. It presents the idea that humanity is saved in the humanity of Jesus and is not rescued from being human (see Hann, "Election, the Humanity of Jesus, and Possible Worlds," 297).

160. The biblical text emphasizes that the baby to come from this union, John, is of priestly stock and in the great heritage of Israel's prophets (see Fitzmyer, *Gospel According to Luke I–IX*, 317).

161. Significantly, Elisheba (Elizabeth) was the name of Aaron's wife (Exod 6:23) (Nolland, *Luke*, 26).
To be a priest's daughter and to be married to a priest were considered a double distinction; a colloquial expression describing an excellent woman was this: She deserves to be married to a priest (Geldenhys, *Gospel of Luke*, 62).

162. Luke 1:5–6. The division of Abijah is the eighth (Morris, *Luke*, 75).

163. According to tradition, Elizabeth and Zechariah lived in Ein Karem about five miles west of Jerusalem and eighty miles from Nazareth (Holy Apostles Convent, *Life of the Virgin Mary*, 119).

164. The biblical text emphasizes the couple's integrity, faith, and advanced age. The uprightness of Zechariah, Elizabeth, and Mary shines; the three lack any trappings of wealth, fame, or power (see Dean, *Luke*, 22). Green observes that the description of Zechariah and Elizabeth introduces the readers to the world of "first-century Palestinian Jewish piety" because of its "references to prayer, worship, fasting, and expectant waiting" (*Gospel of Luke*, 61).

165. Bauckham thinks that Zechariah and Elizabeth were not of high status but were among the many priests who lived among the peasant population (*Gospel Women*, 71). He argues that Luke 1:36 points dubiously to Mary's connection to the priesthood, especially since priestly descent came through the male line (ibid.).

166. Zechariah and Elizabeth represent the best of Israel; they show that true piety, based not on meticulous legalism but on practiced prayer, existed in Israel (Dean, *Luke*, 20; Luke 1:5–6). Nonetheless, the couple's barrenness seems to indicate that "God seemed to have neglected their dogged fidelity to him" (Wansbrough, *Luke*, 17)—at least at first glance. Because of their advanced ages, no doubt their neighbors and society treated them as "'has-beens,' ready to sink into decrepitude and oblivion" (ibid., 19).

167. Conflict in this dramatic monologue "results from a cause and effect relationship between events" (Lostracco and Wilkerson, *Analyzing Short Stories*, 19).

168. Achtemeier, ed., *Harper's Bible Dictionary*, 161; see Gen 20:18.

169. Luke 1:7. Barrenness is the essential social fact about Elizabeth and her great, ongoing disgrace (Bauckham, *Gospel Women*, 51, 72). Barrenness is an Old Testament pattern present in the stories of Sarai/Sarah, Rachel, Hannah, and the wife of Manoa; see Gen 18:11; Gen 30:1–22; 1 Sam 1: 1–20; Judg 13:2 (Nolland, *Luke*, 25).

170. Ryken posits a number of reasons for suffering. Sometimes suffering is for the sake of righteousness. Sometimes sin causes suffering. Sometimes suffering results from the sins of others. "And sometimes God allows us to suffer because he wants to be

glorified through our suffering" (Ryken, *Luke*, 18). It would seem that the suffering of this couple, Zechariah and Elizabeth, allows God to be glorified.

171. See 1 Sam 1. Elizabeth's story also resembles that of Sarah who longed for a child and conceived when she was eighty-nine or ninety, well past childbearing years (Gen 18:1–15).

172. Morris (*Luke*, 75) writes that "their childless state (was) hard for them to understand, for people believed that God would bless faithful servants by giving them children."

173. The text presents Zechariah "as an Abraham-like figure" (R. E. Brown, "Annunciation to Zechariah," 483).

174. In an earlier exegesis of Zechariah's encounter with Gabriel I wrote, "Zechariah's prophecy exudes joy. This is amazing, because Luke introduces Zechariah as something of an old grump" (Branch, "Exegetical Perspective," 2009: 35). In this monologue, I imagine what it must have been like to live with him as his wife. Zechariah is a round character, for he changes from the time of his encounter with Gabriel to the time of his prophetic song.

175. The encounters in Luke 1 smack of realism and theological insights. Theology—technically the study of God—expands with the stories in Luke 1. Steuernagel points out that theology begins with unexpected encounters, encounters set in the messy confines of day-to-day lives. Luke 1:8–9 ("Doing Theology with an Eye on Mary," 103).

Notice, please, that in recounting Luke 1:5–25 I, as a writer, pause frequently. Pausing avoids the tendency in reading and reciting to race through a text. As a writer, I hear Gabriel's encounters first with Zechariah and then with Mary as lasting longer than the ten or fifteen seconds or less it takes to read each aloud. The biblical text in both testaments is known for its brevity. A dramatic monologue presents human reactions that are normal, possible, and/or implied in the text. Human reactions take time.

176. Nolland, *Luke*, 27. Geldenhys gives several insights on priests and their duties (*Gospel of Luke*, 62–63). Evidently at the time of Zechariah, there were thousands of priests, and a priest was not allowed to burn incense more than once in his lifetime. Incense was offered twice a day, in the morning and then again at 3 p.m. As an officiating priest, Zechariah could enter the holy place, the space inside the Temple and just in front of the Holy of Holies. The high priest alone was permitted to enter the Holy of Holies only once a year, on the Great Day of Atonement.

Barclay (*Gospel of Luke*, 3, 4) also outlines Zechariah's priestly duties: Every morning and evening, sacrifice was made for the nation of Israel. The sacrifice involved a burnt offering of a male lamb, a year old and without spot or blemish. Before the sacrifice was made, incense was offered enabling the sacrifices to ascend to God as a sweet-smelling savor.

177. Zechariah, in prayer and doing his duty, nonetheless listened as well. He gave himself the chance to hear God's voice. Barclay notes that God's voice comes to those who listen for it, as did Zechariah (*Gospel of Luke*, 5).

178. It was the apex of Zechariah's career; once a priest was chosen for Temple service, he was not eligible to serve again (Ryken, *Luke*, 20).

Fitzmyer gives the time as the afternoon (*Luke* I–IX, 317–18). A priest could serve throughout his life without serving in the Temple; but if the lot fell to him, it was the highlight of his life. Zechariah certainly "was thrilled to the core of his being," Barclay comments (*Gospel of Luke*, 4).

Green says that Zechariah was singularly chosen by God for this special and blessed honor (*Gospel of Luke*, 69).

179. Fitzmyer, *Luke I–IX*, 323–24. Incense was offered at the table of incense; the table was stationed "in the holy place before the curtain separating the holy place from the most holy place (Exod 30:1–6)" (Nolland, *Luke*, 27–28).

180. Morris (*Luke*, 76) comments that since directions in the Bible often are given from the standpoint of someone facing to the east, it is possible that the angel stood between the altar of incense and the golden candlestick.

Angelic visitations announcing births are common throughout the Old Testament (see Gen 16:10–11; 17:15–19; 18:10–15; 25:23; Judg 13:3–21) (Bock, *Luke*, 36).

181. Luke 1:12. Zechariah is facing a crisis. A crisis is an element in drama. A play is the actualization of a segment, a slice of life, in a set time; it is brought to life by characters who act and speak in ways relevant to the situation—often a crisis—in which they have been caught and which is happening to them right now (Ehrensperger, *Religious Drama*, 23).

182. Conrad ("Annunciation of Birth," 660–63) explores Old and New Testament texts containing "Fear not." The phrase is used to comfort a dying woman in labor (Gen 35:17; 1 Sam 4:20). God addresses Abram with the phrase in the vision recorded in Gen 15; similarly, the same words are used by Gabriel to Zechariah in Luke 1. Conrad says that "Fear not" in the New Testament "seeks to eliminate the fear aroused not only by the appearance of the numinous but also by other circumstances associated with the announcement of the birth of a son" (ibid., 661)

These normal anxieties could include the life of the mother during gestation and labor, the reputation of the mother, the reaction of the general populace, and the responsibilities of parenting a child with a divine destiny. Conrad (ibid., 663) sees Gabriel's declaration to Zechariah to "Fear not" (Luke 1:13) as a word of comfort similar to that of the Lord to Abram in Gen 15:1.

183. Gabriel mentioned Elizabeth by name, a fact suggesting that Zechariah was praying for her (Ryken, *Luke*, 21).

Several centuries before this, Gabriel appeared to Daniel (see Dan 9:20–21). R. E. Brown ("Annunciation to Zechariah," 485) writes, "There can be little doubt, then, that Luke intends us to see a parallelism between Gabriel's appearance to Daniel and his appearance to Zechariah." Luke 1:11–17.

184. As the officiating priest representing the people of Israel, his prayers were to include prayers for Israel's spiritual redemption (Geldenhuys, *Gospel of Luke*, 63).

Green points out that the need of Zechariah and Elizabeth for a son parallels the need of divine intervention by God for Israel (*Gospel of Luke*, 62).

185. The name John indicates the child will be graced by God (see Fitzmyer, *Luke I–IX*, 325). His name means God has been gracious and its cognate means prayer for favor (Nolland, *Luke*, 29).

According to Bede, "Whenever in the Scriptures a name is imposed or changed. . .by God, it is indicative of great praise and virtue" (Just, *Luke*, 9). Ambrose writes that the angel announced not greatness of body but of soul regarding John (ibid.).

186. Green notes the escalation of the angel's remarks about John (*Gospel of Luke*, 74). John will be of import to Zechariah, then to many, and finally in the sight of the Lord. Eventually, John's importance "can be appreciated only against the backdrop of what God has been doing, and how God is even now bringing his aim to its consummation in part through his human agent John" (ibid., 112).

187. Bock says that the major message of Gabriel's visit to Zechariah and to Luke's readers "is that God will do what he promises in his own way" (*Luke*, 37).

188. The area's common strong drink was barley beer (Fitzmyer, *Luke I–IX*, 326).

189. As well they should be because the angel heaped accolade upon accolade and blessing upon blessing on the couple and this child (Ryken, *Luke,* 23)!

190. John will not be a reincarnation of Elijah but will be like that firebrand prophet in temperament, mannerisms, and unequivocal message (see Fitzmyer, *Luke I–IX*, 321).

191. The angel's description of John's role indicated he would "do much more than an ordinary prophet," Geldenhuys rightly says (*Gospel of Luke*, 65; Luke 1:16–18).

192. Zechariah, like his wife Elizabeth, is a dynamic character in this monologue. Often what a character says is more revealing than are his or her actions (Lostracco and Wilkerson, *Analyzing Short Stories*, 17). Significantly, Zechariah does not believe Gabriel, God's representative, that a restorative miracle could happen to himself and to his wife Elizabeth in their old age (Branch, "Exegetical Perspective," 35, 37).

193. Surely Nolland understates the enormity of Zechariah's statement when he writes about "the impropriety of Zechariah's question" (*Luke*, 33)

194. Morris observes that Gideon and Hezekiah (Judg 6:36–39; 2 Kgs 20:8) likewise asked for a sign—but Zechariah's tone and spirit were different (*Luke*, 78). Speaking from unbelief, Zechariah "reminds the angel that both he and his wife are old (his *I* is emphatic). Babies are not born to people like them. The angel retorts with an emphatic *I* of his own as he discloses his name," Morris (ibid.) says.

195. One view about Zechariah's response to Gabriel is that Zechariah's own faith worked against him. He did not believe himself worthy—although Gabriel and his sender, God, did—and was punished for his skepticism (Holy Apostles Convent, *Life of the Virgin Mary*, 126).

Green comments that here in the story the tables turn on Zechariah in favor of Elizabeth (*Gospel of Luke*, 63). She is introduced as barren and disgraced but becomes pregnant and is restored to a position of honor at the close of the chapter.

196. Branch, "Exegetical Perspective," 35. Wright puts it this way: "We can almost see the angel putting his hands on his hips and telling Zechariah off for presuming to doubt his word" (*Luke for Everyone*, 7).

197. Zechariah was struck mute, arguably as was Daniel (Dan 10:15–17; see R. E. Brown, "Annunciation to Zechariah," 487). Gabriel's name means "man of God" (Geldenhuys, *Gospel of Luke*, 67) or, according to Bede, "strength of God" (Just, *Luke*, 13).

198. Silence descends immediately upon Zechariah, and he is unable to pronounce the priestly blessing, as Elizabeth soon recounts (Nolland, *Luke*, 33).

199. It was customary for an officiating priest to bless the worshippers. Zechariah, because of his muteness, could not pronounce the blessing (see Fitzmyer, *Luke I–IX*,

320).

200. Ryken rightly sees the humor in the situation (*Luke,* 25). He comments: "Poor Zechariah! He had just heard the greatest news that anyone had heard in about four centuries, but he wasn't able to tell anyone about it. All he could do was make hand signals. But just imagine trying to play charades with Gabriel's prophecy!" (ibid., 26).

201. Luke tells the story of two miraculous births: "Zechariah and Elizabeth, in their old age and despite their barrenness, conceive a child in a natural way. Jesus will be born of a virgin" (Card, *Luke,* 38).

202. Luke does not say why Elizabeth decided to hide herself in seclusion, but she expresses joy that the disgrace of her barrenness is being removed (Bock, *Luke,* 38). Green says that "Elizabeth's five months of seclusion remain a mystery" (*Gospel of Luke,* 81). Ambrose believes it was because of modesty (Just, *Luke,* 11). Nolland views her withdrawal from the community as showing "a sense of privacy about the precious and intimate way that God has dealt with her in her old age" (*Luke,* 33).

However, I see Elizabeth's voluntary seclusion as ending up reinforcing the prophetic word to Mary about Mary's own pregnancy. Mary is the only one, besides Zechariah, to know of Elizabeth's pregnancy, and Elizabeth is the only one, besides her fetal son and Zechariah, to know of Mary's pregnancy.

203. Elizabeth did not withdraw in order to hide her pregnancy, Geldenhys believes, but in order to glorify God and worship him for the miracle she was experiencing (Luke 1:21–25; *Gospel of Luke,* 69).

204. John's conception involves a miracle because of the ages of Zechariah and Elizabeth, but it is the result of human intercourse; on the other hand, the conception of Jesus in Mary is a "divine creative action without human intercourse" (R. E. Brown, "Annunciation to Mary," 252).

205. Elizabeth's miraculous pregnancy served as a sign to Mary and serves as a sign to all subsequent believers that Mary's pregnancy, impossible as it seems, is not impossible (Luke 1:36–37) (Fitzmyer, *Luke I–IX,* 321). God often blesses his people with signs and miracles, thereby increasing their faith.

206. Wansbrough (*Luke,* 22) sees Mary's visit to Elizabeth as an expression of Mary's kindness to her aging relative and as an expression of support to her during the exciting and worrisome time of her pregnancy. However, I believe Kershner ("Advent Sermon," 20) is more accurate by saying that Mary came immediately to her cousin Elizabeth's house "because she did not know where else to go."

207. Nolland also sees the "everything happening all at once" sequence; the child's movements and Elizabeth's prophetic words bump into and overlap each other amid much rejoicing (*Luke,* 67).

208. Luke 1:39–40 addresses Mary's visit this way: "At that time Mary got ready and hurried to a town in the hill country of Judea where she greeted Elizabeth." Swanson ("Magnificat and Crucifixion," 101) thinks that Mary, whom he calls Mariam, "ran, perhaps in flight." He senses an urgency in her coming to Elizabeth, an urgency that perhaps indicates she was fleeing for her life.

209. Tradition surrounds the kinship link between Elizabeth and Mary (Holy Apostles Convent, *Life of the Virgin Mary,* 120). Elizabeth, by tradition, is the daughter of

Anna's sister Zoia. Joakim and Anna, by tradition parents of Mary, waited fifty years for Mary's birth. Consequently, if this tradition is correct, Mary follows in the line of special children and long-awaited deliverers of Israel: Isaac (Gen 21); Joseph (Gen 37); Moses (Exod 1–2); Samson (Judg 13); Samuel (1 Sam 1–2); and Judith and Esther of the books bearing their names.

210. The legends about Mary including her delayed birth, her holiness, her childhood, and her participation with other virgins in making the veil of the Temple are not mentioned in this drama, but for a fascinating account of them, read Holy Apostles Convent, *The Life of the Virgin Mary*, especially 1–73.

211. The normal age for betrothal for a girl was soon after her twelfth birthday; for boys, the betrothal age was about sixteen (Wansbrough, *Luke*, 20). The normal engagement time was about a year.

212. Luke 1:40–41. The mother of the Lord greeted the mother of his prophet (Holy Apostles Convent, *Life of the Virgin Mary*, 122–23).

213. Origen, writing on the significance of Elizabeth's prophecy, notes that "Elizabeth prophesies before John. Before the birth of the Lord and Savior, Mary prophesies. Sin began from the woman and then spread to the man. In the same way, salvation had its first beginnings from women" (Just, Luke, 24).

214. Bede notes that Elizabeth had "a great voice because she recognized the great gifts of God"; she rejoiced and "was on fire" because of the visit of the Son of God (in the womb) to her (Ibid., 21, 22).

215. Elizabeth blessed Mary by reinforcing what the angel had already said. Elizabeth blessed Mary and blessed the child she was carrying and would bear (Luke 1:42) (see Holy Apostles Convent, *Life of the Virgin Mary*, 121). Luke 1:42.

Wansbrough (*Luke*, 21) sees God's choice of Mary in this way: "It is the unmerited favour of an all-powerful ruler, who needs to justify his deeds to no one; he simply chooses his favourites unpredictably and showers his gifts upon them as he will. Primarily it is the personal relationship, the choice and the love, and only secondarily the gifts, the graces which follow. So God simply fixed his choice upon Mary, quite arbitrarily, not for any merits of hers."

Martin ("Luke 1:39–47," 396) offers an interesting clarification about Elizabeth's words. He points to Jesus' words to a woman who blesses the womb that bore him and the breasts he suckled. He replies, "Blessed are those rather who hear the word of God and keep it" (Luke 1:27–28). Yes, Mary is blessed not only because she is pregnant with the Son of God but also because she hears the word of God and keeps it.

Fitzmyer (*Luke I–IX*, 358) notes that Elizabeth gives a blessing and a beatitude over her young kinswoman; first, Mary is blest (*eulogeme*) among women because of whom she carries in her womb, and second, she is blessed (*makaria*) because of her faith.

B. E. Wilson ("Pugnacious Precursors and the Bearer of Peace," 436–56) links three women the biblical text calls blessed: Jael (Judg 5:24), Judith (Jdt 13:18); and Mary (Luke 1:42). While the first two were blessed because they acted as deliverers and saved Israelite lives, Mary, linking verses 42 and 48, believes she is blessed because God has looked with favor on the lowliness of his servant (ibid., 448). "Unlike Jael and Judith, Mary is called blessed not for any act of violence but for her acceptance of God's word: 'Here am I, the servant of the Lord; let it be with me according to your word' (1:38)," B. E. Wilson (ibid.,

449) writes. Unlike Jael and Judith, exemplary women warriors, "Mary is presented as a woman disciple, a peaceful hearer and doer of God's word," B. E. Wilson (ibid., 449) says.

216. Elizabeth speaks as a prophet (Dean, *Luke*, 23).

217. One view regarding Elizabeth's loudness and outbursts is that they teach humanity to cry out to Mary (Holy Apostles Convent, *Life of the Virgin Mary*, 122). I, however, see her loudness and words as the energizing of and power from the Holy Spirit. Furthermore, Elizabeth acknowledges that her words are not from herself but that she is filled with the Holy Spirit. Therefore, she believes Mary because of what the Holy Spirit did in and through her; Mary's words and rendition of her story simply fill in the details. Similarly, an angel encounters a doubting Joseph in a dream. This divine encounter verifies Mary's words and gives Joseph the clear moral leeway to continue the marriage proceedings and to marry his betrothed (Matt 1:18–25).

218. The meeting of the four—the two mothers and their two sons—produces "a new tradition of a super-hero's birth" (Brenner, "Female Social Behaviour," 269).

Landry ("Narrative Logic in the Annunciation to Mary," 78–79) uses an interesting verb, *congratulates*, as he sums up the meeting between the kinswomen: Elizabeth's speech "congratulates Mary for believing that there would be a fulfillment of what was spoken to her from the Lord." The scene certainly carries tones of exuberance, celebration, joy, anticipation, loudness, and singing!

219. Themes common in an account of a super-hero's birth, Brenner continues, are the barrenness of one mother and the unmarried social status of the other mother (Brenner, "Female Social Power," 269). Significantly, there is a lack of rivalry—on issues like status, beauty, ambition, age—between Elizabeth and Mary. Instead, the women are mutually supportive and share the commonality of faith. Brenner points out that the good will of the mothers, Mary and Elizabeth, sets the tone for the relationship of their sons by eliminating the possibility of power struggles between them in the future and by promoting, instead, good will (ibid., 270).

220. Praise acknowledges God's goodness and actions and brings attention to God (Bock, *Jesus according to Scripture*, 45).

221 Elizabeth could have felt resentful, and Mary could have exhibited pride, yet neither emotion marks the relationship of these two women. Instead, they celebrate God (see Wright, *Luke for Everyone*, 16).

222. Elizabeth willingly takes second place; she acknowledges that her young kinswoman has received from the Lord more honor than has she (Geldenhuys, *Gospel of Luke*, 83). Elizabeth's action is part of a tradition of such in Scripture: Jonathan knows David will be king (1 Sam 20); Barnabas lets Paul take the lead midway through the first missionary journey (see Branch, "He Is Risen!").

223. Luke 1:45. Mary accepts the miraculous blending of the divine and the human (Dean, *Luke*, 23). Mary is blessed and unique because of her faith and the child she carries (see Bock, *Luke*, 43–44).

"Blessed is she who has believed" gives the essence of a proper response to God: Trust that what God says is true and live joyfully in light of that truth (ibid., 44).

224. Holy Apostles Convent, *Life of the Virgin Mary*, 122.

225. As a pregnant, older woman, Elizabeth is a sign for Mary of faith and the

certainty of miracles; God's work in Elizabeth's life indicates God is at work in Mary's life, too (see Martin, "Luke 1:39–47," 397).

226. Acting on the hint supplied by Gabriel, Mary comes to her kinswoman, Elizabeth. It was natural to want to be around someone who also was experiencing a miracle (Geldenhuys, *Gospel of Luke*, 82).

227. Nolland observes that the "three months of Mary's stay may allude to the three months in 2 Sam 6:11 of the ark's remaining in the house of Obed-edom" (*Luke*, 77).

228. Mary may well have needed sanctuary. According to Swanson ("Magnificat and Crucifixion," 104), "When Mariam was in danger and overwhelmed and needed someone to take her in, feed her, and tell her stories that would protect and stabilize her in the coming months and years, she went to Elisheva, her auntie."

229. Isa 7:14. Matt 1:23.

230. Drane (*Introducing the New Testament,* 55–57) discusses the difficulties modern readers have with the concept of a virgin birth. "To be a virgin and pregnant is a contradiction in terms," he begins (ibid., 55), and that concept was "quite unacceptable in any form to orthodox Jews" (ibid., 57). Matthew seems to draw from the LXX version of Isaiah, which translates 7:14 as *virgin* while in the Hebrew text the term may refer to a *young woman* (ibid., 56–57). Both Luke and Matthew present the material about Jesus' birth in the same way that they present other material about Jesus: Straightforwardly and without elaboration.

In terms of textual structure, Mary's virginity parallels Elizabeth's barrenness: Neither is an obstacle for God in terms of a promised child (see Nolland, *Luke*, 49).

231. Throughout the ages, Mary has remained both fascinating and mystifying. Although the biblical text indicates her humility and contentment with lowly things, the Lord called her to greatness and exalted her (Holy Apostles Convent, *Life of the Virgin Mary*, 128).

232. Mary is widely considered both the first disciple and a model disciple because of her obedience (Wansbrough, *Luke*, 27).

233. It's interesting to note that what has come to be known as the Magnificat of Mary (Luke 1:46–55) may indeed have been spoken by Elizabeth! While Mary is the designated speaker in all Greek manuscripts, Elizabeth is the speaker in three copies of the Old Latin (*Vetus Latina*) versions; significantly, Irenaeus credits her as the speaker (Fitzmyer, *Luke I–IX*, 365). Morris, however, says that "the textual evidence in support of *Mary* is overwhelming" (*Luke*, 83; italics original).

Mary's song resembles that of Hannah (1 Sam 2:1–10). Mary, Hannah, and Elizabeth are all women, mothers-to-be, whom God uses in his ongoing actions of salvation. The theme of God's faithful love runs through both Mary's song and Zechariah's song (Wansbrough, *Luke*, 25).

234. Luke 1:46–55. Her hymn emphasizes God's present movements. God is acting *now* and has pledged himself to act *forever* on Israel's behalf (see Kuist, "Sources of Power in the Nativity Hymns," 291).

235. O'Day points out that Mary's mention of *low estate* does not really mean Mary's humility but Mary's poverty ("Singing Woman's Song," 207).

236. Luke 1:46–49. Mary links what is happening to her with the history of God's workings with Israel when she sings, "the Mighty One has done great things for me" (ibid., 208).

237. One tradition is that the annunciation occurred when Joseph was absent from his home and working his trade as a builder (Holy Apostles Convent, *Life of the Virgin Mary*, 71).

238. Luke 1:26–38. Significantly, Gabriel came with an announcement of what God was going to do; it was not a command (Geldenhuys, *Gospel of Luke*, 7). Notice that Mary was not looking for God, but the angel Gabriel was sent to her.

239. Roman Catholics generally interpret the phrase, "full of favor," to mean she can confer favor; Protestants, on the other hand, see the phrase as meaning she has received favor (ibid., 75).

240. The greatness of this Son is unequalled; his greatness will exceed everything. In Greek, the phrase is "Son of the Highest"; it contains no articles, a grammar technique indicating "the absolute uniqueness and highness of His divine Sonship" (ibid., 76).

241. Ryken writes that "Mary did not ask this question in unbelief. Here Luke is drawing a contrast between Zechariah's doubt and Mary's faith" (*Luke,* 34).
In Luke 1:34, Mary may be seen as knowing that she cannot have intercourse until Joseph takes her home and normal sexual relations begin as husband and wife. Landry ("Narrative Logic in the Annunciation to Mary," 69) translates Mary's words in this way: "How will this be, since I do not have sexual relations with my husband?" Landry says that "Luke has Mary ask the question for no discernible reason other than to give the angel the further opportunity to speak of the child's identity" (ibid., 69). However, Smith sees Mary's question, "How can this be?," as still very much our question, too, especially when we think about Jesus and the promise to mankind that Jesus' story presents ("Exposition of Luke 1:26–38," 417).
Throughout her book, Schaberg, however, argues that Luke presents the conception of Jesus as an illegitimate conception (*Illegitimacy of Jesus*). This argument is not generally accepted. One who differs with it throughout his article is Landry ("Narrative Logic in the Annunciation to Mary").

242. The concept of *theotokos* (literally *God-bearer*) is not to give glory to the mother but to verify that the life of Jesus—from the very beginning—was God's action.

243. Mary realizes that "she would bear a child without the intervention of a man, perhaps even that conception would be immediate" (Morris, *Luke*, 81).
By her consent, "Mary is here a pattern for the Christian faith but also much more: she responds to a call that is unique in human history" (Nolland, *Luke*, 59).
Mary realized, by her acceptance, that she was chosen for a great task. Barclay provides telling comments: "The piercing truth is that God does not choose a person for ease and comfort and selfish joy but for a great task that will take all that head and heart and hand can bring to it. *God chooses that person to use that person.* When Joan of Arc knew that her time was short she prayed, 'I shall only last a year; use me as you can'" (*Gospel of Luke*, 8; italics original).
Steuernagel, however, gets pretty basic when he says that if you want to understand theology, follow Mary and offer your womb ("Doing Theology with an Eye on Mary," 104)! Such an offer entails many sighs. Steuernagel (ibid., 104) envisions Mary sighing

as she considers the craziness of her offer and its cost to her reputation and later as she grapples with Joseph's confusion (Matt 1:18–19).

244. Wright notes that Mary, when asked to be the mother of the Messiah, and although not yet aware of what this involves, "says the words which have rung down the years as a model of the human response to God's unexpected vocation: 'Here I am, the Lord's servant-girl; let it be as you have said'" (*Luke for Everyone*, 12).

Mary's response echoes the readiness of Abigail (1 Sam 25:41) and Sarah (Gen 21:1) and Hannah (1 Sam 1:11) (see Nolland, *Luke*, 57).

Mary's statement shows she exhibits faith immediately in three ways: She believes the angel's words, willingly lets God use her, and hurries to visit another, Elizabeth, who also is being used amazingly by God (Luke 1:38; see Bock, *Luke*, 44).

Ambrose sees it this way: Mary "did not deny the faith, she did not refuse the duty, but she conformed her will, she promised obedience" (Just, *Luke*, 17).

Irenaeus contrasts Eve and Mary. He writes that "the former was seduced to disobey God and so fell, but the latter was persuaded to obey God, so that the Virgin Mary might become the advocate of Eve" (ibid., 19).

245. Daniel ("Borne in Perplexity," 26–28) emphasizes Mary's perplexity. Calling Luke 1:26–38 a "news flash," she writes "that the most important woman in the world, the one who is about to give birth to the son of God, the one who will have to tell her beloved news of a pregnancy that will bring scandal to their new life, the one who will sit at the foot of the cross heroically suffering her son into eternity, the one who now as a young girl will have to have the strength to travel long distances in miles and even greater distances in faith, begins her adventure *in a state of perplexity*. From the moment the angel greets her, she is confused" (ibid., 26; italics original).

246. In contrast to Zechariah who does not initially believe, Luke presents Mary as a model of someone who, in her own particular life, fully and responsibly accepts the will of God (R. E. Brown, "Annunciation to Mary," 259).

247. Ryken offers these telling comments: "How rare it is to find someone who is willing to trust God for the impossible and then obey him without hesitation or qualification" (*Luke*, 38)

248. What I call Mary's courage, Ryken sees as her faith (*Luke*, 39). He writes that Mary "trusted God for all of it—her relationship with Joseph, her reputation in town, her physical suffering, and the anguish of her soul. Mary believed in God and followed him with trusting obedience" (ibid.).

249. All people should be amazed at God's plan as revealed in Zechariah, Elizabeth, and Mary (see Bock, *Luke*, 43).

250. The betrothal meant that the couple was treated as married; however, there had not been a consummation. Consequently, matters of inheritance, death, adultery and divorce were handled according to the law. A betrothal, as with a marriage, could not be dissolved except by divorce (Holy Apostles Convent, *Life of the Virgin Mary*, 69; see also *m. Ketub.* 1:2; 4:2; and Hagner, *Matthew 1–13*, 17). See Matt 1:18–25.

251. Swanson ("Magnificat and Crucifixion," 102, 105) points to the penalties in the Talmud for pregnancies outside of marriage. Granted, we do not know if these penalties were in force in Mary/Mariam's time. However, they are sobering. Talmud *Kethuboth* 44b–45a says that if a girl plays the harlot in her father's house, she is to be stoned at the

entrance of her father's house. If witnesses testify she has played the harlot in his house, she is to be stoned at the entrance of the gate of the city. If Mary/Mariam has priestly blood, as may be the case because Elizabeth is a daughter of Aaron, then she could be burned. The Talmudic tractate *Sanhedrin* 9:1 states that if the daughter of a priest plays the harlot, she deserves the capital punishment of burning. Swanson (ibid., 103) writes that her name, *Mariam*, means sea of bitterness. Here is the biblical reference for death by stoning: Deut 22:20–24.

252. Luke and Matthew report that "Jesus did not have a father in the ordinary way, and that this was because Mary had been given special grace to be the mother of God's incarnate self" (Wright, *Luke for Everyone*, 10).

253. For the law on adultery and other marriage issues see Deut 22:13–30. Bailey (*Jesus through Middle Eastern Eyes*, 44, 46) picks up on Joseph's anger when he learns of Mary's pregnancy (Matt 1:18–19). Bailey asserts that a better translation of "he considered" is "while he *fumed* over this matter" (Matt 1:20; ibid., 46, italics original). A significant attribute of this just man, however, was that he was able "to reprocess his anger into grace" (ibid., 47).

This drama does not agree with the view that Mary retained her virginity after her marriage to Joseph. However, for a fine summary of those who hold to this view, see Holy Apostles Convent, *Life of the Virgin Mary*: "Annunciation of the Mother of God and Ever-Virgin Mary," 74–118.

254. Mary returned home (Luke 1:56), but Luke gives no indication of whether that meant her parents' home or the home of Joseph (see Fitzmyer, *Luke I–IX*, 369).

255. Abraham was the first prophet in Scripture, Gen 20:7. Moses, who delivered the Hebrew slaves from Egypt and led them for forty years in the wilderness, is acknowledged as Israel's greatest prophet. John was beheaded by Herod (Matt 14:1–12; Mark 6:14–29; Luke 7:24–35).

256. One of the most beautiful aspects of the infancy narratives is that God deals on micro and macro levels. While preparing to deal with sin, as he promised, through the birth of his son, Jesus, God honors an honorable, obedient, faithful couple with granting them their hearts' desire, a son named John. Wright correctly states that God "takes care of smaller human concerns as well" (*Luke for Everyone*, 8).

257. Barclay (*Gospel of Luke*, 11) recounts that in Palestine at that time, musicians and friends gathered at a house for a birth. If the child was a boy, a great celebration ensued; if a girl, well, the musicians went away silently and in sorrow. "So in Elizabeth's house, there was double joy," Barclay says, because at last their neighbor had a child and that child was a son (ibid.)! Luke 1:57–66.

258. Her "No!" is emphatic (Morris, *Luke*, 86).

259. With the birth of John "God vindicates Elizabeth and, coincidentally, provides a prophet of the coming of the Lord," Green writes (*Gospel of Luke*, 107).

260. The name *John* is a shortened version of *Jehohanan* and means *God is gracious* (Barclay, *Gospel of Luke*, 12)

261. Perhaps he could now hear, too, for the text hints that Zechariah also was deaf (Luke 1:20, 62) (Branch, "Exegetical Perspective," 35). The specialness of the child is attested by the miracle of Zechariah's sudden speech. He, like Elizabeth, is filled with the

Spirit and becomes "the mouthpiece of God" (Fitzmyer, *Luke I–IX*, 382).

262. Maximus of Turin sees the timing of the baby's being named John and Zechariah's sudden ability to speak again as miraculous and symbolic because the child "gave his father back his voice, he restored the faculty of speech to the priest . . . John unloosed the mouth that the angel had bound. What Gabriel had closed, the little child unlocked. When John is born, the father suddenly becomes a prophet or priest, speech attains its use, love receives an offspring, the office recognizes the priest" (Just, *Luke*, 29).

263. The events leading up to John's circumcision and what took place at the circumcision show that God is moving again among his people and in Israel's history (see Fitzmyer, *Luke I–IX*, 309).

264. The horn of salvation (Luke 1:69) expresses not only joy but also might, strength, and power, all attributes of the God of Israel. Here, designating an agent of God's salvific power in David's line, it becomes "in a loose sense a messianic title" (Fitzmyer, *Luke I–IX*, 383). Luke 1:67–79.

265. Consider this logic: Since God saved Zechariah from his unbelief, he surely can save Israel from her enemies (see Branch, "Exegetical Perspective," 37).

266. Zechariah's prophetic song breaks neatly into two parts. Verses 68–75 offer praise to the God of Israel; verses 76–79 provide a broad job description for his son, John (ibid., 33).

267. Wright believes that the song shows Zechariah as one "who has pondered the agony and the hope for many years, and who now finds the two bubbling out of him as he looks in awe and delight at his baby son" (*Luke for Everyone*, 18). Morris (*Luke*, 89) observes that "we might have expected that Zechariah's song would be all about his little boy. He surprised us by beginning with the Messiah whom God was about to send."

268. Zechariah and Elizabeth both realize that their son's role was not the main one in the drama. Granted, he was to be honored as "the prophet of the Most High," but he was not the "Son of the Most High," Luke 1:76, 32 (Dean, *Luke*, 25). John will be like the servant in Isa 49:5—and a servant with a daunting task: Restoring Israel to God (Nolland, *Luke*, 35–36).

269. Luke 1:76–77. Elizabeth and Zechariah's son John will proclaim God's salvation and Mary's baby will be the salvation (Bock, *Luke*, 5). Zechariah's prophetic words emphasize restoration. Barclay (*Gospel of Luke*, 13–14) rightly emphasizes the key aspect of forgiveness: Yes, it entails looking again at the penalty but also and more importantly it aims to restore a relationship, I believe. Significantly, this restoration begins at the instigation of the one wronged; the one wronged is God.

270. Kuist puts it this way: "Because of God's heart of mercy, 'the day-spring from on high' was at hand" ("Sources of Power," 298).

271. Ryken sees the condition of Israel before the birth of Christ as dark days and indeed that darkness "is the situation we are all in until we are saved" (Card, *Luke*, 64).

272. Card writes that Zechariah sings "a song about a new world where the condition in which one will serve God is love and faithfulness and joy." In the old world order, the predominant emotion in the service of God was fear (*Luke*, 44).

273. Nolland prefers the word *fear* to *awe* because "a totally unlikely pregnancy, a

strange insistence on a completely unexpected name, and the subsequent instantaneous recovery of Zechariah combine to produce that involuntary response of fear of the divine activity which Luke is so fond of noting (cf. 5:26; 7:16; 8:37; etc.)" (*Luke*, 81).

274. See Bock, *Luke*, 43.

275. The monologue is ending. Elizabeth summarizes what she hopes the guests to her home, the audience, have learned from her action of sharing her life. A monologue, a subcategory of creative drama, is an effective teaching tool because it involves participation and imagination (see Barragar, *Spiritual Growth through Creative Drama*, 15). For example, Jewish children can tell the story of the Exodus from Egypt because they have heard it and enacted it yearly throughout their lives. Drama certainly is not a new technique for conveying spiritual truths (ibid., 13). Drama engages one's God-given gift of imagination.

276. In a very real sense, this monologue incorporates worship, for it explains the biblical text. Long defines worship as follows: A service allows "*the drama already present in worship to be brought to the surface and to be more deeply experienced*" (*Beyond the Worship Wars*, 43; italics original).

277. Holy Apostles Convent, *Life of the Virgin Mary*, 123. Doriani et al. (*Incarnation in the Gospels*, 69) are incorrect when they write that John was the first to recognize Jesus as the Christ. Furthermore, they entirely ignore the contributions of Elizabeth.

278. Darden seems to note the joy of those throughout the ages who wish to communicate the Good News to others when he writes, "Here's the wonderful thing—we are part of that story! We play an important role in God's Great Plan. This is our story! The Bible is our roadmap and our cast list. Knowing how these stories are used, how they're important, and what to watch for is important so we will know our parts in this great cosmic comedy/drama" (*Reluctant Prophets and Clueless Disciples*, 13).

279. The monologue was designed to be fun (in the sense of viewing and acting) but academic (in the sense of solid research). It is not devotional, although during the many times I have presented it, both men and women have wept. This monologue was designed to encourage a deeper awareness of formative events in the lives of Elizabeth, Zechariah, and Mary in the ongoing, wonderful work of God in history (cf. Ratcliff, "Social Contexts of Children's Ministry," 129–130).

The monologue and Luke 1 emphasize the prominence of the upcoming Davidic king and acknowledge the importance of "his prophetic precursor, John" (Nolland, *Luke*, 24).

280. See Psalm 1, for example.

281. While characteristics like *blameless* and *upright* describe Zechariah and Elizabeth, the designation *virgin* describes Mary. Mary becomes the first model disciple in the new order. Luke 1 shows her as calm, obedient, full of worship, courageous, willing to take God at his word, willing to experience the unknown, willing to believe past her natural understanding, and even a good song writer! Likewise, Elizabeth is a model of how to react. Believing and joyful, she is an "amazed saint" (Bock, *Luke*, 43).

282. Luke 1:25, 43.

283. Elizabeth's monologue has sought to create an experience in which the audience has listened to how God is moving and has moved in a mighty way in the lives of ordinary people; it is hoped that the audience can reflect upon her words in fruitful and

creative ways (see McNabb and Mabry, *Teaching the Bible Creatively,* 51).

284. According to tradition, and the writings of Church Fathers Epiphanius, Basil, and Cyril of Alexandria, Zechariah died a martyr and was killed in the Temple between the porch and the altar. Herod ordered his death because he refused to disclose the location of his son (Thurston and Attwater, *Butler's Lives of the Saints,* 4:267). Nothing is known about Elizabeth's death. Their shared saint's day is November 5 (ibid.).

285. Worship is essentially a public, corporate, and dramatic event. Consider this definition: A worship service allows "*the drama already present* in worship to be brought to the surface and to be more deeply experienced" (Long, *Beyond the Worship Wars,* 43; italics original). This Acts play clearly makes use of the drama already present in Scripture. In addition, drama illuminates Christian theology (von Balthasar, *Theo-Drama,* 1:25).

286. The elementary school child by nature is an explorer; a propensity toward adventure naturally readies a child to move on toward new horizons and accept new ways of doing things (Fritz, *Child and the Christian Faith,* 145). The Acts play offers children and adults a chance to explore the meaning of their faith and to see the Scriptures presented in an interactive, noisy, exuberant way (ibid.).

According to Wheeler, characteristics of the audience, ages six to thirteen, are as follows: A six year old can understand the concepts of space, time, and the material world. (Wheeler, *Creative Resources,* notes from the inside cover). Children ages seven to eleven begin to develop an awareness of logical necessities; they can appreciate a symbolic knowledge that allows for generalization. Children from ages ten and up can form hypotheses, make assumptions, and draw conclusions. Furthermore, elementary school children are able to remember facts, know the sequence of events, and discover meaning in both (Stonehouse, *Joining Children on the Spiritual Journey,* 162).

287. The play is an appropriate resource for a worship service because it communicates in an established, known way. Children and adults are familiar with television news. This effort at familiarity emphasizes a chord in child evangelism: A child must feel he belongs; this "belongingness" will then lead a child into new areas of learning (Fritz, *Child and the Christian Faith,* 147).

288. A version of this play was published. Branch, "He is Risen!" (2010). This chapter acknowledges Professor de Klerk's service to the Lord and the joy and honor his life exemplifies.

289. Not all experiences in church are equally educative for all age groups of people in a congregation. In other words, a monologue sermon, the regular means of conveying the biblical message in Protestant circles, may not work for all age groups all the time. There can be positive and negative aspects to public, corporate worship and drama (D. Brown, *God and Mystery in Words,* 178). I wrote the Acts play as an attempt to create an experience for the children and their teachers on which they could later fruitfully and creatively reflect (McNabb and Mabry, *Teaching the Bible Creatively,* 51).

As I wrote it, I kept in mind the insights and definitions that Quash gives: "Drama displays *human actions* and *temporal events* in *specific contexts.* Theodramatics concerns itself with human actions (people), temporal events (time), and their specific contexts (place) *in relation to God's purpose*" (*Theology and the Drama of History,* 3–4; italics original).

290. Research shows that dramatization helps a child to learn a story and get inside

another person (Clark et al., *Childhood Education in the Church*, 544). Dramatization, especially one in which a child participates, helps a child to understand his/her reactions to something and the reactions of other people, too (ibid.).

McNabb and Mabry stress that the Bible is an understandable book for children; the job of a teacher is to present it as understandable and timeless (*Teaching the Bible Creatively*, 22). They add that Bible stories are open to interpretation and contain various levels of truth. "There is often more than one valid way of looking at a particular passage" (ibid., 23.) Drama offers one such way.

Some teachers, however, hesitate to use drama. Two reasons given are that it's a waste of time and control of a classroom may be in jeopardy. But perhaps those who refuse to use drama and plays in which a child participates as an actor or viewer display a lack of trust in their young charges and in themselves (see Clark et al., *Childhood Education in the Church*, 545).

Over the centuries the Christian church has developed many different orders of worship. However, according to Long, who stresses its public and liturgical aspects, any order can be considered a good avenue of worship if "worship is an acted-out story, a piece of community theater" (*Beyond the Worship Wars*, 47–48).

291. Perhaps a reason for the play's good reception and the fact that the children left smiling was because it was easily understood. Many children shyly shook my hand; their teachers hugged me as they said their thanks. One theology student in the audience stayed seated as everybody left. He was weeping. He told me later he cried because he saw how the play reached the children.

The positive feedback indicated the play's success. The play's dialogue is upbeat, short, and kept its first audience—primarily children and their teachers—in mind. Similarly, Pulitzer Prize winner Frank McCourt decided to write his memoir, *Angela's Ashes*, like a child. "Children are almost deadly in their detachment from the world," he commented in an interview. "They tell the truth, and somehow that lodged in my subconscious when I started writing the book" (McCourt quoted in Grossman, "Milestones: Frank McCourt," 21).

Similarly, this Acts play was written with a detachment from the text and with children in mind. It contains short sentences, active verbs, questions, exclamations, rowdiness, wonder, and a sense of live action.

292. Creativity must have its place in Sunday School and in larger church settings. Creativity is a gift given by God to all in some measure, not just to a few. I believe it is a sin to neglect God's gift. A good working definition of creativity is that it combines something old with something new and the product is something different (Clark et al., *Childhood Education in the Church*, 545). Above all, creativity allows one to look at something old, like the biblical text, with new eyes and present a wonderful, timeless truth in a new and appropriate way.

293. The children and their teachers expected that a Christian message would be presented. Aldrich lists seven guidelines with subsets about gearing a message of evangelism to an unsaved person; some of his guidelines apply to a group and to children. I considered the following two in writing the play:

What did I know of the children's background? *I knew the children were black South Africans, English speakers, and that their teachers were primarily white women. The children arrived in an orderly way, and I complimented them on their good manners in my opening remarks.*

What signs of openness to the gospel are seen? *I knew the children knew Christian songs and would sing them as part of the service* (see Aldrich, *Lifestyle Evangelism*, 192).

B. W. Anderson adds something that guided my writing and study. To be sure, the Bible is the record and the witness of events that climax the life, death, and resurrection of Jesus Christ. To be a Christian, Anderson maintains, "is to understand one's existence in this dramatic context" (*Unfolding Drama of the Bible*, 11).

294. In teaching children, it is important to stress that the Bible is not only a positive book but also a book that is fun (McNabb and Mabry, *Teaching the Bible Creatively*, 21). McNabb and Mabry add that most kids (erroneously!) see the Bible as a book of rules to keep them from having fun; but the Bible is not only Good Advice but also Good News (ibid.)!

Why is it fun? The Bible contains lots of adventure stories, many of them in the book of Acts. In the story that this play depicts, the disciples see something amazing: Jesus, whom they had seen die, is alive and rises into heaven! They greet these miracles with wonder and joy. Truly, the Ascension of Jesus sets them off on the adventure of their lives!

295. McCorkindale suggests the children's song "He brought me to his banqueting table" as a singing aid for a Sunday between Easter and Pentecost It is suitable for Ascension Day. Sometimes the song is called "His banner over me is love." Verses include these:

He rose from the dead, and He is alive. (His banner over me is love.)

Jesus went up into heaven. (His banner over me is love.)

We are his hands, and we are his feet. (His banner over me is love.)

He calls on us to love one another. (His banner over me is love.)

He is the shepherd, and we are the sheep. (His banner over me is love.)

He is the vine, and we are the branches. (His banner over me is love.) (McCorkindale, "Children's Ministry between Easter and Pentecost," 293).

296. Von Balthasar asserts that theater is an illumination of existence, "and a central one at that" (*Theo-Drama*, 1:259). The stark setting of this play invites audience members to fill in the blanks—outside trees and rocks—by using their imagination.

297. The Acts play is neither an allegory nor a typology. But it does seek to integrate contemporary experience—a news format—into patterns inherent in the biblical text and into a pericope that lends itself to enactment (O'Keefe and Reno, *Sanctified Vision*, 73; for an excellent explanation of typology and allegory, see ibid., 69–113).

298. McNabb and Mabry (*Teaching the Bible Creatively*, 25–27) offer these tips on how to approach a Bible study with children:

Find the passage's main point.

Consider the passage's context.

Use the canonical principle of letting Scripture interpret Scripture.

Look at how to apply the passage to one's daily life.

299. I assumed that the children did not know the stories in Acts, for on the whole, people are largely ignorant of the stories in the Bible (Hunter, *How to Reach Secular People*, 55). I wanted to put everybody in the audience on the same footing and knowledge level. Reading the text aloud does that.

300. There are two Ascension stories (Acts 1:1–12 and Luke 24:36–53, specifically verses 50–53). This play concentrates on the Acts narrative. A. Wilson maintains the Ascension stories are one and the same and must be read together ("Ascension," 49). I agree.

301. Vanhoozer sees three benefits to "knowing God theatrically": Theo-drama re-invigorates what Vanhoozer terms "our anemic imaginations, diluted as they are by the mess of pottage we are fed by contemporary culture" (*Drama of Doctrine*, 79–80).

A theatrical metaphor enables people (the actors, the writer, the congregation/audi-ence) to see their ordinary and daily lives as replete with urgency, vibrancy, tension, and importance. The ordinariness of daily life is a window for God's intervention.

The metaphor of theatrical direction enriches both biblical authority and theology by providing "a complex yet concrete model for conceiving the relationship between text and interpretation." This concrete model is *performance*, he says (ibid., italics original).

302. Wall, "Acts of the Apostles," 8.

303. Neil, *Acts of the Apostles*, 25. Quash stresses the value of what he calls a "'theo-dramatic' conception of history"; he defines this as "a way of thinking theologically about (the) historical process and the historical character of human agents and environments that emphasizes their dramatic features" (*Theology and the Drama of History*, 1).

304. Wall concludes his list with these two reasons:

Acts, because of its stories, deepens the faith of new believers or people thinking about converting like Theophilus—and maybe like you! A person is born a Jew or a Gentile, an American or a South African. One *becomes* a Christian.

Acts, like many of the books in the Bible, was written in response to crises. One crisis the book of Acts addresses is what to do about the newcomers, the Gentiles. Acts wel-comes the newcomers who believe in Jesus, the Gentiles, equally with those Jews who also believe in Jesus (Wall, "Acts of the Apostles," 8–10).

305. Acts 27:27–44; 28:1–10; 3:1–10; 9:36–43.

306. Marshall, *Acts of the Apostles*, 17.

307. A child's active imagination is a great tool and strength to work with for a teach-er intent on training a child in the faith (Stonehouse, *Joining Children on the Spiritual Journey*, 158).

308. The Acts play is designed to be fun, but it also is based on solid research. It en-courages the awareness of a formative event in Christian history; it exposes the audience to a different view of the text, an eyewitness account; it seeks to educate the children and others in the audience about the Ascension as recorded in Acts in a way that combined scholarship and fun (cf. Ratcliff, "Social Contexts of Children's Ministry," 129–130).

309. I was mindful of a couple of Spurgeon's rules for teachers of children: I must be taught by God myself before I can teach; I must ask God to use me as a teacher; and I must respect my audience (Spurgeon, *"Come Ye Children,"* 92, 93). First and foremost, children must be taught morality (ibid., 87).

Furthermore, children are socialized within or without faith, and exposure to faith is a requirement for acceptance of belief, but how socialization into faith takes place can make the difference between acceptance or rejection of it; passing on the faith is a re-quirement for covenant believers and a crucial concern for religious education (Ratcliff, "Social Contexts of Children's Ministry," 119). The tripod for passing on the faith is the family, school and community.

310. Marshall, *Acts of the Apostles*, 19, 20, 23.

311. Young children are dramatic and playful by nature, spending hours acting out

the events their imaginations create (Stonehouse, *Joining Children on the Spiritual Journey*, 156). Children express a love of the dramatic, are comfortable with mystery, and desire to explore and investigate things themselves; that is how they learn (ibid.).

The use of the medium of a play for Ascension Day recognized that an unusual presentation of a text can deepen a child's engagement with the Bible (D. Brown, *God and Mystery in Words*, 184).

312. What I call "imagination hats," Berryman calls "the wondering" ability (Berryman, *Teaching Godly Play*, 37). Children, already so good at "wondering," must be guided and supported by the storyteller. I was very conscious of that as I wrote the play and as I portrayed the SABC news reporter. I hoped to catch the wonder of the biblical text passage via the excitement of the disciples and their truthfulness. The disciples were role models these children could trust and emulate. My young audience participated avidly. Because by nature children pretend and wonder easily, children do not have to be taught how to imagine (Clark et al., *Childhood Education in the Church*, 543).

It is the teacher's responsibility in a group's "wondering" to genuinely enter the lesson himself or herself (Berryman, *Teaching Godly Play*, 38). The unspoken part of the lesson is the authentic participation of the teacher, who is moving toward discoveries appropriate to himself or herself. There is no talking down to children as they wonder, or boiling down of Scripture's profound depths to a thin "kiddy religion."

Correctly done, a successful lesson for children "makes them joyful" and gives the children "something they deeply need . . . This is not the elation that entertainment might give. It is the happiness that the satisfaction of the soul's wholeness can give" (ibid.).

313. Imagination is at work in the forming of faith. Stonehouse writes: "As children stretch to understand God's involvement in their experiences and in their world, they call on their imagination to provide explanations or answers for questions they had never thought about before. Often their explanations are magical" (*Joining Children on the Spiritual Journey*, 154).

314. My hope in writing the play was that it would help the audience to find meaning in the passage (cf. Hunter, *How to Reach Secular People*, 57). A film, video, or play shows a teacher plans a lesson; all three are contemporary ways of communicating the Christian faith in a way that will continue to live in the minds of students (cf. McNabb and Mabry, *Teaching the Bible Creatively*, 52).

Vanhoozer writes that his book "insists that God and humanity are alternately actor and audience" (*Drama of Doctrine*, 37). He sees life as a divine and human interactive theater. He maintains that "theology involves both what God has said and done for the world and what we must say and do in grateful response" (ibid., 37–38). The disciples in this play clearly act in a joyful and grateful way to the commands of the risen, alive, and ascending Jesus.

315. Marshall, *Acts of the Apostles*, 62. Drama has several advantages including the following:
Enacting a story makes it more real.
A drama may show honest feelings that one may skim over when reading the text.
Interactions within a drama promote new friendships and let a teacher and students get to know each other in new ways.
Ideas and feelings expressed become part of the actor.
Enacting a story helps an actor to think outside himself or herself.

Enacting a story gives the actor, via imagination, insights into another person's think-ing and actions (cf. Clark et al., *Childhood Education in the Church*, 545–46).

Just as Christ says he can be encountered in many ways—as one poor, naked, hun-gry, or in prison (Matt 25:31–40)—so likewise the biblical text can be encountered in many guises (Stevenson-Moessner, *Prelude to Practical Theology: Variations on Theory and Practice*, 22). The pericope of Acts 1:1–12 can be treated in a conventional way as a straight sermon or, as I did, presented as a play.

316. Mark 15:27; John 19:16–18.

317. Luke 5:12–16; 8:40–56; 9:10–17.

318. Luke 23:1–3; John 18:28–37.

319. Luke 23:44–56.

320. Because the character of the SABC news reporter was not a believer, knew noth-ing about the new movement, and was "professionally neutral" in her questions, there was no possibility that the audience would feel lectured or demeaned (cf. Hunter, *How to Reach Secular People*, 61).

321. SABC stands for the South African Broadcasting Corporation. If the play is per-formed elsewhere, use the television network most familiar to a young audience.

322. Why a play? Drama conveys ideas, values, beliefs, and attitudes and provokes us as readers, hearers, and viewers to analyze what is portrayed on stage (DiYanni, *Litera-ture*, 901). A play is meant to be experienced both intellectually and emotionally (ibid.).

Drama is a staged art; in this it is unique (ibid., 899). The purpose of writing a play is to have it performed successively in front of audience after audience. A play may be a vehicle for persuasion (ibid.). In other words, it may have an agenda. Playwrights Shake-speare, Ibsen, Elliott, Shaw, Sondheim, Miller, and Bernstein presented issues, propa-gated ideas, and maybe at times even pummeled an audience with words.

323. I wanted to teach and bless those whom Spurgeon calls "young in grace" (*"Come Ye Children,"* 5). I saw the invitation to present the service on Ascension Day as a way to do that by using a medium the children knew, television, in a positive way. The ac-tors in the play were a special blessing to me. Spurgeon characterizes those who work with children this way: "If you want big-souled, large-hearted men or women, look for them among those who are much engaged among the young, bearing with their follies, sympathizing with their weaknesses for Jesus' sake" (ibid., 10). The seven volunteers who worked so hard on the play—Godwin Mushayabasa, Nikolaas Pienaar, Danie Potgieter, Johann Engelbrecht, Carlo Wright, Gideon Semakuezi, and Albert Coetsee—truly are that!

324. The actors were instructed to keep the action moving; avoid a monotone voice; speak clearly; smile often; avoid "walking" on another's line; allow for pauses, wonder, and laughter; and avoid sounding pompous or know-it-all (cf. Childers, *Performing the Word*, 93–95). I was impressed with the unselfishness of those I came to call "my disci-ples." The actors were what Childers calls unselfish performers (ibid., 95). Consequently, the resulting performance of the Acts play was "full of the voice and life of the text" and "full of the voice and personality" of each actor (ibid.).

325. Stevenson-Moessner defines exegesis as "to lead out" or "to interpret" (*Prelude to Practical Theology*, 20). She observes that this definition evokes an image of leading

from one location to another, "as from experience to text or from text to experience" (ibid.). The play's actors and the play's audience were about to experience the retelling of eyewitness accounts of the ascension of Jesus.

B. W. Anderson seems to be smiling when he writes that "the Great Dramatist is apt to lure us from the spectator's balcony and put us into the act" (*Unfolding Drama of the Bible*, 15). The purposeful action of putting on "imagination hats" brought the audience into the drama in a non-threatening and gracious way.

326. When a play is performed, one is first struck by its *representational* quality. Drama is *mimetic* art—art that imitates and reflects life, emotions, and experiences (DiYanni, *Literature*, 900).

327. Dialogue in a play functions on two levels: First, what the words mean and second what they reveal and suggest about the characters' behavior, backgrounds, feelings, ethics, motivations (DiYanni, *Literature*, 901). Drama entertains, "offers provocative ideas about the life it portrays, and it provides an imaginative extension of its possibilities" (ibid.).

328. In the Acts play, the disciples express their faith and its progressions. As such, the Acts play seeks to create an environment where those in the audience can investigate the ideas and images they are forming about God (cf. Stonehouse, *Joining Children on the Spiritual Journey*, 159). Indeed, stories are at the heart of faith development, because stories capture and communicate theology (ibid., 161). In their elementary school years, children start taking ownership of the stories, beliefs, and religious rituals esteemed by those in the faith community to which they belong (ibid., 162).

329. Matt 27:33. The play emphasized the memorization of lines. This was teaching by example on a subliminal level. Consider this insight: "Words once understood become a part of the stuff of which concepts are formed and may be a strong influence in the child's later choices and decisions as well as his conduct" (Fritz, *Child and the Christian Faith*, 149).

330. From here on in the play, only Scripture references that are not part of Acts 1:1–12 are mentioned.

331. Matt 27:57–66.

332. The resurrection can be seen as one of the many interventions of an active God breaking into time (von Balthasar, *Theo-Drama*, 1:26).

333. Matt 28:1–10; Mark 16:108; Luke 24:1–10.

334. The pattern of the church fathers was to interpret the Ascension as the climax of the resurrection (Kapic and Van der Lugt, "Ascension of Jesus," 26).

335. The phrase "into heaven" occurs four times in Acts 1:10–11 (Maile, "Ascension in Luke-Acts," 55). The disciples were not looking "toward heaven" but actually were looking "into heaven" (Fuller, "Life of Jesus after the Ascension," 392); Acts 1:11 says they actually saw Jesus go into heaven.

336. John 21:1–14.

337. Clouds are associated with God's presence: Exod 13:21; Pss 68:4, 33; 104:3 (cf. A. Wilson, "Ascension," 49).

338. The Bible records numerous comings and goings of the Lord Jesus during the

forty-day period between the Resurrection and the Ascension (Grant, "Christ Ascended for Us," 39).

339. Anyone associated with young children knows they love stories (Stonehouse, *Joining Children on the Spiritual Journey*, 156). They especially like stories which strongly state good and evil and in which the good prevails (ibid., 157). In the Acts play, good prevails: The crucified and dead Jesus comes back from death, is alive, and rises into the air!

340. John 20:24–31.

341. In Acts 1:3, Luke relates that Jesus showed himself alive to the apostles, "after his passion, by many infallible proofs, being seen of them forty days, and speaking of the things pertaining to the kingdom of God." The infallible proofs seem to mean interviews and communications with people (Robinson, "Resurrection and Ascension," 31).

342. Neil, *Acts of the Apostles*, 64.

343. Ibid., 65; Luke 24:43; possibly Acts 1:4.

344. While it is possible that some in the audience identified with the SABC Eye-Witness News Reporter as a seeker or as someone who did not know anything about Christianity, others may have identified with one of the disciples. Each disciple portrayed himself as someone with dignity and a responsibility to share the good news of Jesus with others (Hunter, *How to Reach Secular People*, 62).

345. While writing the play, I attempted to address questions the children might have through the questions of the SABC reporter (cf. ibid., 59). Furthermore, a benefit of the play was that the children were exposed to six fine young men as role models what Hunter (ibid.) calls credible Christians—students in the Faculty of Theology at North-West University.

346. Wall, "Acts of the Apostles," 41.

347. Matt 6:5–8; Luke 11:1–4.

348. Matt 6:9–10. What is commonly known as the Lord's Prayer continues through verse 14.

349. John 20:15.

350. There are six reasons the Ascension is important:
It is the confirmation of the exaltation of Christ in his present Lordship.
The Ascension is the explanation of the continuation of the ministry of Jesus and the church.
It is the culmination of the resurrection appearances.
The Ascension is the prelude for the sending of the Holy Spirit.
It is the foundation of the Christian mission.
The Ascension is the pledge of the return of Christ (Maile, "Ascension in Luke–Acts," 56–58).

351. Spence and Exell, *Acts & Romans*, 12.

352. Ibid., 12.

353. Ibid., 13.

354. The intent of the baptism of the Holy Spirit is the empowerment of the mission

of the church (Weissenbuehler, "Acts 1:1–11," 62).

355. The teaching of Jesus is strongly relational (Grant, "Christ Ascended for Us," 40).

356. Acts 1:13–15.

357. The disciples do not react with a sense of extreme loss; they experience joy (Shore, "Living by the Word," 21).

358. Neil, *Acts of the Apostles*, 64.

359. Acts 1:7 in essence says this: It is God's business and not yours. The disciples are correct, however, in thinking that the restoration of all things does include the restoration of Israel (Weissenbuehler, "Acts 1:1–11," 63).

360. Neil, *Acts of the Apostles*, 66.

361. Spence and Exell, *Acts & Romans*, 13.

362. The drama portrayed here in Acts 1:1–12 and indeed throughout the entire Bible is always at God's initiative (von Balthasar, *Theo-Drama*, 2:53).

363. Neil, *Acts of the Apostles*, 25.

364. Ibid., 63.

365. The important direction in the Ascension story is not *up* but *out* (Shore, "Living by the Word," 21).

366. While Jesus is in heaven, he passes beyond our realm of vision, but this does not reduce our assurance in his existence (Fuller, "Life of Jesus after the Ascension," 392).

367. Using Psalm 68 as a cross-reference for the Ascension, G. W. Charles notes that the Rider of the clouds becomes the Climber of the cross and the Ascender into the clouds (G. W. Charles, "Rider of the Clouds," 15–16).

368. The two men in white underscore the connection between the Resurrection and the Ascension (Weissenbuehler, "Acts 1:1–11," 64).

369. *NIV Study Bible*, 1995:1647n.

370. Cf. Gen 16:7; 22:11; 2 Sam 24:16; 1 Kgs 19:7; 2 Kgs 19:35.

371. Luke 24:1–12.

372. The angels' question points to the obvious: "You have your orders! Get on with them!" (A. Wilson, "Ascension," 51).

373. The Ascension means these four things:
Jesus now continues his mission in the world through the apostolic witness of believers.
In changing places, so to speak, Jesus exercises lordship over the church in the Spirit.
The Ascension presupposes the coming of the Holy Spirit.
The Ascension bears witness to the inevitability of the return of Jesus to complete what is now being accomplished (Weissenbuehler, "Acts 1:1–11," 65).
A. Wilson adds this important point: The Ascension establishes the whereabouts of Jesus: Jesus is in heaven ("Ascension," 50).

374. Marshall, *Acts of the Apostles*, 61.

375. Ibid.

376. The Ascension is not the last word: He will come again (A. Wilson, "Ascension," 51; cf. Ps 68:18).

377. Neil, *Acts of the Apostles*, 66. Effective evangelism takes place over a time span. The Good News includes the love of God, the grace of God, the Kingdom of God, forgiveness of sins, new birth, reconciliation, sanctification, justification, and holiness (Hunter, *How to Reach Secular People*, 103). The play included mention of many of these concepts. They were defined as the play progressed by the characters' actions and words.

Effective communication involves telling stories, especially the kind of stories that enable people to discover the point for themselves (ibid., 105). Effective Christian communication may involve word plays, proverbs, and drama (ibid., 104); these tools stick in one's memory bank.

378. Jesus now intercedes for us in heaven, but the Holy Spirit intercedes for us in our hearts here on earth (Rom 8:26; McGowan, "Ascended Jesus Interceding for Us," 52–53). The play follows Spurgeon's dictum about teaching children: Teach children the absolute necessity of a change of heart (*"Come Ye Children,"* 90).

379. Deut 29:29.

380. God describes himself in Exod 34:6–7. The play communicates what Spurgeon cites as a necessity of child evangelism: Teaching children the joy and blessedness of becoming and being Christians (Spurgeon, *"Come Ye Children,"* 91).

381. Neil, *Acts of the Apostles*, 67.

382. It is generally held that children learn their behavior from others. The Acts play intends to show that accepted behavior is excitement about the Good News of Jesus. Furthermore, excited people convey this message: Jesus is alive, is risen, and will come again!

383. In the account of Luke 24:50–53, Jesus departs and blesses his disciples at the same time. Kapic calls this "a profound portrait of the ascending Christ" ("Receiving Christ's Priestly Benediction," 252). The disciples now know Jesus as the One who not only promised peace but is Peace. As High Priest, Jesus not only pronounced a benediction over his disciples in the Luke account, but also became the benediction. Kapic concludes his observations with this astonishing theological statement: "Those who saw the ascension *witnessed the personification of Aaron's benediction in Jesus Christ*"; cf. Num 6:24–26 (ibid.; italics added).

384. Rev 1:8; 22:12–13.

385. Shore, writing in contemporary language, notes that the "ascension is not a picture of a risen Christ who leaves the disciples and goes into retirement (as if the Son sinks down into a throne at the right hand of the Father and says, 'Whew, am I glad that job is done'). Instead, the ascension gives us a picture of Jesus as an advance worker for his own followers" ("Living by the Word," 21).

Darden agrees with the disciples' exuberance. Writing to those wishing to communicate the Good News he says, "Here's the wonderful thing—we are part of that story! We play an important role in God's Great Plan. This is our story! The Bible is our roadmap and our cast list. Knowing how these stories are used, how they're important, and what to watch for is important so we will know our parts in this great cosmic comedy/drama" (*Reluctant Prophets and Clueless Disciples*, 13).

386. Jer 29:11–13. A purpose of the play was to show children that the church, the body of believers, is a powerful force in the world (Fritz, *Child and the Christian Faith*, 145).

387. John 10:14.

388. John 6:35; 8:12.

389. John 10:7.

390. John 11:25.

391. John 14:6. Stonehouse postulates that when "those who stand for good win, children are assured that they, too, will have the strength to win over danger and evil" (*Joining Children on the Spiritual Journey*, 157). Yes, indeed.

392. John 15:1. John 1:43. A focus of the play was to honor children and to recognize that the Holy Spirit could also use them for high purposes and noble ends. Quite possibly the children could do what the apostles were doing: Telling others in the neighborhood the Good News that Jesus saves (cf. Spurgeon, *"Come Ye Children,"* 138).

393. Neil, *Acts of the Apostles*, 25.

394. Wall, "Acts of the Apostles," 38.

395. Matt 10:1–4.

396. Wall, "Acts of the Apostles," 37.

397. Ibid., 37–38. The idea of Good News means change; the Bible calls it *metanoia*, conversion (D. Brown, *God and Mystery in Words*, 157). The biblical text by nature is confrontational. The Acts play by its nature challenges its audience by role play to either be a disciple (one charged with telling the Good News of an ascended Jesus) or a hearer like the SABC reporter (one who listened to the disciples' excited story for the first time). It is quite possible that identifying with either role left someone in the audience uncomfortable. But a feeling of being uncomfortable is commonly acknowledged throughout the biblical text when a message is presented because again, the biblical message is confrontational (ibid., 158).

398. A goal of the play was to show model disciples—disciples who had witnessed something extraordinary, were excited about their mission, and loved being together. The Acts play shows disciples as role models who are excited about their new assignments and the work ahead of them; they love the Lord Jesus and each other (cf. McNabb and Mabry, *Teaching the Bible Creatively*, 32).

399. Neil, *Acts of the Apostles*, 25.

400. John 3:16. On earth, Jesus was both God and man in one person, and now as the ascended Lord, he continues to be both God and man in one person (Needham, "Christ Ascended for Us," 42).

401. Marshall, *Acts of the Apostles*, 29.

402. Matt 4:43–47.

403. A positive worship experience is to let the text presented produce a result in a congregation's life and in an individual's life (cf. Stevenson-Moessner, *Prelude to Practical Theology*, 15). The SABC EyeWitness News reporter summarizes for the audience that

she and they can expect to hear more from these excited disciples.

404. Marshall, *Acts of the Apostles*, 25. People who commit their lives to child evangelism use a variety of techniques to hold the interest of their young audiences. Two such
ministers were Willard and Margaret Grant who retired in 1980 after thirty-five years
of crossing America holding conferences for children. Their conferences, streamlined
into seventy-five minutes a night or day, incorporated visualized singing and visualized
Scripture so that the children could remember the words and the biblical truths. There
was a time of prayer in which the children were encouraged to participate. The Grants
included missionary adventure stories and marionette dramas. The couple dressed up
in costumes as models of whatever theme they were using—nautical, Viking, American
West, China (M. J. Anderson, *A Miracle Ministry to Children*, 19). The Grants emphasized participation by the children. they provided costumes for the children. Everything
presented was researched, showed God's love, and was of high quality (ibid., 15). Usually
their conferences were a week long at a church. The conferences gave the children time
to make individual commitments to Christ.

This Acts play incorporated research and contemporary methods. It was performed as
a church worship service and not part of a week-long conference. In looking back, a way
the worship service could have been improved was to engage the audience in more participation. For example, with their "imagination hats" still in place, the SABC reporter
could have asked the students to follow the disciples' words and wonder what it was like
to see Jesus rise up into the air.

In a venue other than a worship service, a follow-up with the children could incorpo-
rate questions like the following:

What part of the story did you like best?

What part of the story do think is the most important?

Which character was the most like you?

How did the story make you feel?

What did the story make you think about?

Is there any part of the story we could leave out?

Does anybody know what happened next in the story? (Berryman, *Teaching Godly
Play*, 40–41).

This kind of "wondering" or imagination requires time and, it is hoped, leads the
children more deeply into examining their personal responses (ibid., 41).

405. Goals of religious education are establishing faith and, from that position of
faith, looking at the text in an informed way. The Acts play seeks to supplement cat-
echism classes the children may already attend (Ratcliff, "Social Contexts of Children's
Ministry," 133, 136).

406. What works in child evangelism? Hunter offers the following observations and
my comments follow in italics:

A theology that works remains consistent with the "faith of the fathers" throughout
the Bible and history. (*The Acts play faithfully presented the biblical text.*)

The claims of Christianity are not effectively communicated by merely parroting
a tradition. These claims must be interpreted meaningfully for an audience, honor its
members' culture and life situation, and give the explanation of the gospel in ordinary
language. (*The play did that.*)

It is necessary to acknowledge that secular people may relate better at first to the
humanity of Jesus. (*The play mentioned Jesus before his death, after his resurrection, and*

during his ascension. The play stressed, as the Acts text does, the aliveness of Jesus.)

Remember that the kingdom of God is a complex subject to modern ears. *(The play emphasized that the kingdom of God is a reality, is also a mystery, and presents no fear to a believer because God is good and his good purposes will prevail.)*

Remember that every person has a calling. *(The play emphasized the upcoming work of the excited disciples: To share the good news of Jesus.)*

In evangelism, present a positive image of Christianity (Hunter, *How to Reach Secular People*, 91–97). *(The play presented the concept of a loving God who reaches out to the whole world, a world inhabited by sinners.)*

Although the play ends quite naturally with bows by the actors, the worship service purposefully added a postscript. Albert Coetzee stepped forward and talked about the meaning of the disciples' excitement. They knew Jesus was alive and wanted above all to tell others. The disciple actors, and Coetzee himself, had given their lives to Jesus. Coetzee explained in simple language how to do that. In this way, the worship service—which incorporated a welcome, an invitation to put on "imagination hats," an explanation of the book of Acts, a dramatization of Acts 1:1–12, and an invitation to become an exuberant disciple—involved what von Balthasar calls "integrated interplay" (*Theo-Drama*, 2:91). The audience members were invited to involve themselves in God's ongoing drama.

407. This play is dedicated to the Rev. Evelyn Lupardus, my friend from seminary, who blesses the Body of Christ as a funny bone.

408. *Funny Bone* is a Christian drama containing humor and music. First Corinthians 12:12–27 contains humor because of its incongruities (see Arbuckle, *Laughing with God*, 2). Edyvean writes that Christian drama presents ideas like human responsibility, Christ's centrality, confession, forgiveness, fellowship, and hope (*This Dramatic World*, 18–19).

409. A version of this play was published. Branch, "Funny Bone finds a home: A musical featuring the Body of Christ," *In die Skriflig* 47 (2013); http://www.indieskriflig. org.za/index.php/skriflig/article/view/113/2367.

410. See Arbuckle, *Laughing with God*, 9. Iverson believes that while we laugh at Jesus' disciples who forgot to take bread on the boat (even though they had witnessed a miraculous feeding of four thousand [Mark 8:1–21]and clearly the joke is on them), "we end up laughing at ourselves as well" ("Redemptive Function of Laughter").

411. Theology contains sacred experiences that are "accessible to the contemporary heart and mind" (Wells, *Improvisation*, 35–36). I agree with McNabb and Mabry who state that a Bible teacher's job is to present the text in an understandable way (*Teaching the Bible Creatively*, 22). *Funny Bone* follows Loader's lead in pausing to reflect on the 1 Cor 12 text with imagination but remaining within its parameters (*New Testament with Imagination*, ix).

412. As a writer of a musical based on the biblical text, I see God's dramatic involvements throughout Scripture (see Pitzele, *Scripture Windows*, 221–24; Branch, *Jeroboam's Wife*, 181–84).

413. Brueggemann argues that preaching can provide an "alternative imagination"; *Funny Bone* preaches in a way that certainly does that ("Preaching as Reimagination," 21).

414. Loader invites readers to see the New Testament in "a new way: through

imagination" (*New Testament with Imagination*, ix). He guides imagination with facts about New Testament times, social customs, farming practices, taxation, unemployment, et cetera.

415. John Chrysostom outlined principles for preaching that included these: Be straightforward, biblical, and down to earth (see Stott, *Between Two Worlds*, 20–21). *Funny Bone* employs allegory and is a straightforward teaching tool.

416. *The Book of Common Worship* (vi) notes that the Presbyterian Church has always emphasized its liberty and has left its ministers free as to the form and order of worship.

A suggestion is to have the passage taught in a traditional sermon during the morning worship and then explained in *Funny Bone* that evening. A minister could open the service by reading 1 Cor 12:12–27 and thereby introduce the play.

417. *The Book of Common Worship* (vi) notes that people in congregations want a more active participation in Christian worship, "which was the custom in the Early Church and is the heritage of the Protestant Reformation."

418. In this I follow Stott who notes there is a freshness and vitality about every sermon born of study (*Between Two Worlds*, 180).

419. *Funny Bone* and four others have been published (see Branch in bibliography).

420. Brueggemann, "An Imaginative 'Or,'" 51.

421. A play's standard elements include plot, character, dialogue, setting, staging, and theme; the musical acknowledges symbolism, irony, and repetition as well as teaching and writing tools (DiYanni, *Literature*, 920–35).

422. Hill and Walton (*Survey of the Old Testament*, 575) note that a literary analysis focuses on character development; features the use of motifs, vocabulary, syntax and literary elements; and excludes avenues like historical and archaeological background. I look at the text in its final, canonical form, its composite whole, and consider it Scripture (ibid., 575).

423. See DiYanni, *Literature*, 918.

424. Brueggemann "Preaching as Reimagination," 17.

425. Trueblood, *Humor of Christ*, 15.

426. Arbuckle provides a helpful list of humor as a teaching method that Jesus employed that includes this and other insights like a parent giving his child a stone instead of bread (*Laughing with God*, 33–34; Matt 7:9).

427. I agree with Stott's belief that good preaching is essential to the healthy growth of a healthy church and add that good teaching is, too (*Between Two Worlds*, 9).

Stott mentions a difficulty preachers face: The rift between the biblical and modern world (ibid., 38). I wrote *Funny Bone* as a way of putting Paul's teaching, which I hold to be inspired, in a contemporary setting. As a teacher, I know that songs help my students to memorize. So I included songs as another teaching tool. A good sermon has variety; so does a good musical.

428. Trueblood, *Humor of Christ*, 32.

429. In this I follow the Presbyterian resource book, *Service for the Lord's Day* (7). Additionally, *Funny Bone* concentrates on two of Osmer's guidelines regarding practical

theological interpretation: It incorporates theatre art and presents a particular situation in Corinth in a contemporary way (*Practical Theology*, 4).

430. "Our bodies have members," writes Dever ("The Church," 94). Membership is basic to human communities. Funny Bone believes she has served her apprenticeship as a volunteer with the established members of the Body of Christ.

431. All Scripture verses are from the New International Version, with the exception of Prov 17:22, which is from the King James Version.

In this 1 Corinthians passage, Paul "takes in the totality of the individual members, refers to the body, and demonstrates its basic unity," Kistemaker writes (*1 Corinthians*, 429). Smalley adds that 1 Corinthians 12 covers spiritual gifts "not in isolation but in relation to the church as the body of Christ" ("Spiritual Gifts and 1 Corinthians 12–16," 31).

432. *The Random House Dictionary of the English Language*, 575. A *funny bone* is located at the end of an elbow. But *funny bone* also is associated with a good sense of humor.

433. *Funny Bone*, with its cast of allegorical characters, continues a tradition of Christian drama that includes the Dorothy Sayers' radio play, *The Man Born to be King* (D. Brown, *God and Mystery in Words*, 174).

434. An actor recreates the author's character with gestures, tone, pauses, and costumes (see von Balthasar, *Theo-Drama*, 1:284). In *Funny Bone*, each character at times stars, leads, and commands center stage.

435. A minimal stage allows the writer to verbalize a scene (see Pitzele, Scripture Windows, 39). Ten people and a piano crowd the stage; furniture should be of good quality, sturdy, and in levels like a bar table and two high chairs.

436. I agree with Long, who views a worship service as a play performed in a kind of community theater with God as the audience and the worshipers as actors (*Beyond the Wordship Wars*, 44).

437. Long acknowledges the controversies surrounding drama's role in worship (ibid., 43–44). Worship is not a spectacle but inherently a participatory event with willing and joyful assemblers (ibid., 44).

Good teaching, like good preaching, seeks to honor and engage the audience and to combine ideals and reality (see Stott, *Between Two Worlds*, 29, 10).

438. Von Balthasar writes that "dramatic action is possible and meaningful only within a given situation" and setting (*Theo-Drama*, 1:343). *Funny Bone* follows Brueggemann's view that the audience "interprets the text in the here and now of the members' lives; the text does not operate in a vacuum" ("Preaching as Reimagination," 19).

439. The play permits *ad libbing*. Through improvisation, actors may put themselves into the story (see B. W. Anderson, *Unfolding Drama of the Bible*, 15).

440. *Funny Bone* follows this idea presented by Bolte and McCusker (*Short Skits for Youth Ministry*, 5, 6): A play provides a snapshot on an issue and is a good teaching tool for youth and adults.

441. Smiles increase one's "face value" (see Swindoll, *Laugh Again*, 17). I agree with McNabb and Mabry who see the Bible not only as a positive book but also as containing

lots of fun (*Teaching the Bible Creatively*, 21).

442. Paul affirms that congregation members are equal, wanted, and needed (see Kistemaker, *1 Corinthians*, 440).

443. *Funny Bone* may also be considered bibliodrama. Bibliodrama begins with the ability to read the text creatively and see "the text is given a voice and answers me back," Pitzele writes (*Scripture Windows*, 26, 28).

444. Drama concentrates on actions but comedy directs attention to gestures (Bergson, *Laughter*, 143).

445. McNabb and Mabry (*Teaching the Bible Creatively*, 21) maintain the Bible needs to be seen not as a tool that keeps people from having fun but as a way of discovering, in community, "the greatest news ever heard."

446. The characters exhibit a pride Paul sees as destructive (1 Cor 11–14) (Loader, *New Testament with Imagination*, 80).

447. Paul shows the Eye wants "to be independent of the other parts of the body" (Kistemaker, *1 Corinthians*, 435).

448. Loader invites readers to imagine Paul as he wrote the letter's drafts that included attacks on idolatry, hypocrisy, and the self-righteous pride that Eye introduces here (*New Testament with Imagination*, 70).

449. Hand presents not only a theatrical moment but also a theological truth based on experience. Vanhoozer sees several benefits to "knowing God theatrically," including reinvigorating "our anemic imaginations" and seeing he ordinariness of daily life as a window for God's intervention (*Drama of Doctrine*, 79–80).

450. Eslinger writes that most first-person stories in a sermon do not serve their intended purposes of demonstrating solidarity with the congregation or making a point immediately ("Story and Image," 175).

451. Head, Ear, and Heart's evangelism stories indicate pride in themselves more so than joy in spreading the Gospel message. Bailey outlines several aspects of Paul's view of evangelism in 1 Cor 12:22–24: Evangelism involves personal relationships, needs a long-term commitment, and must be motivated by love (*Paul through Mediterranean Eyes*, 344–45).

452. If the Corinthian congregation contains those who are high-status society members, they may look down on members like Unpresentable Parts they deem to be "lower class." Unpresentable Parts represents those who are poor in the congregation at Corinth. Paul emphasizes that these members, who may be an embarrassment, must be seen with dignity and honor (Hays, *First Corinthians*, 215–16). A theme in 1 Corinthians is the lack of charity toward the poor on the part of the rich (see Ramelli, "Spiritual Weakness, Illness, and Death in 1 Corinthians 11:30," 145).

453. What Foot calls the Good News, Vanhoozer may call theology (*Drama of Doctrine*, 37–38); theology is, first, what God has said and done, and, second, the response of human beings to his ongoing actions.

454. Nose states another textual theme: the passage talks about the Body—not the church—of Christ, an unexpected wording (see Fisk, *First Corinthians*, 79).

455. DiYanni (*Literature*, 923), writing on the essential nature of characters, states that characters bring a play to life.

456. Funny Bone, an attractive character, smiles, worries about nothing, prays about everything, and relaxes (see Swindoll, *Laugh Again*, 199–201).

457. Studies find that humor and "the telling of stories and jokes occurs with almost equal frequency and are human characteristics shared by both sexes," write Peter and Dana (*Laughter Prescription*, 115). Funny Bone displays what Arbuckle calls "laughter of the heart," an interior peace and joy (*Laughing with God*, 2).

458. Laughter makes a person human. Aristotle in *Poetics* defines man as "a rational animal capable of laughter," suggesting that man is the only animal who does laugh (Welsh, "Homo Ridens," 95).

459. Arbuckle says negative laughter includes irony, which is saying one thing and meaning another; mockery; and scoffing (*Laughing with God*, 8, 23, 9). Arbuckle calls caricature "risky" and urges caution when using it (ibid., 9). Satire criticizes, sarcasm expresses ridicule, and parody impersonates with exaggeration (ibid., 10–11).

On the positive side, wit makes subtle plays on words, and humor serves as a "lubricant" for social situations and enables people to learn concepts in a successful way (ibid., 13, 16).

460. Von Balthasar writes that "laughter is as much a part of life as weeping" (*Theo-Drama*, 1:436).

461. Foot and others resent Head for misusing his gifts of leadership and organization and for overlooking others' gifts. Wells comments that the underwritten patriarchal social experience of the winners, the men in charge, has "inhibited women's freedom, experience, voices, ministries, lives" (*Improvisation*, 36).

462. Conflict is expressed as rudeness and confrontation. Conflict, a significant literary tool drawn from the plot and the central idea, occurs when competing or opposing forces collide (Lostracco and Wilkerson, *Analyzing Short Stories*, 19). Reading canonically, conflict appears throughout the New Testament. Consider Jesus' conflict with the chief priests and elders over authority (Matt 21:23–27); Saul's conflict with the early church (Acts 9:1–2); and divisions in Corinth regarding whom to follow (1 Cor 1:10–17).

463. By covering an awkward social situation with laughter, Unpresentable Parts follows what Welsh ("Homo Ridens," 97–99) considers laughter's essential element: A relaxed rather than an intense attitude.

464. The audience will laugh frequently throughout the play. It is well known that the fuller the theater, the more the laughter (Bergson, *Laughter*, 6–7).

465. Arbuckle argues that humor pervades the Bible because of God's pursuing and forgiving love of fickle humanity (*Laughing with God*, 40, iii).

466. Glavich, *Catholic School Kids*, 106.

467. Multifaceted laughter can be an act of reflection, occur spontaneously, comment on something in a tit-for-tat fashion, and/or punish recognizable human failings (Bergson, *Laughter*, 197–98).

468. Laughter has many helpful byproducts. Cousins used laughter to combat an illness and was "convinced that creativity, the will to live, hope, faith, and love have

biochemical significance and contribute strongly to healing and to well-being" (*Anatomy of an Illness*, 86, 87). Laughter and imagination form tools for training a congregation in the faith (see Stonehouse, *Joining Children on the Spiritual Journey*, 158).

469. Funny Bone's request forms the central idea of the drama. Lostracco and Wilkerson say a story's central idea "reveals the author's point of view on some aspect of life" (*Analyzing Short Stories*, 1).

470. Funny Bone stresses what Paul does: Christ, rather than the church. The passage's usual interpretation is that all Christians have gifts which they must contribute to and share with the Church (see Wright, *Paul for Everyone: 1 Corinthians*, 158).

471. The characters' reactions are consistent with Scripture, for Paul's use of the human body and its comparison with Christ is a surprise; one expects Paul to compare the body and the church (Kistemaker, *1 Corinthians*, 429).

472. B. W. Anderson believes there are two ways to approach a study of the Bible: Academically in a classroom and as an "attempt to *stand within* the Bible and to look out at the world through the window of biblical faith" (italics original) (*Unfolding Drama of the Bible*, 9–10). *Funny Bone* uses the latter.

473. Funny Bone's declaration represents a dramatic moment: a new, controversial thought is introduced. Long says that dramatic worship involves flow and pacing (*Beyond the Worship Wars*, 48).

474. A tool in bibliodrama is echoing (see Pitzele, *Scripture Windows*, 47).

475. Throughout *Funny Bone*, keep in mind what Wells calls a "creative fidelity" to the text (*Improvisation*, 61).

476. Dever defines formal membership as a commitment of Christians in the name of God to one another ("The Church," 98).

477. The tune to "Home on the Range" is in the public domain; see http://www.justanswer.com/intellectual-property-law/2pdiq-song-home-range-public-domain.

478. Berryman comments that laughter is a legitimate use of power in religious education. As a teacher, I find that my students learn more when smiling ("Laughter, Power, and Motivation," 358).

479. Funny Bone makes laughter a habit. The Orthodox Church believes Easter should be a day of laughter and hilarity (for it showcases God's triumph) and sets it aside as such (Copenhaver, "Laughter at Easter," 15, 17).

480. Copenhaver correctly writes that comedy is closer to the deep springs of the Christian religion than is tragedy (ibid., 17).

481. *Funny Bone* is intended to be sung and enjoyed (see Murfin and Ray, *Bedford Glossary of Critical and Literary Terms*, 286).

482. Welsh finds 250 biblical references to laughter and varieties of it in the biblical text ("Homo Ridens," 102).

483. Stevenson-Moessner writes that in the twenty-first century, there is a wider acceptance of new and different culture voices. *Funny Bone* exemplifies this (*Prelude to Practical Theology*, 20).

484. Great theatre means that the actor experiences a kind of self-forgetting; the actor becomes so absorbed in what he or she says that the "hows" and "whys" of the performance recede (Childers, *Performing the Word*, 96).

485. Theology can be studied as a range of sacred experiences "accessible to the contemporary heart and mind" (Wells, *Improvisation*, 35–36). *Funny Bone* looks at Paul's theology and arguments in 1 Cor 12 with honor, honesty, and humor. Church tradition includes such open discussion (see Acts 15).

486. In 1 Cor 12:21 Paul turns to personification. Those who view themselves as superior see themselves as able to get along without others (see Fee, *First Epistle to the Corinthians*, 612).

487. Jesus identifies himself completely with the church; see Acts 9:4 (Kistemaker, *1 Corinthians*, 429).

488. Using their imagination and knowledge of Jesus, Rice and Yaconelli posit that the Master may have used skits especially to illustrate parables (*Greatest Skits on Earth*, 7).

489. McNabb and Mabry outline a mentor's qualities as listening, not needing to be perfect, guiding, and loving a person younger in faith or experience toward Christian maturity (*Teaching the Bible Creatively*, 177–80).

490. Bergson (*Laughter*, 4) writes that comedy contains an absence of feeling because laughter needs indifference; laughter's greatest foe is emotion.

491. Berryman presents four categories of laughter: Superiority, Incongruity, Relief, and Pleasant Psychological Shift ("Laughter, Power, and Motivation," 364–68). Head portrays the Superior model; the response is guffaws, muted laughter, grimaces, and sarcasm.

492. The tune to "God the Omnipotent" is in the public domain (*Pilgrim Hymnal*, 446, 554).

493. Deut 28:13.

494. Head does not see his own arrogance. Bergson provides good comments: "Profoundly comic sayings are those artless ones in which some vice reveals itself in all its nakedness: how could it thus expose itself were it capable of seeing itself as it is?" (*Laughter*, 146–47).

495. The words and actions of the Body of Christ show the members' good and bad attitudes (see Lostracco and Wilkerson, *Analyzing Short Stories*, 28).

496. Laughter, joy, and kindness are all attitudes of choice, ones a wise person selects (see Swindoll, *Laugh Again*, 45).

497. Puns, an aspect of humor, can intensify "the active experience of reading the text" (Pitzele, *Scripture Windows*, 11–12).

498. The tune to "Onward, Christian Soldiers" is in the public domain (*Pilgrim Hymnal*, 382, 553).

499. Foot ends strongly with an emphasis on Jesus as King (see Wright, *Paul for Everyone: 1 Corinthians*, 159).

500. Rough, earthy humor in drama can bring understanding smiles regarding our shared humanity. For examples of this from Scripture see D. Brown, *God and Mystery in Words*, 161.

501. Steuernagel ("Doing Theology with an Eye on Mary," 103) points out that theology begins with unexpected encounters often set in the messy confines of day-to-day lives.

502. Head, Foot, and Eye face uncomfortable truths about themselves. Members of the audience may feel uncomfortable, too. Theatre, however, succeeds when a spectator is compelled "to face the concrete dramatic dimensions of his own life," writes Von Balthasar (*Theo-Drama*, 1:265).

503. Words reveal the characters' motivations, attitudes, cover-ups, hopes, fears, loves, hates (see DiYanni, *Literature*, 901).

504. Foot is responsible for his behavior and happiness (see Swindoll, *Laugh Again*, 71).

505. H. W. Robinson's advice for good preaching applies to good teaching: Present concepts clearly (*Biblical Preaching*, 79–80).

506. Here I show that Foot's behavior addresses a theme in 1 Corinthians, namely that some in the congregation "have used their new sense of freedom to live in ways which seem to ignore moral values and the need to let faith affect the way" they live (Loader, *New Testament with Imagination*, 81).

507. Jude 9.

508. The play shows that the Body of Christ knows this: Funny Bone chooses joy and cultivates a sense of humor (Swindoll, *Laugh Again*, 77).

509. Glavich, *Catholic School Kids*, 96.

510. Eslinger, writing on the efficacy of concrete images in good preaching, notes they are helpful for a communal identity ("Story and Image," 176). *Funny Bone's* characters clearly portray both strengths and weaknesses and are therefore good teaching tools.

511. The tune to "Row, Row, Row Your Boat" is in the public domain; see www.pdinfo.com.

512. Biblically-based theatre helps open people's "hearts to the good news of the scandalous love of God for his people" (Cloninger, *Drama for Worship*, 2:11).

513. Heart, with a military step, leads a disorganized line through the audience. Bergson notes that *"attitudes, gestures and movements of the human body are laughable in exact proportion as that body reminds us of a mere machine"* (*Laughter*, 29; italics original).

514. H. W. Robinson encourages reading, teaching, and preaching 1 Corinthians 12–14 in context (*Biblical Preaching*, 60). Love, as Heart indicates, is central to Paul's teaching (1 Cor 13).

515. Arends writes that laughter resembles a glue "that attaches us to the goodness that inhabits this world and to the gladness that hints of the world to come" ("Carbonated Holiness," 74).

516. Head certainly shows no fear of public speaking. The Corinthians may have

taken sides in judging who was the best public speaker among Peter, Paul, and Apollos (Loader, *New Testament with Imagination*, 81).

517. The tune to "Tenting Tonight on the Old Camp Ground" is in the public domain. See www.pdinfo.com.

518. Unpresentable Parts, because she shares her struggles, shows emotion, extends gracious acceptance, displays anger, and at times reflects on the words and actions of the other characters, is what Lostracco and Wilkerson call a dynamic character (*Analyzing Short Stories*, 13).

519. Paul makes this point: Both modesty and decency should be Christian characteristics (see Kistemaker, *1 Corinthians*, 437).

520. Unpresentable Parts expresses unexpected joy at Heart's gift (see Arends, "Carbonated Holiness," 74).

521. A mentor gives someone younger in the faith meaningful opportunities to express faith (McNabb and Mabry, *Teaching the Bible Creatively*, 180).

522. Via Unpresentable Parts, Paul encourages the congregation's privileged members "to respect and value the contributions of those members who appear to be their inferiors" (Hays, *First Corinthians*, 213).

523. The tune to "Mine Eyes Have Seen the Glory" is in the public domain (*Pilgrim Hymnal*, 443, 554).

524. See Pss 30:3; 40:2; 103:4.

525. Eye's attitude and song create conflict. Conflict "results from a cause and effect relationship between events" (Lostracco and Wilkerson, *Analyzing Short Stories*, 19).

526. Eye's elitist behavior illustrates Paul's point that diversity—not uniformity—is essential for a healthy church (Fee, *First Epistle to the Corinthians*, 583).

527. Paul disdains Eye's and Head's independent attitudes (see Kistemaker, *1 Corinthians*, 435). Perhaps the great error Paul seeks to correct is an arrogant self-sufficiency and the demeaning way of thinking, "I do not need you" (see Fee, *First Epistle to the Corinthians*, 612–13).

528. The cycle of discontent common in Corinth prevails today. After an initial welcome wears off, a member may express envy and jealousy and carry grudges (see Kistemaker, *1 Corinthians*, 434).

529. Phil 2:3.

530. John 15:12.

531. See 1 Cor 4:18, 19; 8:1.

532. Peter and Dana (*Laughter Prescription*, 113) write that "adding a ridiculous element, such as an exaggeration, is often a way to express empathy with another," as when Nose extends his hand and receives rejection.

533. Bonhoeffer (*Life Together*, 84–85) comments that we pray, guided by Scripture, asking for preservation from sin, growth in sanctification, and faithfulness in our work. Nose's prayer concentrates on sanctification.

534. The tune to "Danny Boy" is in the public domain. See www.pdinfo.com.

535. Via his song, Nose leads the Body of Christ in worship, a dramatic corporate event (see Long, *Beyond the Worship Wars*, 43). Von Balthasar adds that drama illuminates Christian theology (*Theo-Drama*, 1:25).

536. A theme in 1 Corinthians is freedom in Christ. The Corinthians understood this (erroneously) to mean, as Allard writes, a freedom from all restraints ("Freedom on Your Head," 400). They thought that they were free to eat meat dedicated to idols (1 Cor 8:1–13) and engage in sexual liaisons with prostitutes (6:15); that a man could have sexual relations with his father's wife (5:1); that women could disrupt a service (14:34); and that women need not wear veils (11:2–16) (ibid.). Nose correctly sings, "There is no health among us anymore."

537. Nose clarifies Paul's message of freedom: Believers are set free to serve their neighbors, for "service is the motif of the gospel" (see ibid., 401, 402).

538. Quash provides some valuable insights that apply to *Funny Bone's* tone: "Drama displays *human actions* and *temporal events* in *specific contexts*. Theodramatics concerns itself with human actions (people), temporal events (time), and their specific contexts (place) *in relation to God's purpose*" (*Theology and the Drama of History*, 3–4; italics original).

539. Jas 5:16. 1 John 1:19. Prov 28:13.

540. Paul mentions that a person who has received the gift of healing (which often is done by the laying on of hands), cannot say to the rest of the body, "I have no need of you" (see Kistemaker, *1 Corinthians*, 436).

541. Titus 2:8

542. Jer 17:9.

543. Ear, Eye, and Head are pretentious and therefore "inherently humorous," as Trueblood (*Humor of Christ*, 83–84) observes.

544. The tune "I've Been Workin' on the Railroad" is in the public domain. See www.pdinfo.com.

545. Ear incorporates a basic principle of worship: Confession. Confession and pardon fulfill the idea of the reality of sin in personal and communal life (see *Book of Common Worship*, 35).

546. Lawsuits between and among believers in the Corinthian community are an issue (1 Cor 6:1–11) (Grams, "Shaping of Christian Convictions," 12). Paul condemns this, saying that "the very fact that you have lawsuits among you means you have been completely defeated already" (v. 7a).

547. Prov 16:28.

548. Prov 11:13.

549. See Prov 20:19.

550. Ear repents, an action showing change. This play, an accompaniment to traditional preaching, may well empower godly change in some lives (see Brueggemann "Preaching as Reimagination," 25).

551. While Heart recommends forgiveness, Paul presents another possibility. Paul asks instead, "Why not rather be wronged, why not rather be defrauded?" (1 Cor 6:7; see Grams, "Shaping of Christian Convictions," 12).

552. According to von Balthasar (*Theo-Drama*, 3:150), the highest qualification of Jesus, who said these words, is that he is the Son of God and the Father's Beloved Son.

553. Luke 11:4.

554. Matt 18:22.

555. See Matt 5:23–24.

556. Bureaucrats like Head and Hand "do not appreciate having their nonresponsiveness exposed to the public eye" (Peter and Dana, *Laughter Prescription*, 141).

557. Members of the Body of Christ often insult each other. If an insult cannot be ignored, it must be topped; if it cannot be topped, it must be laughed at; if it cannot be laughed at, then probably it is well deserved (ibid., 151).

558. Members of the Body of Christ bicker the same way the disciples jealously disputed who would be the greatest (Luke 22:24–27); Jesus corrects them by introducing the paradox that serving leads to greatness in his new world order (see Trueblood, *Humor of Christ*, 87–88).

559. Corinthian women may have abandoned modest dressing and may even be dressing as men (Loader, *New Testament with Imagination*, 82).

560. Funny Bone does not like the qualities she sees the Body of Christ expressing. Characters may or may not appeal to us, and may or may not remind us of ourselves (see DiYanni, *Literature*, 922).

561. Here the members of the Body of Christ childishly fight, openly showing their divisions (see 1 Cor 3:1–3). Paul chides his beloved Corinthians "for failing to allow what they had known and realized to be true to inform their on-going Christian life" (Francis, "As Babes in Christ," 57).

562. Trueblood (*Humor of Christ*, 92) observes that some hard problems—whether in exegesis or in life—are "soluble only in the acids of humor."

563. Rom 3:23.

564. Instead of boasting in our accomplishments, we should boast of "preferment of one another in love," Francis observes ("As Babes in Christ," 57).

565. Rom 7:24–25.

566. John 8:36; Luke 13:16; Mark 5:1–20.

567. B. W. Anderson correctly sees the Bible as an unfolding story of our lives and God as the great dramatist and storyteller (*Unfolding Drama of the Bible*, 100, 104).

568. Rhyne writes that "though the Corinthians may be spiritual, their behavior reflects an unspiritual approach to the faith . . . They are acting like infants rather than (as) grown-ups in Christ" ("1 Corinthians 3:1–9," 175–76).

569. Themes organize a play (see DiYanni, *Literature*, 934). *Funny Bone's* themes are disunity/unity; each member's self-importance; and the absurdity of "going it alone"

without others.

570. Biblical examples of those who are weak but essential and even invaluable to the Body of Christ are Dorcas/Tabitha (Acts 9:32–43), the woman who befriended widows in Joppa and was raised from the dead by Peter; and the woman who anointed Jesus at the home of Simon the leper (Mark 14:1–9), a prophetic act Jesus commends.

571. Unpresentable Parts believes members of the church are joined together (see Fisk, *First Corinthians*, 81).

572. The tune to "Sweet Betsy from Pike" is in the public domain. See www.pdinfo.com.

573. Phil 4:3.

574. Jefferson writes that Paul "possessed the joy of feeling that he was working with God. God has far-reaching plans, and Paul is helping him to carry them out" (*Character of Paul*, 285).

575. Hand recognizes Funny Bone's gifts of teaching and friendship. Jefferson writes that Paul experienced "the full joy of friendship" and that Paul "feasted on the joy of helping others" (ibid., 283–84)

576. Childers, observing that preaching and theatre are events, adds that performance in preaching is a valuable exegetical tool (*Performing the Word*, 45, 49).

577. See 1 Cor 12:12–27. Funny Bone, as she begins to teach, follows Stott's advice that preaching entails an open-minded, comprehensive, and expectant approach to looking at a text (*Between Two Worlds*, 182–87).

578. 1 Cor 12:12.

579. Regarding *baptized* in 1 Cor 12:13, the multi-dimensional and figurative word probably here means Jesus' baptism into death on the cross (1 Cor 10:2; Acts 1:5; see Kistemaker, *1 Corinthians*, 430).
Throughout writing the play, I bore in mind the view of B. W. Anderson, who affirms that via the Holy Spirit, "God appears in the cast" (*Unfolding Drama of the Bible*, 13).

580. 1 Cor 12:13.

581. Perhaps behind Paul's argument is that male and female together reflect God's image (Gen 1:26–28) (Wright, *Paul for Everyone: 1 Corinthians*, 164).

582. Regarding the 1 Corinthians 12 passage, Fisk writes: "Paul's point is that *all* such distinctions—of race, class, wealth, gender—must no longer divide those who have been drawn together into the singular, Spirit-empowered body of Christ" (*First Corinthians*, 79). The immersion in the Holy Spirit makes all believers one (Hays, *First Corinthians*, 214).

583. The phrase, *into one body*, takes into account the unity in diversity of the body of Christ that was already present in Corinth in terms of racial, cultural, sexual, social, economic, and other differences (see Kistemaker, *1 Corinthians*, 430, 431).

584. 1 Cor 12:14.

585. Because of the equality between different parts that have different functions, there is "no room for social, cultural or 'spiritual' elitism or snobbery within the church,"

Wright maintains (*Paul for Everyone: 1 Corinthians*, 164–65).

586. Brueggemann writes that the church is either a like-minded group of people who exclude all others or a group harboring a generous spirit and a minimum but clear bar of admission ("An Imaginative 'Or,'" 61).

587. 1 Cor 12:15.

588. Kistemaker (*1 Corinthians*, 434) comments that a single-unit body "may be a unit but it is unable to function as an organic body. An entity without any differentiating parts can be as useless as a lump of discarded clay."

589. 1 Cor 12:16.

590. 1 Cor 12:17a.

591. A body that is just one part—be it nose, ear, or eye—is a monstrosity, Fee (*First Epistle to the Corinthians*, 611) correctly observes.

592. 1 Cor 12:17b.

593. Comic breakthrough celebrates with kindness, smiles, and understanding—but only "if we let it expose our mortal vulnerabilities, and are willing, lovingly, to embrace them" (Miller, "Laughter and the Absurd Economy of Celebration," 230).

594. Laughter echoes (Bergson, *Laughter*, 5).

595. Funny Bone's spontaneity encourages the audience to laugh. D. A Charles comments that "spontaneous theatre forms . . . unmistakably share a common and pervasive audience response: laughter" ("Power of the Carnival Satirist," 11).

596. 1 Cor 12:18.

597. 1 Cor 12:21a.

598. Eye's apology illustrates that the 1 Corinthians text argues against a member becoming a duplication of another member in order to feel a sense of belonging (see Troupe, "One Body, Many Parts," 40).

599. 1 Cor 12:21b.

600. In my research on laughter, I found these insights from Welsh to be up-to-date: We laugh at the unexpected. Someone's slipping on a banana peel is funny when it happens to someone else. Laughter requires a relaxed rather than intense attitude. Laughter serves a social function, for it binds together age groups ("Homo Ridens," 97–99).

601. Using parts of the body, Paul sees the Body of Christ in a new way. The Body of Christ's more significant, visible members must respect and value those parts considered less so (Fisk, *First Corinthians*, 79).

602. 1 Cor 12:22–23. The weaker body parts present a surprise: They are indispensable (ibid., 80)!

603. 1 Cor 12:24.

604. The kindness of God leads to repentance (Rom 2:4; Eph 2:7; Titus 3:4).

605. H. W. Robinson provides a good rule for writing a sermon or play: Let supporting material restate, repeat, and explain a pericope's parts (*Biblical Preaching*, 243).

606. The Greek word *perichoresis* describes the happy fellowship of the Father, Son, and Spirit. Arends likens the word to being worn out with gladness ("Carbonated Holiness," 74).

607. The passage emphasizes unity. B. W. Anderson writes that the biblical text, in contrast to Greek dramas, which think of history in terms of cycles, moves toward an end in which God's purpose will be realized (*Unfolding Drama of the Bible*, 81; see 1 Cor 15:24–28).

608. See 1 Cor 12:25a; 3:1–9. One division was "parties"—some claimed to belong to Paul or Cephas or Apollos or Christ (1 Cor 3:4–5; see Rhyne, "1 Corinthians 3:1–9," 174).

609. 1 Cor 12:25b.

610. Ramelli notes that "disease and death can be understood in a spiritual sense" and indeed are understood in this way "by most ancient exegetes" ("Spiritual Weakness, Illness, and Death," 146).

611. 1 Cor 12:26a. Kistemaker says this passage "describes the effect genuine care can have on members in the Christian church" (*1 Corinthians*, 438).

612. Paul stresses that the Corinthians must behave rightly toward each other to recover spiritual health and life and to avoid judgment (Ramelli, "Spiritual Weakness, Illness, and Death," 163).

613. Bailey observes that Paul reminds his beloved congregation that members of the Body of Christ are clothed in splendor and honor and that they are bound to one another in life's ups and downs of suffering and honor (*Paul through Mediterranean Eyes*, 347).

614. 1 Cor 12:26b.

615. Funny Bone begins teaching in a contemporary way with a rap. Drama is a tool enabling both young and old to remember biblical teachings and act upon them (McNabb and Mabry, *Teaching the Bible Creatively*, 21).

616. While writing the rap, I bore in mind Childers' view that the foundation of a careful, skilled oral performance (whether for preaching or teaching or acting) contains four elements: Rate, pitch, volume, and pause (*Performing the Word*, 80). Proper emphasis transforms a dead reading or a dead performance into an enlivened event (see ibid., 84).

617. McNabb and Mabry give guidelines about interpreting any passage: Find its main point; consider the context; look at the whole book and read the individual part in light of the book and scripture as a whole; and consider how the passage applies to life today (*Teaching the Bible Creatively*, 25–26). *Funny Bone* gives audience members a nonthreatening and humorous way to see strengths and weaknesses in themselves.

618. Dever writes that indeed we are "obliged to love one another" ("The Church," 97).

619. John 15:12.

620. How is this love meant to be expressed? By active sympathy among the members; by members going out of their way to care for others and in seeking to carry others' burdens (ibid., 98).

621. Gal 5:13.

622. Gal 6:10. Tone, language, and repetition—a playwright's tools and present in literary analysis—overlap throughout the play (see Lostracco and Wilkerson, *Analyzing Short Stories*, 40).

623. Prov 10:12; Jas 5:20; 1 Pet 4:8.

624. In a performance, I encourage my actors to stress the fun of this rap and the joy of being forgiven. *Pilgrim Hymnal* contains a Percy Dearmer hymn, "The Whole Bright World Rejoices Now" (194). Notice its emphasis on hilarity. Here the Latin adverb *hilariter* means "cheerfully," "joyfully," and even "merrily." Dearmer's hymn captures these characteristics of God and encourages God's followers to respond in kind.

> The whole bright world rejoices now, Hilariter, Hilariter;
> The birds do sing on every bough, Alleluia, Alleluia.
> Then shout beneath the racing skies, Hilariter, Hilariter.
> To him who rose that we might rise, Alleluia, Alleluia.
> And all you living things make praise, Hilariter, Hilariter;
> He guideth you on all your ways, Alleluia, Alleluia!
> He, Father, Son, and Holy Ghost, Hilariter, Hilariter;
> Our God most high, our joy and boast, Alleluia, Alleluia!

625. Laughter, as *Funny Bone shows,* is individual and social, physiological and psychological, caused and causative (Welsh, "Homo Ridens," 96).

626. Again Head takes charge, but Troupe asks, "Who decides who should be the head?" (Troupe, "One Body, Many Parts," 44).

627. A prop like a rug helps "the where" of a scene (see Lostracco and Wilkerson, *Analyzing Short Stories*, 31).

628. I incorporated the idea of a huddle from church polity. This huddle is a congregational meeting. Although enacted with humor, it nonetheless conveys the sense of discussing the issue that is before the Body of Christ.

Making 1 Cor 12 a musical comedy has several advantages including the following (cf. Clark et al., *Childhood Education in the Church,* 545–46): Enacting a story makes it more real and gives the actor, via imagination, insights into another person. A drama may show honest feelings.

629. The tune to "Yankee Doodle Dandy" is in the public domain. See www.pdinfo.com.

630. *Funny Bone* involves entrances and exits, characters and plot, scenes and settings, tone and dialogue, pauses and monologues (see Vanhoozer, *Drama of Doctrine,* 41).

631. "The church can afford to take the risk of the humorous and ephemeral, because the joke is God's and the laughter is divine," Wells writes (*Improvisation*, 69). Laughter keeps Funny Bone involved with people (Swindoll, *Laugh Again*, 225).

632. Eye and Heart appreciate Funny Bone's ability to fuss at them with a twinkle in her eye. Trueblood sees the same in Jesus. He writes that a person "who reads the Synoptic Gospels with a relative freedom from presuppositions might be expected to see that Christ laughed, and that He expected others to laugh, but our capacity to miss this aspect of His life is phenomenal" (*Humor of Christ*, 15).

633. Here are some meanings of humor present in *Funny Bone* (Arbuckle, *Laughing with God*, 2):

- Humor, or the comic, helps us cope with the vicissitudes of life.

- Humor is negative when it degrades a person. Humor is positive when it respects a person's dignity.

- Positive humor evokes two types of laughter. The first response is audible; you can hear a laugh. The second is an interior laughter, a laughter of the heart, if you will, which manifests itself in joy and peace.

634. Trueblood calls Jesus' humor "deliberately preposterous" (*Humor of Christ*, 47); that phrase applies to portions of *Funny Bone* which exaggerate to make a point.

635. Jefferson links Paul's character and joy: "In the outer courts of his soul there is often pain and sometimes agony, but in the inner court there is always the sound of music and dancing. Underneath the surface of his letters there runs a strain of deep and solemn gladness. Again and again it is hidden from the eye and ear, but it keeps breaking through . . . He knew the joy of hope. Hope always wears a radiant face" (*Character of Paul*, 280–82).

636. Jesus was gregarious and so often in fellowship with so-called questionable characters that he was termed "a wine-bibber and gluttonous man" (Welsh, "Homo Ridens," 103).

637. Song 4:1–7. Brueggemann challenges preachers (and playwrights!) to see a text in a new way that is "credible and evocative of a new humanness, rooted in holiness and practiced in neighborliness" ("Preaching as Reimagination," 25).

638. DiYanni writes that a playwright arranges incidents (*Literature*, 921). For example, each character's song allows for smiles and a relaxation of intensity, but the church fight of shoving and poking may cause some uncomfortable feelings in the audience.

639. McNabb and Mabry categorize teaching as promoting creativity or engaging in ordinariness (*Teaching the Bible Creatively*, 164). *Funny Bone* falls in their creative category.

640. Cousins gives his own version of this verse: "A merry heart works like a doctor" (*Anatomy of an Illness*, 83).

641. *Funny Bone* was written for enjoyment and teaching purposes. A spectator's pleasure in watching a play "remains a reference to that delight that underlies and sustains all life's seriousness, a delight in being privileged to share in existence," writes Von Balthasar (*Theo-Drama*, 1:267).

642. Studies show people retain ten percent of what they read and hear but that "direct purposeful experiences" like acting produce a ninety percent retention (McNabb and Mabry, *Teaching the Bible Creatively*, 42).

643. Duckworth correctly writes that a "skit can brighten a worship service with humor and, at the same time, drive home a serious point" (*High-Impact Worship Dramas*, 5).

644. The tune, "All People that on Earth Do Dwell, 'Old Hundreth,'" is in the public domain (*Pilgrim Hymnal*, 4, 550).

645. Bonhoeffer, *Life Together*, 21.

646. Ibid.

647. Ibid., 23.

648. Ibid., 24.

649. The author thanks Pam Walker, librarian at Victory University in Memphis, Tennessee, for her help in verifying that *Funny Bone's* tunes are in the public domain. The author thanks Dr. George Fluitt and Dr. Clarice Fluitt, pastors of the Eagle's Nest Church in Monroe, Louisiana, for their encouragement of song, dance, creativity, and member participation during worship services and other church activities in the 1980s. My idea for the musical *Funny Bone* started because of church skits that used laughter to teach biblical principles.

Bibliography

Achtemeier, Paul J., ed. *Harper's Bible Dictionary.* San Francisco: Harper & Row, 1985.

Aldrich, Joseph C. *Lifestyle Evangelism: Learning to Open Your Life to Those around You.* Sisters, OR: Multnomah, 1993.

Allard, Robert E. "'Freedom on your Head' (1 Corinthians 11:2–16): A Paradigm for the Structure of Paul's Ethics." *Word & World* 30 (2010) 399–407.

Anderson, Bernhard W. *The Unfolding Drama of the Bible.* 4th ed. Minneapolis: Fortress, 2006.

Anderson, Margaret Jennine. *A Miracle Ministry to Children.* Turlock, CA: Kincaid, 1983.

Arends, Carolyn. "Carbonated Holiness: Laughter is Serious Business." *Christianity Today* April 1, 2008, 74.

Arbuckle, Gerald A. *Laughing with God: Humor, Culture, and Transformation.* Collegeville, MN: Liturgical, 2008.

Bailey, Kenneth E. *Paul through Mediterranean Eyes: Cultural Studies in 1 Corinthians.* Downers Grove, IL: InterVarsity, 2011.

————. *Jesus through Middle Eastern Eyes: Cultural Studies in the Gospels.* Downers Grove, IL: InterVarsity, 2008.

Balthasar, Hans Urs von. *Theo-Drama: Theological Dramatic Theory.* Vol. 5, *The Last Act.* Translated by Graham Harrison. San Francisco: Ignatius, 1998.

————. *Theo-Drama: Theological Dramatic Theory,* Vol. 3, *The Dramatis Personae: The Person in Christ.* Translated by Graham Harrison. San Francisco: Ignatius, 1992.

————. *Theo-Drama: Theological Dramatic Theory.* Vol. 2, *The Dramatis Personae: Man in God.* Translated by Graham Harrison. San Francisco: Ignatius, 1990.

————. *Theo-Drama: Theological Dramatic Theory.* Vol. 1, *Prolegomena.* Translated by Graham Harrison. San Francisco: Ignatius, 1988.

Barclay, William. *The Gospel of Matthew.* Vol. 1. Daily Study Bible Series. Philadelphia: Westminster, 1958.

————. *The Gospel of Luke.* Daily Study Bible Series. Philadelphia: Westminster, 1956.

Barker, Kenneth, ed. *NIV Study Bible.* Grand Rapids: Zondervan, 1995.

Barragar, Pam. *Spiritual Growth through Creative Drama for Children and Youth.* Valley Forge, PA: Judson, 1981.

Bauckham, Richard. *Gospel Women: Studies of the Named Women in the Gospels.* Grand Rapids: Eerdmans, 2002.

Beechick, Ruth. *Teaching Juniors: Both Heart and Head.* Denver: Accent, 1981.

Bergson, Henri. *Laughter: An Essay on the Meaning of the Comic.* Translated by Cloudesley Brereton and Fred Rothwell. New York: Macmillan, 1924.

Berryman, Jerome W. "Laughter, Power, and Motivation in Religious Education." *Religious Education* 93 (1999) 358–78.

———. *Teaching Godly Play: The Sunday Morning Handbook*. Nashville: Abingdon, 1995.

Bock, Darrell L. *Jesus According to Scripture: Restoring the Portrait from the Gospels*. Grand Rapids: Baker Academic, 2002.

———. *Luke*. IVP New Testament Commentary Series. Downers Grove, IL: InterVarsity Press, 1994.

Bolte, Chuck, and Paul McCusker. *Short Skits for Youth Ministry*. Loveland, CO: Group, 1993.

Bonhoeffer, Dietrich. *Life Together*. Translated by John W. Doberstein. New York: Harper & Row, 1954.

The Book of Common Worship. Philadelphia: Office of the General Assembly, United Presbyterian Church in the United States of America, 1946.

Branch, Robin Gallaher. "Astonishment and Joy: Luke 1 as Told from the Perspective of Elizabeth." *In die Skriflig* 47 (2013b). http://www.indieskriflig.org.za/index.php/skriflig/article/view/77/2017.

———. "Exegetical Perspective: Luke 1:68–79." In *Preaching the Revised Common Lectionary: Feasting on the Word. Year C, Volume 1*, edited by David L. Bartlett and Barbara Brown Taylor, 33, 35, 37. Louisville: Westminster John Knox, 2009.

———. "Funny Bone Finds a Home: A Musical Featuring the Body of Christ." *In die Skriflig*, 47 (2013c). http://www.indieskriflig.org.za/index.php/skriflig/article/view/113/2367.

———. "He Is Risen! A Play Based on Acts 1:1–12." *In die Skriflig* 44 (2010) 229–58. http://dx.doi.org/10.4102/ids.v44i1.145.

———. *Jeroboam's Wife: The Enduring Contributions of the Old Testament's Least-Known Women*. Grand Rapids: Baker Academic, 2010a.

———. "Life's Choices: A Play Based on Eight Characters in Proverbs." *Christian Higher Education: A Journal of Applied Research and Practice* 4 (2004) 57–69. Also published in *Society of Biblical Literature, SBL Forum for February/March* (2006) 8pp. http://www.sbl-site.org/publications/article.aspx?articleId=488.

———. "When Mary Tells Joseph: A Play Based on Matthew 1:18–19." *In die Skriflig* 47.1 (2013a). http://www.indieskriflig.org.za/index.php/skriflig/article/viewFile/92/2097.

Brenner, Athalya. "Female Social Behaviour: Two Descriptive Patterns within the 'Birth of the Hero' Paradigm." *Vetus Testamentm* 36 (1986) 257–73.

Brown, David. *God and Mystery in Words: Experience through Metaphor and Drama*. Oxford: Oxford University Press, 2008.

Brown, Raymond E. "The Annunciation to Zechariah, the Birth of the Baptist, and the Benedictus (Luke 1:5–25, 57–80)." *Worship* 62 (1988) 482–96.

———. "The Annunciation to Mary, the Visitation, and the Magnificat (Luke 1:26–56)." *Worship* 62 (1988) 249–59.

———. *The Birth of the Messiah: A Commentary on the Infancy Narratives in Matthew and Luke*. New York: Doubleday, 1979.

Brown, R. M. *Unexpected News: Reading the Bible with Third World Eyes*. Philadelphia: Westminster, 1984.

Brueggemann, Walter. "An Imaginative 'Or.'" In *A Reader on Preaching: Making Connections*, edited by David Day, Jeff Astley and Leslie J. Francis, 51–64. Explorations in Practical, Pastoral, and Empirical Theology. Burlington, VT: Ashgate, 2005.

————." Preaching as Reimagination." In *A Reader on Preaching: Making Connections*, edited by David Day, Jeff Astley and Leslie J. Francis, 17–29. Explorations in Practical, Pastoral, and Empirical Theology. Burlington, VT: Ashgate, 2005b.

Burge, Mary M., Lynn H. Cohick, and Gene L. Green. *The New Testament in Antiquity: A Survey of the New Testament within Its Cultural Contexts*. Grand Rapids: Zondervan, 2009.

Card, Michael. *Luke: The Gospel of Amazement*. Biblical Imagination Series. Downers Grove, IL: IVP Books, 1985.

Cawley, Arthur. C., ed. *Everyman and Medieval Miracle Plays*. New York: Dutton, 1959.

Ceroke, Christian P. "Luke 1:34 and Mary's Virginity." *Catholic Biblical Quarterly* 19 (1957) 329–42.

Charles, David A. "The Power of the Carnival Satirist: Taking Laughter Seriously." *Journal of Theater and Performance* 2 (2005) 11–28.

Charles, Gary W. "Rider of the Clouds: Ps. 68:1–10, 32–35." *Journal for Preachers* 31 (2008) 14–16.

"The Cherry Tree Carol." In *The New Oxford Book of Carols*, edited by Hugh Keyte and Andrew Parrott, 440–43 (#128). Oxford: Oxford University Press, 1992.

Childers, Jana. *Performing the Word: Preaching as Theatre*. Nashville: Abingdon, 1998.

Clark, Robert E., Joanne Brubaker, and Roy B. Zuck. *Childhood Education in the Church*. Rev. ed. Chicago: Moody, 1986.

Cloninger, Curt. *Drama for Worship: Contemporary Sketches for Opening Hearts to God*, Vol. 2. Cincinnati: Standard Publishing, 1999.

Conrad, Edgar W. "The Annunciation of Birth and the Birth of the Messiah." *Catholic Biblical Quarterly* 47 (1985) 656–63.

Cooper, Stephen A. "Luke 1:39–45 (46–55): Exegetical Perspective." In *Feasting on the Word: Preaching the Revised Common Lectionary. Year C, Volume 1: Advent through Transfiguration*, edited by David L. Bartlett and Barbara Brown Taylor, 93, 95, 97. Louisville: Westminster John Knox, 2009.

Copenhaver, Martin B. "Laughter at Easter: Matthew 28:1–10." *Journal for Preachers* 30 (2007) 15–18.

Cousins, Norman. *Anatomy of an Illness as Perceived by the Patient: Reflections on Healing and Regeneration*. New York: Bantam, 1979.

Craddock, Fred B. *Luke*. Interpretation. Louisville: Westminster John Knox, 1990.

Daniel, L. "Borne in Perplexity: Luke 1:26–38." *Journal for Preachers* 29 (2005) 26–28.

Darden, Robert. *Reluctant Prophets and Clueless Disciples: Introducing the Bible by Telling Its Stories*. Nashville: Abingdon, 2006.

Dean, Robert J. *Luke*. Layman's Bible Commentary 17. Nashville: Broadman, 1983.

Dever, Mark. "The Church: A Summary and Reflection." In *Understanding the Times: New Testament Studies in the 21st Century*, edited by Andreas J. Kostenberger and Robert W. Yarbrough, 87–103. Wheaton, IL: Crossway, 2011.

DiYanni, Robert. *Literature: Approaches to Fiction, Poetry, and Drama*. Boston: McGraw-Hill, 2008.

Doriani, Daniel M., Philip Graham Ryken, and Richard D. Phillip. *The Incarnation in the Gospels*. Phillipsburg, NJ: P&R, 2008.

Drane, John. *Introducing the New Testament*. 3rd ed. Minneapolis: Fortress, 2011.

Duckworth, John L. *High-Impact Worship Dramas: Quick-Prep Message Boosters for Pastors & Church Leaders*. Loveland, CO: Group, 1999.

Edyvean, Alfred R. *This Dramatic World: Using Contemporary Drama in the Church*. New York: Friendship, 1970.

Ehrensperger, Harold. *Religious Drama: Ends and Means*. New York: Abingdon, 1962.

Epstein, I., ed. *Babylonian Talmud*. 35 vols. London: Soncino, 1935–1952.

Eslinger, Richard L. "Story and Image in Sermon Illustration." In *A Reader on Preaching: Making Connections*, edited by David Day, Jeff Astley, and Leslie J. Francis, 175–78. Burlington, VT: Ashgate, 2005.

Evans, Craig A. *Fabricating Jesus: How Modern Scholars Distort the Gospels*. Downers Grove, IL: IVP Books, 2006.

Faley, Roland J. Review of J. F. Craghan's *Mary, the Virginal Wife and the Married Virgin: The Problematic of Mary's Vow of Virginity*. *Catholic Biblical Quarterly* 30 (1968) 437–38.

Fee, Gordon D. *The First Epistle to the Corinthians*. New International Commentary on the New Testament. Grand Rapids: Eerdmans, 1987.

Fisk, Bruce N. *First Corinthians*. Interpretation Bible Studies. Louisville: Geneva, 2000.

Fitzmyer, Joseph A. *The Gospel According to Luke I–IX*. Anchor Bible 28. New York: Doubleday, 1981.

Forde, Nigel. *Theatercraft: Creativity & the Art of Drama*. Wheaton, IL: Shaw, 1990.

France, R. T. *Matthew*. Tyndale New Testament Commentaries. Grand Rapids: Eerdmans, 1989.

Francis, James. "'As Babes in Christ'—Some Proposals Regarding 1 Corinthians 3:1–3." *JSNT* 7 (1980) 41–60.

Fritz, Dorothy B. *The Child and the Christian Faith*. Richmond: Covenant Life Curriculum, 1964.

Fuller, George C. "The Life of Jesus after the Ascension (Luke 24:50–53, Acts 1:9–11)." *Westminster Theological Journal* 56 (1994) 391–98.

Geldenhuys, Norval. *The Gospel of Luke*. New International Commentary on the New Testament. Grand Rapids: Eerdmans, 1979.

Glavich, Mary Katherine. *Catholic School Kids Say the Funniest Things*. New York: Paulist, 2002.

Globe, Alexander. "Some Doctrinal Variants in Matthew 1 and Luke 2, and the Authority of the Neutral Text." *Catholic Biblical Quarterly* 42 (1980) 52–72.

Gomes, Peter J. *Sermons: Biblical Wisdom for Daily Living*. New York: Morrow, 1998.

Grams, R. G. "The Shaping of Christian Convictions and the Avoidance of Ideology: Paul's Contribution to a Vexing Issue in 1 Corinthians." *Baptistic Theologies* 3.1 (2011) 1–14.

Grant, Jamie. "Christ Ascended for Us—'I have gone to prepare a place for you.'" *Evangel* 25 (2007) 39–42.

Green, Joel. B. *The Gospel of Luke*. New International Commentary on the New Testament. Grand Rapids: Eerdmans, 1997.

Greenblatt, Stephen. *The Norton Anthology of English Literature*. New York: Norton, 2006.

Grossman, Lev. "Milestones: Frank McCourt." *Time*, Aug. 21, 2009, 3, 21.

Gundry, Robert H. *A Survey of the New Testament*. 4th ed. Grand Rapids: Zondervan, 2003.

Hagner, Donald A. *Matthew 1–13*. Word Biblical Commentary 33A. Dallas: Word, 1993.

Hann, Rrobert R. "Election, the Humanity of Jesus, and Possible Worlds." *Journal of the Evangelical Theological Society* 29 (1986) 295–305.

Hare, Douglas R. A. *Matthew*. Interpretation. Louisville: Westminster John Knox, 1993.

Hays, Richard B. *First Corinthians*. Interpretation. Louisville: John Knox, 1997.

Hill, Andrew E., and John H. Walton. *A Survey of the Old Testament.* Grand Rapids: Zondervan, 2000.

Holy Apostles Convent. *The Life of the Virgin Mary, the Theotokos.* Buena Vista, CO: Holy Apostles Convent, Dormition Skete, 1989.

Hospodar, Blaise. "*Meta spoudes* in Luke 1:39." *Catholic Biblical Quarterly* 18 (1956) 14–18.

Hunter, George G., III. *How to Reach Secular People.* Nashville: Abingdon, 1992.

Iverson, Kelly R. "The Redemptive Function of Laughter: Performance and the Use of Humor in the Gospel of Mark." Paper presented at the annual meeting of the Society of Biblical Literature, San Francisco, 19–22 November 2011.

Jefferson, Charles Edward. *The Character of Paul.* New York: Macmillan, 1924.

Just, Arthur A., Jr., ed. *Luke.* Ancient Christian Commentary on Scripture. Downers Grove, IL: InterVarsity, 2003.

Kapic, Kelly M. "Receiving Christ's Priestly Benediction: A Biblical, Historical, and Theological Exploration of Luke 24:50–53." *Westminster Theological Journal* 67 (2005) 247–60.

Kapic, Kelly M., and Wesley Vander Lugt. "The Ascension of Jesus and the Descent of the Holy Spirit in Patristic Perspective: A Theological Reading." *Evangelical Quarterly* 79 (2007) 23–33.

Karris, Robert J. "Luke's Soteriology of With-ness." *Currents in Theology and Mission* 12 (1985) 346–52.

Kershner, Shannon Johnson. "Advent Sermon: Luke 1:39–55." *Journal for Preachers* 31 (2007) 20–22.

Kistemaker, Simon J. *1 Corinthians.* Grand Rapids: Baker Books, 2002.

Kuist, Howard Tillman. "Sources of Power in the Nativity Hymns: An Exposition of Luke 1 and 2." *Interpretation* 2 (1948) 288–98.

Landry, David T. "Narrative Logic in the Annunciation to Mary (Luke 1:26–38)." *Journal of Biblical Literature* 114 (1995) 65–79.

Loader, William. *The New Testament with Imagination: A Fresh Approach to Its Writings and Themes.* Grand Rapids: Eerdmans, 2007.

Long, Thomas G. *Beyond the Worship Wars: Building Vital and Faithful Worship.* Bethesda, MD: Alban Institute, 2001.

Lostracco, Joe, and George Wilkerson. *Analyzing Short Stories.* 7th ed. Dubuque: Kendall/Hunt, 2008.

Maile, John F. "The Ascension in Luke–Acts." *Tyndale Bulletin* 37 (1986) 29–59.

Marshall, I. Howard. *The Acts of the Apostles: An Introduction and Commentary.* Grand Rapids: Eerdmans, 1989.

Martin, J. P. "Luke 1:39–47." *Interpretation* 36 (1982) 394–99.

Marx, Steven. *Shakespeare and the Bible.* Oxford: Oxford University, 2000.

McCorkindale, Donald. "Children's Ministry between Easter and Pentecost." *Expository Times* 117 (2006) 293–94.

McGowan, Andrew. "The Ascended Jesus Interceding for Us." *Evangel* 25 (2007) 51–53.

McNabb, Bill, and Steve Mabry. *Teaching the Bible Creatively: How to Awaken Your Kids to Scripture.* Grand Rapids: Zondervan, 1990.

Miller, Jerome A. "Laughter and the Absurd Economy of Celebration." *Cross Currents* 45 (1995) 217–33.

Morris, Leon L. *Luke: An Introduction and Commentary.* Downers Grove, IL: IVP Academic, 1988.

Murfin, Ross C., and Supryia M. Ray. *The Bedford Glossary of Critical and Literary Terms.* Boston: Bedford, 1997.

Murphy, Frederick J. *An Introduction to Jesus and the Gospels.* Nashville: Abingdon, 2005.

Needham, Nick. "Christ Ascended for Us—Jesus' Ascended Humanity and Ours." *Evangel* 25 (2007) 42.

Neil, William. *The Acts of the Apostles.* New Century Bible. London: Oliphants, 1973.

Nolland, John. *Luke 1–9:20.* Word Biblical Commentary. Dallas: Word, 1989.

O'Day, Gail R. "Singing Woman's Song: A Hermeneutic of Liberation." *Currents in Theology and Mission* 12 (1985) 203–10.

O'Keefe, John J., and R. R. Reno. *Sanctified Vision: An Introduction to Early Christian Interpretation of the Bible.* Baltimore: Johns Hopkins University, 2005.

Osmer, Richard R. *Practical Theology: An Introduction.* Grand Rapids: Eerdmans, 2008.

Packer, J. W. *Acts of the Apostles.* Cambridge Bible Commentary. Cambridge: Cambridge University Press, 1966.

Peter, Lawrence J., and Bill Dana. *The Laughter Prescription: The Tools of Humor and How to Use Them.* New York: Ballantine, 1982.

Phipps, W. E. "Blake on Joseph's Dilemma." *Theology Today* 28 (1971) 170–78.

Pilgrim Hymnal. Boston: Pilgrim, 1966.

Pitzele, Peter A. *Scripture Windows: Towards a Practice of Bibliodrama.* Los Angeles: ALEF Design Group, 1998.

Protoevangelion: The Lost Books of the Bible. New York: Meridian, 1966.

Public Domain Information Project (PD Info). *List of public domain music.* http://www.pdinfo.com/Public-Domain-Music-List.php

Quash, Ben. *Theology and the Drama of History.* Cambridge Studies in Christian Doctrine. Cambridge: Cambridge University Press, 2005.

Ramelli, Ilaria L. E. "Spiritual Weakness, Illness, and Death in 1 Corinthians 11:30." *Journal of Biblical Literature* 130 (2011) 145–63.

Ratcliff, Donald E. "Social Contexts of Children's Ministry." In *Handbook of Children's Religious Education,* edited by Donald E. Ratcliff, 119–42. Birmingham, AL: Religious Education Press, 1992.

Rhyne, C. Thomas. "1 Corinthians 3:1–9." *Interpretation* 44 (1990) 174–79.

Rice, Wayne, and Mike Yaconelli. *The Greatest Skits on Earth: Skits with a Message.* Grand Rapids: Zondervan, 1987.

Robinson, Edward. "The Resurrection and Ascension of Our Lord." *Bibliotheca Sacra* 150 (1993) 9–34.

Robinson, Haddon W. *Biblical Preaching: The Development and Delivery of Expository Messages.* Grand Rapids: Baker Academic, 2001.

Ryken, Philip Graham. *Luke: Volume 1, Luke 1–12.* Phillipsburg, NJ: P & R, 2009.

Schaberg, Jane. *The Illegitimacy of Jesus: A Feminist Theological Interpretation of the Infancy Narratives.* San Francisco: Harper & Row, 1987.

The Service for the Lord's Day: The Worship of God. Supplemental Liturgical Resource 1. Philadelphia: Westminster, 1984.

Shakespeare, William. *The Tragedy of Othello.* In *Literature: Approaches to Fiction, Poetry, and Drama,* edited by Robert DiYanni, 1012–97. Boston: McGraw-Hill, 2008.

Shore, Mary Hinkle. "Living by the Word: Sunday May 20, Luke 24:44–53." *Christian Century* 124 (May 1, 2007) 21.

Smalley, S. S. "Spiritual Gifts and 1 Corinthians 12–16." *Journal of Biblical Literature* 87 (1968) 427–33.

Smith, D. Moody. "Exposition of Luke 1:26–38." *Interpretation* 29 (1975) 411–17.

Spence, H. D. M., and Joseph S. Exell. *Acts & Romans*. Pulpit Commentary 18. Grand Rapids: Eerdmans, 1950.

Spivey, Robert A., D. Moody Smith, and C. Clifton Black. *Anatomy of the New Testament*. 6th ed. Minneapolis: Fortress, 2010.

Spurgeon, Charles H. *"Come Ye Children": A Book on the Christian Training of Children*. Warrenton, MO: Child Evangelism Fellowship, ND.

Steuernagel, V. R. "Doing Theology with an Eye on Mary." *Evangelical Review of Theology* 27 (2003) 100–112.

Stevenson-Moessner, Jeanne. *Prelude to Practical Theology: Variations on Theory and Practice*. Nashville: Abingdon, 2008.

Stein, Jess, ed. *The Random House Dictionary of the English Language*. New York: Random House, 1973.

Stonehouse, Catherine. *Joining Children on the Spiritual Journey: Nurturing a Life of Faith*. Grand Rapids: Baker, 1998.

Stott, John. *Between Two Worlds: The Challenge of Preaching Today*. Grand Rapids: Eerdmans, 1982.

Strauss, Mark L. *Four Portraits, One Jesus: An Introduction to Jesus and the Gospels*. Grand Rapids: Zondervan, 2007.

Swanson, Richard W. "Magnificat and Crucifixion: The Story of Mariam and Her Son." *Currents in Theology and Mission* 34 (2007) 101–10.

Swindoll, Charles R. *Laugh Again*. Dallas: Word, 1992.

Talbert, Charles H. "Luke 1:26–31." *Interpretation* 39 (1985) 288–91.

The Theology and Worship Ministry Unit. *Book of Common Worship*. Louisville: Westminster John Knox Press, 1993.

Thurston, Herbert, and Donald Attwater. *Butler's Lives of the Saints*. 4 vols. New York: Kenedy, 1956.

Troupe, Carol. "One Body, Many Parts: A Reading of 1 Corinthians 12:12–27." *Black Theology: An International Journal* 6 (2008) 32–45.

Trueblood, Elton. *The Humor of Christ*. New York: Harper & Row, 1964.

Vanhoozer, Kevin J. *The Drama of Doctrine: A Canonical-Linguistic Approach to Christian Theology*. Louisville: John Knox, 2005.

Wall, Robert W. "The Acts of the Apostles." In *The New Interpreter's Bible: A Commentary in Twelve Volumes. Volume X: Acts, Introduction to Epistolary Literature, Romans, 1 Corinthians*, edited by Leander E. Keck, 1–368. Nashville: Abingdon, 2002.

Wansbrough, Henry. *Luke. Daily Bible Commentary: A Guide to Reflection and Prayer*. Peabody: Hendrickson, 2007.

Weissenbuehler, Wayne E. "Acts 1:1–11." *Interpretation* 46 (1992) 61–65.

Wells, Samuel. *Improvisation: The Drama of Christian Ethics*. Grand Rapids: Brazos, 2004.

Welsh, W. A. "Homo Ridens: A Preliminary Consideration of Some Aspects of Human Laughter." *Lexington Theological Quarterly* 2 (1967) 95–103.

Wheeler, Russell A. *Creative Resources for Elementary Classrooms and School-Age Programs*. Albany, NY: Delmar, 1997.

Wilson, Alistair. "The Ascension: What Is It and Why Does It Matter?" *Evangel* 25 (2007) 48–51.

Wilson, Brittany E. "Pugnacious Precursors and the Bearer of Peace: Jael, Judith, and Mary in Luke 1:42." *Catholic Biblical Quarterly* 68 (2006) 432–56.

Wright, Tom. *Luke for Everyone*. Louisville: Westminster John Knox, 2004.

Bibliography

———. *Paul for Everyone: 1 Corinthians.* Louisville: Westminster John Knox, 2004.